It was time for the alternate plan the Executioner had suspected they might have to resort to

One of the many things Mack Bolan had learned over the years was that *nothing* ever went exactly as planned. Sometimes it was just a small deviation from the expected. Other times, as the old adage went, "The best plans fall to pieces a soon as the first shot is fired." But this, he suspected, was simply a minor bump in the road. And one which he'd be able to pass over with a little creativity.

Bolan reached behind him, lifting his shirttail slightly and running his fingers along the top of the stiff black leather case sticking up out of his back pocket. He had brought half of what he needed for plan B.

The other half would have to be acquired here, inside the compound.

Don Pendleton's Mack Bolan®

Escalation Tactic

A GOLD EAGLE BOOK FROM

W★RLDWIDE®

TORONTO • NEW YORK • LONDON
AMSTERDAM • PARIS • SYDNEY • HAMBURG
STOCKHOLM • ATHENS • TOKYO • MILAN
MADRID • WARSAW • BUDAPEST • AUCKLAND

Recycling programs
for this product may
not exist in your area.

First edition March 2013

ISBN-13: 978-0-373-61559-9

Special thanks and acknowledgment to
Jeri Van Cook for his contribution to this work.

ESCALATION TACTIC

Printed in U.S.A.

Under current law, there is no additional penalty for someone who enters the United States illegally and then commits either a crime of violence or a drug trafficking offense.

—John Shadegg, b. 1949,
former member of the U.S.
House of Representatives

It matters not what penalties the Feds do or do not mete out. Trangressors come to realize that the only penalty I administer is the terminal kind.

—Mack Bolan

PROLOGUE

The setting was one of peace and tranquility, moderated partially by decor that some might say pushed the envelope between good taste and gaudy. But, regardless of whether one viewed the trappings as classical or garish, they were about to be destroyed.

The wedding was elaborate in a way in which only wealthy members of an underdeveloped country could execute such an event. Although she hadn't yet made her appearance, most of the men and women in attendance knew that the bride would be wearing a gown that would have cost ten Mexican laborers a lifetime of wages. The maid of honor would be decorated almost as expensively, with the dresses of the ten bridesmaids falling only a few pesos short of that.

The husband-to-be, the best man and the groomsmen and ushers wore the latest Parisian tuxedos, which had been recently featured in *GQ*. Even the flower girl's and ring bearer's clothing could have fed a Mexican family of twelve for a month.

The priest officiating the wedding stood on the steps leading up to the stage, looking more like a Latino fashion model than a member of the clergy. His was obviously a wealthy parish, and his parishioners would have never stood for a spiritual leader who reflected poverty.

Red carpets had been rolled down the aisles of the cathedral, and all in attendance—be they friends and family of the bride or groom—stepped carefully on them as the ushers escorted the female guests to their seats with their menfolk following. Candles, set in elaborate gold-and-silver holders mounted to the walls and behind the pulpit, had been lit by young men wearing pristine white robes. More candles burned behind the choir loft, which was filled with men and women spouting eerie and mysterious Gregorian chants as the congregation continued to file into the building. The windows on both sides of the room were of the finest stained glass, with some of them reflecting angels, billowy clouds, a benevolent God on His throne with Christ seated next to Him, and an overall message of the utopia that awaited the saved in heaven.

Finally, when all the guests had been seated, the organist began to play and the bridesmaids and maid of honor strode purposely down the center aisle, followed by the bride. The groomsmen and best man—led by the groom—appeared through a door just to the side of the stage. In addition to their black, Edwardian-cut tuxedos, all wore tremendous smiles, and it became clear to everyone seated in the grand cathedral that neither bride nor groom suffered from cold feet or second thoughts.

Just before the mass was to begin, the doors at the rear of the church suddenly burst open. A heartbeat later a dozen submachine guns fired in unison.

"Nobody move!" shouted a man wearing black army fatigues and a matching ski mask as the other men—dressed identically—raced down the aisles. Those in the congregation who had the presence of mind to look over their shoulders saw that more men in "modern ninja" attire had followed their leaders and now took up guard duty at the doors.

Within the space of five seconds, the church was sealed off and the entire congregation and wedding party had been taken hostage.

The men and women seated in the pews who had thought the wedding was the ultimate in taste dismissed such thoughts. As did the others who had secretly believed the show had crossed the line of class and wallowed in vulgarity.

The man who had spoken earlier now fired a burst into the ceiling of the hallowed room. As soon as the noise died down, he barked out more orders in Spanish. "Everyone! On the ground!"

The people in the pews stood frozen for a moment, and this seemed to irritate the gunman. When he fired this time, he aimed just over their heads. "Down, I said!" he yelled.

This shook the stunned congregation back into reality and most dropped to the floor between the pews. A few were obviously too slow for the masked man now in charge, and his next burst of fire struck a half-dozen men and women in the chests and heads, sending crimson blood, skull fragments and body tissue flying.

As soon as everyone was down—one way or another—the leader of the masked men nodded toward several of his cohorts. Immediately, the intruders began to walk up and down the aisles, occasionally pulling the triggers of their subguns and creating screams and moans of agony. Other times, they stopped, shouting for someone to turn toward them so they could see their victim's face. More often than not when this happened, the face brought on another burst of rounds and more flying blood.

On several occasions, however, after the faces had turned toward the gunmen, there seemed to be some question as to whether they had been predestined to die, then and there. When that happened, the assassins in black called out to their leader—the man who had first ordered everyone to the floor between the pews. He obviously held the final power over life and death and, each time he was summoned, he hurried over to scrutinize the people in question. Then a simple nod brought on a machine-gun obliteration of that face, or a short shake of the head became the captive's salvation and the cold-blooded killers moved on.

Finally, the entire congregation had been scrutinized, and the masked leader looked down to his side where the bride and groom had been forced to half sit, half lie on the steps leading up to the platform. Shifting his weapon to his left hand, he reached down, took the bride's hand and lifted her gently to her feet. Still holding the terrified young woman's hand in his, his eyes moved to the groom.

"Stand up," he growled in a low, menacing voice. "You are coming with us."

The groom did as ordered.

Turning back to face the crowd, the masked leader looked down the red carpet covering the center aisle to where two of his men now held four men from the congregation. All were Hispanics, and their faces had turned a sick-looking gray as they stood with their hands behind their backs. One of the captives stood slightly sideways to the front of the cathedral, and the masked leader saw the glint of steel handcuffs under the overhead lights. He nodded, more to himself than to his men, then pulled his own set of cuffs from a rear pocket of his black fatigues.

A moment later, the groom, too, was cuffed behind his back.

"Forward!" the man in the ski mask ordered the two, and the bride began to retrace her steps down the red carpet. The groom fell in behind. They had gone only a few steps before the nervous groom accidentally stepped on his bride-to-be's train and both almost fell.

The leader of the masked men cursed under his breath and ordered them to halt. In one smooth motion, he pulled a seven-inch fighting knife from the sheath on his hip and began slicing through the bride's train. After several cuts, the cloth lay on the floor looking almost as dead as the people lying still between the pews.

The party moved up the aisle to join the other black-clad, ski-masked men and their prisoners. Then the intruders surrounded their captives and began to leave. The leader was the last to exit, and just before he did, he turned back toward the pews.

"Those of you who still live," he shouted out. "You will carry the story of what has happened here with you to any members of the Morales family who were not in attendance. You will tell them that times have changed. No longer will the Morales Cartel have a monopoly on the drugs and other goods that are shipped north of the Rio Grande. And you will tell them that this—" he waved a hand around the room, indicating the bloody mess in the aisles and between the pews "—is what will happen to any of them who stand in my way."

The crowd had grown perfectly silent as he spoke. And they remained so as the masked man finally turned and left.

By the time he had walked down the steps in the front of the church, his men and the hostages were loaded in six vans. Striding purposefully to the van at the front of the convoy, he opened the front passenger's door and stepped up into the seat. The ski mask remained on his face until they were several blocks from the church.

When he finally pulled the mask from his head, he smiled. The operation had gone well. In one fatal swoop, he had eliminated a significant number of the Morales Cartel leaders. Not all of them by any means, but he had not wanted to completely destroy the organization. He wanted only to diminish their power to the point where they could still operate but would need his assistance to do so.

The smile slowly turned into a frown. His only real regret was that the top man of the cartel, Don Pancho Morales, had been absent from the wedding. An elderly man in his early eighties with a failing heart and pacemaker, "Don Pancho," as he was often called, had been rushed to the hospital while dressing for the occasion.

By the time the wedding was about to begin, however, word had reached the church that the heart attack had been nothing more than indigestion. The Don was recovering nicely, but he wouldn't be attending the ceremony.

As the van convoy drove on, the leader of the attack nodded to himself. His master plan would have gone faster and more smoothly had he been able to kill Don Pancho at the church. And had he learned that the old man would not be in attendance, he would have altered his plans, waiting for another family occasion when the Don would have been present. But while missing the head of the Morales Cartel was a disappointment, he had taken out many of the other top-ranking family figures.

And he had spread terror through the hearts of those he'd left alive. The survivors would spread the word that the assault had been performed by the new group of "mercenary" drug runners rumored to be setting up shop and ready to steal the Morales's business away from them.

A victory by any standards. The smile returned to the man's face. Yes, they would realize this could have been done by no other group than the encroachers who were said to be made up of ex-military and ex-police officers from both Mexico and the United States.

But they wouldn't know the leader's identity.

Now, with the mask in his lap and the convoy speeding down the street toward the highway, the man sat back in his seat and smiled contentedly.

CHAPTER ONE

The last 9 mm magazine for Mack Bolan's Heckler & Koch MP-5 submachine gun had run dry minutes earlier, and he had relied on the sound-suppressed Beretta 93-R ever since. But a pistol—even a machine pistol with 3-round-burst capability such as the Beretta—was hardly the best choice of firepower for the situation in which he found himself.

Bolan, aka the Executioner, let up on the trigger of the 93-R for a moment, taking in his surroundings. He had dropped into a crevice in the rocks, on the side of a mountain in a range he couldn't name. Rifle fire—from the guns of enemies hiding behind boulders and in other crevices over a hundred yards away—continued to pound the rocks above his head and to his sides.

A strange fog also surrounded him, but it didn't seem to be the billowy whiteness from the clouds; they were still too high over the mountains to interfere with his vision. This fog was more of an indefinable, ethereal mist. And somehow, Bolan knew the murky smoke was in his mind rather than outside him, and in sight.

Returning his attention to the fight, Bolan wondered briefly who the enemy was. He didn't know. The only thing he knew was that they were enemies of America and all nations of the free world.

Otherwise, he knew he wouldn't be fighting them.

Bolan spotted the head and one shoulder of a man sticking out from behind a boulder far in the distance. The black silhouette of an AK-47 assault rifle was recoiling in the man's hands, and bullets ricocheted off the rocks next to the crevice. Pebbles and powdered rock dropped over the Executioner's head to join the strange mist.

The Executioner lined up the 93-R's front and rear sights on a spot an inch above the man's head, then lightly squeezed the trigger.

The semijacketed, subsonic 9 mm hollowpoint round arched ever so slightly as it traversed the space between the two men, then fell against the AK-47 itself and flattened as it slid along the rifle's rail. Even in the daylight, sparks could be seen as the copper jacket struck steel, and by the time the bullet left the rifle to penetrate the chest of the man with the Russian weapon it had expanded to almost a full inch of warped and twisted copper and lead.

Even at that distance, Bolan heard the man scream as he fell to his side, away from the boulder that had only partially shielded him.

It was the last round in the first magazine of the Beretta, and the slide locked open. Bolan thumbed the release button, letting the magazine fall to the ground. A split second later, he had jerked a fresh 15-round load from the Kydex magazine caddie under the right side of his shoulder rig and jammed it into the butt of the 93-R. Return fire continued to force him to stay low in

the crevice as he thumbed the slide release to chamber
the first of the new rounds.

The mysterious mist still surrounded him, interfer-
ing with his vision and giving his whole predicament an
otherworldly feel. But the Executioner was used to having to improvise during battle. He had fought thousands
of them, and no two had ever been quite the same. So,
with a deep breath as he moved the selector switch to
3-round-burst mode and pulled down the folding front
grip of the Beretta, he rose slightly and fired three more
9 mm rounds at the rocks across from him.

The rounds hadn't been meant to hit anyone. They
had been fired to create reaction—movement—on the
parts of the enemies who were now better armed than
he. And the ploy worked. Seven heads jerked back behind cover.

Bolan made note in his mind where each man had
hidden. He knew he was taking a chance by not retreating into his own depression in the rocks, but he stayed
where he was, the machine pistol still held in both hands
at arm's length. Taking chances—calculated risks—was
what combat was all about. Nothing ventured, nothing
gained. And Mack Bolan hadn't survived his long career
battling evil in all its forms by being timid.

Seconds later, another AK-47 nosed around a tree
growing at an awkward angle out of the rocks. A face
slowly followed.

Aiming slightly high once more because of the distance, Bolan sent a triple-tap of 9 mm rounds across the
long expanse. At least one of the jacketed missiles found
the face of the enemy, and the Executioner heard another

low moan as the AK-47 fell from the man's hands and tumbled down the side of the mountain.

Four more of the gunners made similar mistakes, and Bolan took them out one by one. But in doing so, he emptied his second magazine and was forced to insert the last one.

Switching the selector to single shot to conserve ammo, Bolan hunkered down lower between the rocks as a new bombardment of fire chipped away at the stone just above him. One tiny chip flew into his eye but he got it out quickly and easily. Once again, he wondered at the strange mist that surrounded him. It gave him the impression that something about this gunfight was, indeed, far different than any he had ever experienced before. But there was little time to ponder the thought.

The explosions that had been coming from over a hundred yards away were getting louder. That meant the men trying to kill him were moving toward him.

The Executioner raised his head slightly, checking all directions. To his left was the flat side of the mountain itself. Without climbing equipment, there would be no escape in that direction. And even if he had the ropes and other gear necessary to traverse the face, he would be exposed like a fly on the wall, and the gunners' rifles would be far faster and more accurate than any flyswatter ever could be. He might as well paint a bull's-eye on his back if he chose that route of escape.

To his right, and rear, were drop-offs. Behind him was at least a five-hundred-foot fall. To his side it was at least one hundred. The rear route meant certain death on its own. He might survive the hundred-foot drop to his right if he could break his fall on the way down by striking the branches of another tree jutting from the bottom. But he'd be unlikely to do so without breaking one, or both, of his legs or sustaining other injuries that would leave him helpless.

And that would mean it would only be a matter of time before the men coming toward him reached where he was now, looked down on him, then riddled his broken body with more of their 7.62 mm bullets.

The roar of rounds coming his way continued to grow in volume, and the Executioner knew he had only seconds to choose his battle plan. The way he saw it, there was only one possibility of escape, and the odds against his surviving it were slim.

Rising to his feet inside the fog that surrounded him, Bolan held the trigger back on the Beretta 93-R, sending 3-round bursts at four men who were leading a pack of about two dozen men. Twelve rounds spit from his machine pistol. And each burst took out one of the four men. A return shot clipped through the strange fog and skimmed over his shoulder, taking with it the epaulet on the shoulder of his camouflage BDU blouse but leaving his flesh unscathed. The final three rounds from the Beretta's magazine all found a home in the chest of a seemingly faceless man a few yards behind the leaders.

Instead of retreating or taking cover, the rest of the two dozen men began to sprint as best they could across the rocky surface of the mountainside. The fog had moved up with the Executioner, and he was surprised to see that none of the enemy coming toward him seemed to have faces. But they all had AK-47s, and all of them were firing on full-auto as they drew ever closer.

Bolan dropped the empty Beretta 93-R and drew the mammoth .44 Magnum Desert Eagle from his hip. Even under the incredible pressure of almost certain death, he took his time, firing a huge .44 at each man as he came, and watching them fall through the hazy mist even as he swung the barrel toward the next. In a few seconds, eight more of the advancing men lay dead on the ground.

But now the Desert Eagle, too, was empty of rounds.

From inside the front right pocket of his BDU blouse, Bolan retrieved the tiny North American Arms 5-shot .22 Magnum Pug minirevolver. So small he could cover it with his palm, he thumbed back the hammer on the single-action wheel gun and pulled the trigger even as his left hand drew the Cold Steel Espada Knife and snagged the opening hook on the pocket of his pants. As small as the Pug might be, the Espada folding knife— based on the ancient Spanish Navaja design—was large, and a second later the 7.5-inch steel blade snapped into place.

The Executioner knew his efforts now would almost certainly be fruitless. But he wasn't the sort of man to surrender, or go down without a fight. So he raised the minirevolver and pointed it at the chest of another of the faceless attackers as they continued their charge forward through the weird mist.

BOLAN WAS ABOUT TO FIRE again when the phone on the nightstand next to his bed suddenly rang.

The soldier's eyelids flipped open and the mist that

had clouded his vision was suddenly gone. So was the mountain range. And so were the men trying to kill him. He glanced down at his empty hands—to his sides, on the bed—then rose to a sitting position and looked across the bedroom toward the desk against the wall.

All his guns, their holsters and the Cold Steel Espada Knife rested on the desktop. And all of them, he knew, were fully loaded.

The phone rang once more and the Executioner grabbed it. As he lifted the receiver, he glanced at his watch. He had been asleep for only three hours after returning to Stony Man Farm after a long mission in Libya. But three hours was more rest than he often got, so he counted himself lucky as he raised the phone to his ear and answered with his usual mission code name.

"Striker," Bolan said.

"Sorry to interrupt your beauty rest." It was the voice of Hal Brognola, director of the Sensitive Operations Group, based at Stony Man Farm on the other end. And the soldier knew the man was calling from an office on the first floor of the Farm's main house.

"I'm not sure I'd call it restful," Bolan answered. "In fact, your call might just have saved my life."

There was a short pause on the other end. Then Brognola said, "Nightmare?"

"No," Bolan said. "Just a pretty average dream."

"Well, for anyone else it would be a nightmare."

"Maybe," Bolan said. "So what's on your mind?"

"How soon can you be in the War Room?" the big Fed asked.

"As soon as you need me," Bolan answered. "If we've got time, I could use a quick shower and shave."

"We've got that much time," Brognola said. "But not much more. Shall we say ten minutes?"

"You're on," Bolan said and hung up.

Five minutes later, the Executioner stepped out of the shower and grabbed a towel. He had shaved using a mirror mounted on the tile inside the stall as the hot water blasted into his back, driving a little of the soreness out of his muscles. The mission in Libya had been long and grueling. But as he drew the towel across his once-again-smooth face, he felt as good as most men feel after ten hours of sleep.

Bolan finished drying himself, combed his hair, then left the bathroom and returned to the bedroom. Realizing he hadn't brought any clean clothing into the room with him, he opened the closet door and looked up at the shelf over the empty hangers. Several stacks of freshly cleaned blacksuits—the formfitting, stretchy, multipocketed and many-featured suits he often used in battle were neatly folded.

The soldier reached up for one, then donned it.

The Beretta's shoulder rig went over the Executioner's arms. The Kydex hip holster for the Desert Eagle was threaded onto a nylon web belt that held extra .44 Magnum magazines, and the NAA Pug minirevolver "hide out" and Cold Steel folding knife went into the slit pockets of the blacksuit. As soon as he was dressed, Bolan stepped out of the bedroom and headed for the elevator at the end of the hall.

He entered the Stony Man Farm War Room with two minutes of his ten-minute deadline to spare.

STONY MAN FARM was like no other installation in the world, known only to the men and women who worked out of the top-secret counterterrorism base, the President of the United States himself and a select few others. On the rare occasions when it became necessary for outsiders to visit the farm, they were blindfolded and flown in by either Jack Grimaldi—Stony Man's number-one pilot—Charlie Mott or a trusted blacksuit pilot. The pilots were masters of their trade and performed so many "loops" and other in-flight methods of disorientation that even visitors with the best sense of direction were totally confused by the time the plane landed.

Bolan had once been an official operative working out of the Farm, but those days were behind him now. Just because he was no longer an official Stony Man agent didn't mean he had cut all ties with the organization. The Executioner still maintained an arm's-length relationship with his brothers-in-arms, and took full advantage of the Farm's computer capabilities, training facilities, cutting-edge armory and other state-of-the-art aspects unique to the installation. He often accepted missions from Hal Brognola when their goals meshed.

So the soldier wasn't particularly surprised to see three unfamiliar faces as soon as he'd punched in the digital code to the War Room, then pushed the door open as soon as the buzzer sounded. The three men were seated toward the end of the long conference table where hundreds of covert actions and surgical strikes had been planned over the years.

And often, the fate of the world was decided.

Hal Brognola, who, in addition to directing operations at the Farm, doubled as a high-ranking official of the U.S. Department of Justice, sat in his usual place at the far end of the table. He glanced up as Bolan walked in.

"Welcome back, big guy," he said.

"Nice to be back," Bolan answered. "Especially in one piece."

Manila file folders lay on the table in front of the men. All were open. The seat just to Brognola's right was empty, and Bolan moved toward it without needing to be told, pulling the chair out and dropping into it. It was obvious that Brognola had been filling in the new people on some aspect of whatever mission they were about to undertake. But now he, too, waited quietly, chomping on the unlit cigar clenched between his teeth, as he waited for the soldier.

As soon as Bolan was settled, the big Fed lifted the open file in front of him to reveal a closed one beneath it. A second later, he slid it along the table to the soldier like some paper shuffleboard disk.

Bolan grabbed the file and opened it to the first page.

"Before we get started," Brognola said, "let me introduce everyone, because you'll be working together on this mission."

Bolan cleared his throat, reminding himself that regardless of the fact that the three new people were present here in the War Room, they would have little to no knowledge of the intricacies and ins and outs of Stony Man Farm.

And he intended to keep it that way. He knew Brognola would be using these men—whoever they were—on a strict need-to-know basis as well.

"A quick question, first," Bolan said.

"Shoot," Brognola replied. Then he smiled. "Not literally, of course. At least not yet."

Bolan folded his hands, rested them on the table in front of him and leaned slightly forward. "Where are the teams?"

Brognola, Bolan knew, would immediately know that he was referring to Phoenix Force and Able Team, the two top counterterrorist units fielded by the Farm. The men sitting at the table didn't need to know about Phoenix and Able.

"Both groups are currently tied up in other parts of the world," Brognola said without missing a beat. "But I think you'll find that these men are more than adequate warriors themselves."

Bolan nodded. He trusted Brognola, both the man's loyalty and judgment. If the Stony Man director said these men were good, then they would be.

But who, exactly, were they? the soldier wondered. He suspected he was about to find out.

"I think introductions are in order," the big Fed stated.

The other men waited patiently.

Brognola pointed two fingers at Bolan. "Gentlemen, this is Matt Cooper. He'll be in charge of the operation. You're to take orders from him just like you would any superior officer, and not question his judgment. Mr.

Cooper's methods are often unorthodox, but they're always effective. He's secure enough to allow you to question his judgment—when there's time. But, of course, when the feces hits the oscillator, and there isn't time for a round-table discussion, you'll be expected to do what he tells you to do. And to do it *right then.*"

Bolan had noted that all three of the unknown men had maintained an erect posture and military bearing ever since he'd entered the room. That told him that they came from a branch of the armed forces. Now, as Brognola spoke, he studied the men's eyes. None of them seemed shocked or even surprised when the Stony Man director warned them that "Matt Cooper" sometimes became creative in order to solve problems. That meant they were used to such approaches, which, in turn, suggested that they came from elite units within the branches in which they served.

The average combat soldier was expected to always do as he was told and never, under any circumstances, question his orders. But the special forces within each arm of the military were of a different breed and, therefore, received different training. They were taught to think for themselves and use their imagination as well as their training and trigger finger. In short, they were encouraged, rather than discouraged, when it came to thinking for themselves.

The man seated just to Brognola's left wore a long-sleeved blue chambray shirt, and what appeared to be a Soviet-era Spetsnaz blue-and-white undershirt beneath it. The sleeves of the chambray shirt had been rolled up to the bottom of his elbows, and the pinstripes below it stood out in bold relief on his forearms and in the V just below his throat. The man's hair was shaved on the sides, but longer on top and standing straight up, held in place by setting gel or some other hair product.

Brognola turned to glance at the man. "Cooper," he said, "this is Richard Nash. Better known as 'Spike,' although I have no idea where that nickname came from." Brognola's eyes rose slightly to the man's prickly hair and he smiled, contradicting his last words and causing the other men to laugh softly.

Then, turning back to Bolan, Brognola went on. "Spike comes to us from Delta Force. He's a small arms and explosives expert. He's also a first-rate historian and has taught military history and theory at West Point."

The Stony Man director removed the chewed cigar from his mouth for a moment, then stuck it back between his teeth. "Spike was born, and grew up, in the Rio Grande Valley of Texas," he added, "so he knows the layout, the land and the people down there. That's one of the reasons he was picked for this mission."

Bolan nodded. Spike Nash was too far away to shake hands unless one of them got up and moved down the table. But there was no need for the ritual to take place. Both men looked into each other's eyes and saw the soul of a fellow warrior looking back at him, which was enough pomp and ceremony for both of them.

Now Hal Brognola turned to his left. Even with the guy sitting down, Bolan could see that he was short— five foot seven or eight at the most. But he was almost as broad as he was tall. The huge, powerful shoulders of a lifelong power weight lifter threatened to split the seams of the olive-drab T-shirt he wore. At the angle at which he sat, Bolan couldn't read the words on the front of the T-shirt, but he could see a silk-screened picture of Popeye squeezing open a can of spinach on the front, and note that some kind of caption was printed below the picture.

"Matt," Brognola said, "this sickly-looking little fellow is John Bryant. U.S. Marine Corps. Recon. And again, I can't imagine where in the world the nickname came from but people call him 'Fireplug.'" This brought another low round of laughter from the other men. From where Bolan sat, he could see that Fireplug Bryant's forearms were as big as most men's biceps, and his chest and torso stretched the Popeye shirt's sides as much as his massive shoulders.

Bryant spoke up for himself now. "I'm sure it's an honor to meet you, Mr. Cooper," he said. "Although I don't have any idea who you really are."

"We don't stand on a lot of ceremony around here," Bolan said as he leaned back in his chair and crossed his legs. "Just call me Matt." He clasped his hands together again but rested them on top of his knee this time. "What are your specialties, Fireplug?" he asked.

"Close-quarters combat," Bryant said without hesitation. "With and without weapons."

"That just might come in handy," Bolan said dryly, and his words brought yet another round of soft laughter from the men. Even Brognola chuckled, because the Stony Man director had yet to see the mission in which Bolan didn't get into multiple situations of close-quarters battle. And like Bryant had said, "Both with and without weapons."

Finally, Brognola looked down the table to the man seated next to Spike Nash on his left. "Lastly," the director said, "let me introduce Raymond 'Shooter' Burton of U.S. Navy SEAL Team Six," he said. "The SEAL rep speaks for itself. Now, without further delay, let's get down to business. Here's the skinny."

He went on to reveal in detail what had occurred at the Morales wedding in Mexico: the intrusion of the masked men, the slaughter of the congregation, and the kidnapping of the bride and groom and other members of the wedding party. Then he summed up the intelligence reports given to him by Aaron "the Bear" Kurtzman, Stony Man Farm's wheelchair-bound computer wizard who could hack his way into all the intel-gathering agencies in the United States and abroad. The consensus appeared to be that the long-established Morales Cartel was being challenged by a new group for dominance of the drug-smuggling operations across the U.S.-Mexican border. No one—not the FBI, CIA, DEA or any of the other agencies whose files Kurtzman had cracked seemed to know much about this new group. But all evidence led the computer expert to believe that the newcomers were a serious threat. His bottom-line analysis was that they were a well-organized group of international mercenaries held together by some unknown "tie" or charismatic leader.

In any case, Brognola went on, the violence, as well as deadly drugs, was spilling across the border into Texas, New Mexico, Arizona and California.

"Just yesterday," the Stony Man director said, "the Texas Highway Patrol stopped a large motor home near Odessa. They found several million dollars in cash hidden in secret compartments built into the vehicle. There's evidence that it's tied to the Morales Cartel." He paused a moment to let it all sink in, then went on. "The motor home was purchased from a dealer in New York City—Brooklyn, actually—but it's registered to a José Morales who has residences in both Juarez and El Paso."

He went on to inform the men that although the Texas Rangers and the New Mexico State Police were keeping as careful an eye on the situation as they could, the fact that the problems originated in Mexico made it difficult to launch counteractions against either the Morales family or the new narcoterrorist organization.

"Which is where our Mr. Cooper and the three of you come in," Brognola said. "You'll be working both sides of the line."

"Excuse me," Spike Nash said, "but this sounds like a police action, at least partially inside the United States. Doesn't that violate the Posse Comitatus Act? I mean, using the military in such a role?"

"Not in the least." Brognola smiled. "You had no way of knowing it because you were blindfolded and on your way here this morning. But while you were in the air, each of you was honorably discharged from your respective branches of the service. You're now civilians."

Another silence fell over the three men at the table, and it was obvious to Bolan that they had mixed feelings. He could understand those feelings—he'd had similar ones when he'd left the Army years ago. These were career military men, warriors through and through. The Army, Marines and Navy were their homes. And those homes had suddenly been taken away from them without either their knowledge or consent.

Bolan wasn't the only one to correctly interpret the silence. Brognola caught on to it, too. After a quick glance at the soldier, he turned back to the three men at his end of the table.

"Relax, gentlemen," he said. "As soon as this is over, you'll be reinstated as if this mission had never happened."

Three faces brightened as one.

"Assuming we survive this mission," Bryant said.

"If you don't, you'll be reinstated posthumously," the big Fed said. "And your families will have all the benefits they'd have if you'd died in official action."

"This is funny," Nash said. "Sounds like the Battle of San Jacinto."

The other four heads in the room turned his way. "What do you mean?" Bryant asked.

"Well," said the former West Point military-history professor, and for the first time Bolan noticed a trace of south Texas twang in his speech.

"Right after the Alamo," Nash said, "Andy Jackson stationed roughly two thousand troops up and down the Louisiana-Texas border in case Mexican general Santa Anna got too big for his britches and decided to move his army into the States. A few days before Houston came onto the Mexican president-general at San Jacinto, a couple hundred of Jackson's soldiers took leave. Others just disappeared—went AWOL. And their names—

or sometimes names that looked suspiciously similar to theirs—showed up on Houston's roster, suddenly bolstering his troops." Nash cleared his throat, then finished with "I know it just sounds like a good story. But there's documentation to the fact."

"Sounds like President Jackson's way of aiding the Texicans without having to go to war with Mexico himself," Bryant said.

"Exactly," Nash said. "Jackson had his eye on Texas becoming part of the U.S. all along. And, of course, after a brief and fairly disastrous period of time as an independent nation, we did. Of course, that was part of the reason for the Mexican-American War, which would come—"

Brognola cleared his throat in such a way that it stopped Nash in midsentence.

"Sorry, sir. I really get off on this stuff. Sometimes the old history teacher in me takes over."

"Well," Brognola said, nodding slightly, "maybe we'll have time for more of it at a later date. But right now, we need to concentrate on our *own* Battle of San Jacinto, and make sure it doesn't turn into an Alamo. Because we're pretty much doing the same thing the Americans did when they went to help Houston—taking you guys out of the U.S. armed forces and inserting you in more of an unofficial police action. The only difference is that there're only three of you instead of a whole army." He took the well-chewed cigar from the corner of his mouth and dropped it into the breast pocket of his sport coat.

The rest of the men, including Bolan, nodded in understanding.

Raymond Burton had kept silent during the brief history lesson, but now he spoke up. "So what's the first leg of this action?" he asked.

Bolan stood, closed his file and picked it up, obviously preparing to leave. "Nash and I are going to Mexico by way of El Paso," the soldier said. "Bryant, you and Burton are headed for New York."

The other men in the room got to their feet. "We aren't going to work with you?" Bryant asked, his face revealing slight confusion.

"You're going to work with me, all right," Bolan said. "We just aren't going to be together all the time."

"You got any other ideas on how to get the ball rolling on this?" Bryant asked.

Bolan nodded. "Somehow, someway, we've got to infiltrate this operation on both ends." His eyes shifted from one man to the next until he'd locked gazes with all three special-unit warriors. "Somehow—I don't know exactly how yet—Nash and I are going to have to hook into the Morales Cartel's drug runs heading north." He paused and stared at each man once more. "Bryant, you and Burton need to find a way to ingratiate yourselves with the motor-home dealership in New York. We can stay in touch through this installation."

"What *is* this installation?" Burton asked.

Bolan smiled. "Don't take this as an insult, but that's information that's given out on a need-to-know basis."

"And we don't need to know," Bryant said, sparing Bolan from having to verbalize the rest of his sentiment.

The soldier nodded. Then, with no further words, all the warriors left the War Room.

CHAPTER TWO

The Learjet's wheels hit the tarmac so smoothly Bolan wouldn't have known they had landed had he not been watching through the front window next to Jack Grimaldi in the pilot's seat. For perhaps the thousandth time, the Executioner marveled at the skill of the man flying the plane. His old friend was the finest flyer Bolan had ever known. What the Executioner was to combat, Grimaldi was to air flight.

The small jet rolled to a halt near the private aircraft terminal, and Bolan turned to the pilot. "Thanks, as always, Jack," he said, sticking out his hand.

Grimaldi grasped it for a moment. "Want me to wait here, or go on into Mexico?" he asked.

Bolan thought for a moment. He had considered that question during the flight from Stony Man Farm and there were pros and cons both ways. They had decided to land in El Paso to avoid going through customs in Mexico and taking the chance that their weapons and other gear might be found. A former Stony Man Farm blacksuit had been contacted, and he would provide a car in which they could cross the border as tourists, who were rarely stopped within thirty miles of the border. Airplanes were a different story. They were checked as a matter of course. In the past, it had been easy to pay off Mexican customs officials. But with the constantly escalating violence from the drug cartels in the past few years, such payoffs had become iffy at best. That was for two reasons: first, the Mexican government was trying harder than ever to hire men and women who weren't as susceptible to bribes as they had been in the past. But second, and probably far more relevant to the fact that payoffs could no longer be counted upon to ensure that officials overlooked contraband in airplanes, was the fact that the cartels themselves spread money throughout the customs officials and police so widely that the small amounts offered by regular air visitors to Mexico were no longer needed.

That brought Bolan back to Grimaldi's question. It would be handier to have the Learjet on the other side of the border, where they could get to it quickly, in case they had to make a fast retreat. And if Grimaldi flew over the river alone, they'd have their weapons and other gear in the car. The plane would be clean.

But the aircraft might still get tied up in bureaucratic red tape on the other side, and that could prove as disastrous as getting caught with illegal firearms.

Bolan made his decision as he opened the door at his side. "Stay here in El Paso, Jack," he said. "If it turns out we have to make a hasty retreat, we'll find a way to cross back on our own."

Grimaldi understood the situation and nodded. "It can't be that hard," he said, smiling. "They tell me hundreds, if not thousands, of illegals do it every time the moon comes up in the sky."

Bolan chuckled. "I'll see if we can find a good coyote," he said.

"Don't forget your rookie," Grimaldi said, hooking a thumb at the seats behind them.

Bolan turned to see Nash grinning. The Delta Force commando might not have been a Stony Man regular, but he was far from a beginner at this sort of mission. So instead of letting the good-natured insult anger him, Nash returned one of his own.

"Thanks for the flight, Mr. Jack," he said, using the only name he'd heard Bolan call the pilot during the flight.

Then he turned to the soldier. "You think maybe we could find someone with a little more flight experience next time? The turbulence he led us into was really bad back here."

The soldier in the passenger's seat couldn't help but grin. Next to Nash, on the unoccupied seat directly behind him, he could see the black blindfold the man had worn during takeoff and across two states before Bolan determined he couldn't possibly pinpoint the location of the Farm and allowed him to take it off.

"I'll see what I can do about that," he said.

"Get out of my airplane, both of you," Grimaldi growled in mock anger. "And when you come back, running for your lives, remember who it is who'll get your butts out of danger just in the nick of time."

Both Bolan and Spike Nash were chuckling as they left the plane.

As his feet hit the tarmac, the Executioner heard the sound of a well-tuned engine coming toward the Learjet from the terminal area. He turned in time to see a nearly new black Buick Enclave slowing to a halt twenty feet away. A moment later, a vaguely familiar face wearing black jeans, a black Western shirt with white pearl snaps, a white cowboy hat and the small star of a Texas Ranger pinned to his shirt stepped out. A wide smile covered the Ranger's face as he strode forward with the slightly bow-legged gait of a man who had spent as much time on horseback as in a car.

As the Ranger neared, Bolan noted that he wore his SIG/Sauer pistol on a separate gun belt from the one threaded through the loops on his jeans. But both belts were secured with the silver-and-gold three-piece Ranger buckles made by prisoners within the Texas Department of Corrections.

Some traditions die hard, Bolan thought, and those among the Texas Rangers would live far longer than most. The man in black also wore a nickel-plated, gold-engraved Government Model 1911 .45 pistol. The grips were of white ivory, and both the white slabs and shiny silver steel reflected the hot rays of the Texas–Mexico-border sun.

"Doug Walker," the man in the cowboy hat said as he stuck out his hand to greet Bolan. "You might not remember. You taught a course in point-shooting when I was…well, *wherever* that was where we were trained."

Bolan shook his hand and nodded.

"Wait a minute," Nash said. "What did you say your name was?"

"Doug Walker," the man repeated as he dropped Bolan's hand and reached for Nash's.

"You've got to be kidding," Nash said. "Ranger *Walker?*"

"That's right," Walker stated. "And no matter what you say next, I've heard it before."

Nash pumped the man's hand up and down. "Well," he said. "The eyes of the Ranger truly are upon us."

"That's probably the one I hear the most," Walker said dryly.

"This our vehicle?" Bolan said, anxious to get back to business.

"It is indeed," Walker replied. "Fully equipped with GPS, a rearview-mirror camera and pretty much automatic everything. We've used it as an undercover vehicle several times. If anyone runs the license plate, it'll come back as registered to a fictitious little old lady in Midland."

"How'd you talk your captain out of that?" Bolan asked.

"I didn't," said Walker. "Sometimes, I've found, it's better to ask forgiveness rather than permission. And considering the fact that the training you guys gave me has kept me alive more than once, I figure you're worth the best. And worth taking the chance of getting some minor disciplinary action if we get caught."

"We'll do our best to get it back to you in one piece," Bolan said.

"Great," Walker replied. "Now, if you could give me a lift back to the parking lot on the other side of the terminal, my partner's waiting for me."

Bolan opened the side storage compartment on the Learjet, and he and Nash began hauling out black ballistic nylon bags and rifle cases and shoving them into the rear of the Enclave. Without needing to be asked, Walker joined them. He lifted a short, almost triangular case that had obviously been made for a submachine gun or folding-stock assault rifle. It also had pockets on the outside that had been devised to carry extra rifle magazines.

Looking down at it, he said, "You guys are crossing over, I take it?"

Bolan had just shoved a similar case into the automobile. "You were trained by us," he said as politely as possible. "So you know, the less you know the better."

Walker nodded. "I understand. I've crossed over armed myself. Dragged a couple of bad hombres back across the river by the light of the moon a time or two. All I'm saying is be careful." He paused behind the Enclave, the black case still in his arms. "In light of all that's going on these days, the Mexican police are shooting first and asking questions later—if ever." Stepping forward, he ducked under the overhead door and dropped the rifle case next to the one Bolan had just loaded.

Nash had hauled a long heavy duffel back to the Buick, and now he shoved it in on top of the rifle cases. "I've been on an op or two in Mexico myself," he said as he stepped back. "I've never known the Mexican cops—*federales, rurales,* customs, or whatever, to handle things any other way than to shoot first." His eyes fell to the fancy .45 in Walker's belt. "And they're the only folks in the world besides you guys who dress their guns up like a rich kid's birthday cake."

Walker laughed out loud. "You're just jealous. We've got style."

"You do have that," Nash said.

When the bags had all been loaded, Ranger Doug Walker handed the soldier the keys to the vehicle. Bolan slid behind the wheel, Nash took the shotgun seat and Walker got into the back. A few minutes later, they were saying goodbye to the Stony-Man-Farm-trained man wearing the five-point star on his chest.

"Like I said, you guys be careful." The Ranger had a genuinely worried look on his face.

Bolan just nodded. He wished there was something he could say to put the man's mind at ease, but there wasn't. They were heading into a world where death could come at the drop of a Texas Ranger's cowboy hat. And he knew Walker's concern was genuine. The men who trained at Stony Man Farm returned to their home agencies when the classes concluded or at the end of their rotation, but they developed a bond. They were all like brothers, and they worried about each other like the family that they were.

After one last handshake with both men, Walker turned and strode toward a dark green Chevy sedan that had its engine running. Behind the wheel sat another man in a white cowboy hat, a slightly confused expression on his face.

Bolan knew that meant he hadn't been a blacksuit trainee, and, therefore, Walker was leaving him in the dark as to what all this was about.

But that was the way it had to be with a top-secret

operation like Stony Man Farm. Sometimes feelings got hurt.

Tough, Bolan thought.

Then, throwing the Enclave into Drive, he glanced at Spike Nash. "Let's go to Mexico," he said.

THE DRIVE INTO JUAREZ from El Paso was as easy as it had ever been, with the impoverished nation wanting, and depending, on gringo dollars in order that the rich might get richer and the poor might stay one tortilla ahead of starvation. Bolan had set the GPS feature in the Enclave to guide them to the church where the Morales massacre had taken place, and now he followed the directions through the streets of the border town.

Soon, they had left the tourist area, then passed through a section of the city where the buildings were crumbling and barefoot children with worn clothing played in the streets with sticks and empty tin cans. From there, they entered a suddenly prosperous neighborhood. Bolan was directed through a complex series of twists and turns, then the vehicle arrived at an elaborate church.

They weren't the only visitors.

A man wearing the uniform and shoulder bars of a Mexican *federale* captain walked toward their car as soon as Bolan had pulled to a halt along the curb. As he strode importantly toward them, he made circles with his hand in front of him, using the age-old hand gesture for them to roll down the window.

Nash was closer to him and he pushed the button, lowering the glass.

The captain, a small man with gray hair sticking out of the sides of his cap, looked to be in his late fifties or early sixties. But he was trim and appeared to have kept himself in good shape. Dark, muscular forearms extended from his short-sleeved khaki uniform shirt as he walked toward them, and his balance was good. Around his waist was a basket-weave belt carrying a military flap holster that hid the grips of whatever handgun he carried. The stainless-steel snap that secured the flap to the rest of the holster gleamed in the sunlight.

As he neared, Bolan, who was bending in front of the wheel to see through the window on Nash's side of the car, noted the name tag opposite the badge on the captain's chest. Garcia, it read.

When Captain Garcia finally reached the Enclave, he bent and looked across the seat to Bolan. "Gringos," he said, his tone reflecting minor frustration. He shook his head and closed his eyes. "I might have known."

Bolan and Nash remained silent.

When Garcia opened his eyes again, he said, "I suppose you are writers. Journalists, no doubt."

That story sounded as good as any to Bolan. He nodded.

"So," the captain said. "You have come to Juarez to capitalize on the misfortunes of the Mexican people who were massacred in this sacred place. You will write stories about our barbaric culture, making money for yourselves and at the same time assuring that the tourist trade is scared away and takes money out of our pockets."

Bolan was still hunched in front of the steering wheel. "No, *señor*," he said, shaking his head. "True, we'll be paid for the articles we write, but not as much as you might think. And we look at the situation differently than the way you stated it. We consider it our duty to inform *norteamericanos* of the dangers they face regardless of where they go."

Bolan had watched the captain's face intently when he spoke, and had seen the man's eyes flicker, then soften slightly when he used the word *"norteamericano"* instead of just American. In truth, Mexicans and Canadians both were part of the North American continent, and many found it arrogant on the part of the United States when they were referred to as the only "Americans."

It was funny, Bolan thought, how the little things sometimes became the determining factor as to whether he received the cooperation from the officials with whom he dealt to successfully carry out a mission.

Garcia sighed. "I will have to see some identification," he said.

Bolan carried a variety of false IDs whenever it was practical, and he had his Associated Press credentials with him. But he had not foreseen a need to present them on this leg of the operation, and they were still packed in one of the black nylon duffel bags with his clothing, in the rear of the Enclave—right alongside rifles, machine guns, pistols, ammunition and other weapons.

So how was he supposed to get the proper ID without Garcia seeing the rest of the "luggage" he was carrying? The Enclave's windows were tinted, so the shapes of the gun cases weren't visible from outside the vehicle. But the captain would surely walk to the back of the automobile with Bolan when the soldier went to get the black leather case in which they were kept.

As soon as the rear door swung upward, the weapons cases would be visible, and they bore no resemblance to luggage in which a man might pack his clothes.

Nash glanced at Bolan. He didn't know about the Associated Press credentials, but he could tell by the atmosphere that had suddenly changed inside the vehicle that a serious problem had just arisen.

"Of course, Captain," Bolan said. "I'll have to get my press ID from the rear of the car."

Garcia nodded, then stood up, his face no longer visible. But what Bolan still could see was the man already moving to the rear of the vehicle as the soldier got out.

An idea suddenly struck Bolan as he went to join Garcia. It was risky, but it was the only thing he could think of that might work. It was based on the old, tried-and-sometimes-true criminal technique of admitting to some minor crime in order to get the authorities' minds off a major one of which you were guilty. So as soon as he reached the rear bumper, Bolan tightened his facial muscles, causing blood to rush into the skin and creating the illusion that he was embarrassed.

"There is something I should tell you, Captain," he said quietly.

Garcia frowned.

"The bag that has my credentials contains a small amount of...well, something that comes from your country but is frowned upon."

For a moment, Garcia looked confused, then it hit him. He shook his head in disgust. "Marijuana," he said through clenched teeth. "You writers. Especially you *norteamericano* writers. You are all alike."

"It is only a small amount," Bolan told him. "Far less than an ounce. Just for our own personal use."

"You are indeed fools," the *federale* captain said. "What kind of man brings marijuana *into* Mexico? It is like taking your own snow to Switzerland."

Bolan affected a short, embarrassed laugh. He reached into his pocket, pulled off two one-hundred-dollar bills from the roll he had there—he didn't want Garcia seeing how much he had. Looking around to make sure no one else was watching, he pushed the money toward the captain. "I know it's not much but it's all we can afford," he said in a whisper again. "Could I convince you to look the other way while I get my identification?"

Garcia snatched the bills from his hand and stuffed them quickly into the shirt pocket just above his name tag. Then he turned and faced the church again.

As quickly as he could, Bolan reached under the door handle, pressed the opening button and waited while the rear door of the Enclave rose automatically. As he had pondered earlier, bribery was no longer a certain thing in Mexico with the cartels spreading money around as if it were peanuts. But that didn't mean it *never* worked anymore. A few years ago, five or ten dollars would have certainly convinced Garcia to ignore a small amount of marijuana. Now, the price had been two hundred.

A moment later, Bolan had retrieved his press credentials and the door was lowering of its own accord again. Garcia heard the noise and turned back. He glanced only briefly at the card with the soldier's picture on it, then said, "You have bought yourself thirty minutes inside the church. Do not touch anything. If you become a problem of any sort, I will arrest you and you will learn that all the horror stories you have heard about Mexican prisons are true." For emphasis on his last statement, he reached down to his side and pulled the flap at the top of his holster away from the stud holding it in place, then lifted it above the butt of the gun.

Bolan thought back to what Nash had said about the fancy guns carried by the Texas Rangers and Mexican cops who could afford them. He'd been right. The .45 pistol in the *federale*'s holster was gold-plated with silver, floral-scrolled grips.

In the "fancy" department, it put Ranger Doug Walker's weapon to shame.

"Thank you," Bolan said. "For everything."

Garcia resnapped the flap at the top of his holster and Bolan heard it click into place. The *federale*'s face reflected the fact that he was being thanked not only for access to the church but also for not arresting them for possession of marijuana. And although he had known it for years, Bolan was reminded that not all threats in the type of missions he undertook came from the barrels of guns, the edges and points of knives, or the shrapnel of bombs and grenades. Just as often he was in danger of finding himself arrested and imprisoned. And in Third World countries, where civil rights were nearly nonexistent, that could mean rotting away for months, years, or the rest of your life without anyone ever knowing where you were.

True, had Garcia refused the money and seen the weapons in the back of the Enclave, Bolan could have probably shot him with the sound-suppressed Beretta beneath his light jacket and driven away before the other *federales* on the church grounds even realized what had happened. But that would have violated the soldier's code of never shooting honest cops—not that a man who could be bribed to ignore illegal drug possession was completely honest. But compared to many of his comrades south of the U.S. border, Garcia was relatively clean.

A moment later Nash, who had turned in his seat to watch the events transpiring at the rear of the Enclave, got out of the car. And a moment after that, Garcia was leading the two men into the church.

LIKE MANY Mexican buildings, the church wasn't air-conditioned. It had been built with ventilation in mind, though, and soft breezes occasionally drifted through the windows and into the shaded nave. Bolan and Nash walked slowly and respectfully into the building, stopping just inside the doors.

Blood was everywhere.

By now, of course, it had dried and taken on an almost black hue. Pools and splotches of what had once been crimson spotted the floor of the aisles that led to the front of the church and the altar. More dark stains had fallen on the tops and seats of the pews themselves, with much of it dripping down the backs to dry in long irregular V-shaped lines.

Bolan glanced around. Several men wearing lab coats

were working between the pews, scraping flecks of the dried blood off the aged wood into plastic evidence bags. The evidence would be tested for blood types, Bolan assumed. Then, if the *federales* had the time, means and inclination, DNA samples might even be matched to the victims whose bodies had obviously been carried out of the building before he and Nash arrived.

Not that the matches were needed to identify the corpses—after all, the bodies themselves were already in a Mexican police morgue. But in the U.S. such practices would be routine, just in case some "surprises" were encountered during the course of the investigation and such matches came in handy. Again, however, in Mexico that wasn't always the case.

Bolan reminded himself that the law-enforcement attitude in this country was somewhat different toward violence between criminal competitors—be they drug cartels or other miscreant organizations—than it was back home. Here, only a scant few miles from the U.S. border, the police looked at such gang wars as beneficial. They viewed them as one evil killing the other off. In the United States, cops rarely lost much sleep when criminals killed other criminals, either. But their view was that it provided not only the deaths of evil men on one side but an opportunity to arrest and convict those who had perpetrated the killings as well.

In essence, it provided for the killing of two birds with one stone.

Followed by Nash, Bolan started slowly down the aisle in front of him, careful to step over and around the dried blood at his feet. In his chest, he felt the slow burn of righteous anger building as he passed not only blood on the sides of the pews, but, here and there, bits of human flesh, brain tissue and other substances that had once been part of human beings. The Morales family, he knew, had the largest drug smuggling operation in Mexico. But not every member of the Morales family was involved in the illegal and immoral trade. And there were sure to have been some innocent men and women attending the wedding who had died to pay for their less reputable brothers' sins.

Reaching the front row of pews, Bolan stopped and looked up at the pulpit. Even there, dried blood covered ninety percent of the front of the wooden podium. But what made his anger rise even further was behind the pulpit, above the choir loft. As he mounted the three steps to the platform, the soldier stared at the life-size crucifix mounted on the wall. It had been carefully carved out of wood, and as he stared at the anguished face hanging from the cross, he saw the letters *INRI* just above the crown of thorns.

Blood had run down from his hands, wrists and feet when Jesus had been nailed to the cross over two thousand years ago. And more blood and water had come out when the Roman centurion thrust his spear into Christ's side. But now, the blood from other people— killed within the last twenty-four hours instead of twenty centuries earlier—also stained the smoothly polished wood, looking as if it had come from Jesus himself.

The ironic blasphemy of a mass murder being committed in this place of worship—a place that honored a man who had been sent to earth to bring peace to hu-

mankind, and was even called the Prince of Peace—
was hardly lost on Bolan. It also reminded him of why
he had been put on this planet.

Bolan's mission in life was to bring as much justice
to the world as he could before he, too, was killed. He
had never lied to himself about how he would meet his
end. Sooner or later, the inevitable would happen and
he would be murdered by the same type of evil men
against whom he fought.

A noise from behind him broke into Bolan's thoughts,
and he turned.

"The animals who did this," Nash said softly, "deserve to die slowly on a cross themselves."

Bolan nodded. Then, turning to face his new partner, he said, "But I suspect we'll have to settle for just
shooting them."

Nash nodded. "Darn shame," he whispered. "But
we'll do just that."

As the soldier nodded again, he felt as if a searing-
hot branding iron had crossed over his right shoulder.
Then the roar of a large-caliber pistol round exploded
from the back of the church.

As he whirled to face the unexpected threat, Bolan's
hand went instinctively inside his jacket to the butt of
the Beretta 93-R. But as his eyes scoured the direction
from which the shot had come, he saw no one. So, thinking that automatically reaching under his jacket might
already have proved to any watching eyes that his "journalist cover" was just that, he dropped his hand to his
side rather than draw his weapon.

Bolan now turned to look down at his right shoulder.

The material from the safari vest he'd worn as part of the photojournalist cover had been ripped away as the bullet screamed past his flesh, just above the skin. The area over which it had passed was hot and felt like an extreme sunburn, but no blood had been spilled.

Leading Nash back up the aisle to the vestibule, Bolan was stopped by Captain Garcia.

"What was that shot?" the *federale* demanded to know.

Bolan shrugged. "I don't know. I was hoping you could tell us."

"Did *you* fire it?" Garcia pressed. "Perhaps I should search you."

The soldier tapped the ripped and torn fabric atop his right shoulder with his left hand. "Do you really think I'd shoot at myself, Captain?" he asked. "And even if I did, do you think I'd miss myself so miserably at the range I'd be shooting at?"

Garcia scowled, but he didn't reply.

"If you've got no further questions," Bolan said, "we've got a story to write." He stepped to the captain's side and started to walk past the man.

Garcia reached out and pressed a hand against the American's chest, stopping him. Bolan halted, looking down at the shorter man and meeting his eyes.

"I do not know exactly who you are," Garcia said, "but I think you are more than just a journalist. And I think I do not like you." He paused to catch a breath of air, then finished with, "If I was you, I would be very careful when you are on my side of the border."

"I'm careful on both sides," Bolan said, then stepped

forward again, watching the *federale*'s outstretched hand fall away as he moved. But the hand wasn't what caught his attention as he looked down. Earlier, Garcia had unsnapped the flap on his holster in order to give Bolan and Nash a dramatic view of his gold-plated .45. But then, the soldier hadn't only watched the captain refasten the flap, he had heard it snap back into place.

Now, however, as Bolan glanced down, he saw that the snap was undone once more.

LOHMAN'S RECREATIONAL and Off-Road Vehicles read the flashing neon sign as John "Fireplug" Bryant and Raymond "Shooter" Burton pulled the rented Mercedes off the thoroughfare onto the access road in Brooklyn, New York. They had been flown to New York by a man wearing an old and worn California Angels baseball cap. Not that they had known that at first. Blindfolded once more, men whom Bryant had noticed were called blacksuits had led them out of the meeting room where they'd met Matt Cooper, then onto the Learjet. The blacksuits had stayed with them during the flight, making sure their blindfolds remained in place until the pilot had, once again, performed so many aerial maneuvers that they'd never be able to pinpoint exactly where the secret installation they'd just left was located. Then, finally, the blindfolds had been allowed to come off.

At first, Bryant had resented the secrecy and all the rest of the clandestine protocol, especially the blindfolds themselves. It had seemed to him that if these mysterious people they were working for didn't trust them, they shouldn't have asked for their help in the first place.

Then, with plenty of time on his hands to think, and no distractions due to the black cloth wrapped tightly around his eyes, the U.S. Recon Marine had begun to look at the situation a little differently.

As a special forces soldier within the U.S. Marine Corps, which was actually a special forces unit in and of itself, Bryant was used to need-to-know policies, and such protocol had little to nothing to do with trust. The fact was that warriors—regardless of who they worked for—were human, and it took only one careless word to a wife, girlfriend, or over a beer in the local tavern, to make an op go south in a flash. And that not only meant failure for the mission, it meant getting good people killed. There was another reason for secrecy, and it had to do with warriors being human, as well—no matter how tough they were.

All men had their breaking point. And if they were captured by the enemy, most of the United States' foes went far beyond water boarding in their interrogation. Eventually, torturers found their captives' weak spots and once they did, they zeroed in and capitalized on them. This meant that sooner or later, the victims of torture began giving up everything they knew.

So it was important that they knew as little as possible.

Bryant glanced to Burton behind the wheel of the luxury automobile. The Navy SEAL had stopped, waiting to make a left turn into Lohman's, but was delayed by a string of Harley-Davidson motorcycles roaring past them in the opposite lane. The men riding the Harleys were hard-looking characters, and all wore the same dirty and weather-beaten leather vests with a variety of outlaw-biker patches on the front. Most were bearded in one way or another, and many had shaved heads or extra-long hair that blew behind them in the wind as they passed. They paid little attention to the two elite warriors whose delay they were affecting, seeming to be far more interested in the motor homes and other vehicles covering Lohman's lot.

Bryant twisted in his seat to get a look at the backs of their black leather vests. Above a highly stylized Tasmanian devil riding a motorcycle in the middle of each back, he saw the top rocker bearing the gang's name: Wildmen. The bottom rocker read simply Brooklyn. Bryant guessed their number to be close to fifty.

As soon as they'd passed, Burton completed his left turn before pulling up to the glass front of the dealership. Before he had even stopped, a group of men—all dressed in bright red polo shirts bearing the Lohman's logo—were jockeying for position to be the first to reach their car and greet them.

Bryant couldn't suppress the grin that spread across his broad face. "Hey, Shooter," he said. "You think they'd be as anxious to help us if we'd driven up in a Volkswagen?"

"I doubt it," Burton said, playing a quick drum solo on the Mercedes's steering wheel with the fingers of both hands. "These guys remind me of my bird dog. The only difference is they smell money and my dog sniffs out quail."

The first man in a red shirt to reach the Mercedes looked to be in his early sixties. He was of slender build, had a seventies-style haircut that fell over his ears and the back of his polo-shirt collar and was brown tinged with gray. Thick, steel-rimmed eyeglasses rested atop his nose.

The embroidered name tag opposite the logo on his chest read Howard.

"Remember what we've got to do," Bryant whispered just before Howard reached the Mercedes. "We've got to subtly convey the idea that we're looking for a motor home to smuggle contraband in but that we aren't very experienced at it, and could use help. But we can't go too far. We don't want to come off as looking so amateurish that these guys are afraid we'll fumble the ball."

"It's a fine line we're walking," Burton agreed.

Howard's arrival on Burton's side of the car ended the conversation. The salesman opened the SEAL's door for him, then reached in to grab Burton's elbow and helped him out.

"Welcome to Lohman's," Howard said with the smile of the career-professional salesman.

Bryant grinned again as he watched the expression on his partner's face change quickly from blank to angry. Burton obviously didn't like the salesman touching him, and he reached over, placed a hand over the fingers on his opposite elbow, twisted slightly and pulled it off.

Bryant did his best to keep from laughing out loud. It was a basic ju-jitsu technique that all soldiers—elite or otherwise—learned in boot camp. But Shooter Burton had followed it only part of the way, stopping just short of breaking the man's wrist. But he'd inflicted enough pain for Howard to get the message that he didn't like being pawed.

And, just as they'd spoken of doing a few seconds earlier, he'd sent out the message that he was no stranger to pragmatic close-quarters combat.

The salesman's hand withdrew and he stepped back, rubbing his wrist, but a little pain wasn't going to get in the way of a big commission. People in Howard's line of work were trained to handle most situations. They would swallow insults if that's what it took to make a sale. They were also amateur psychologists, and they picked up very quickly on who to pressure and who would respond better to a soft sell.

Burton's wristlock had helped the man make up his mind even quicker than most. As he continued to gently rub his wrist, his huge toothy smile beamed again. "My name's Howard, and I'm here to serve you. What can I do first for you gentlemen?"

By now, Bryant had squeezed his bulky frame out of the passenger's side of the Mercedes and walked around the hood to join them. He glanced again at Burton, who still looked as if he wanted to tear the hand that had touched him off Howard's arm.

Bryant decided it might be wise if he took the lead. "We're looking for a new motor home," he said.

"Super," Howard said. By now the pain in his wrist had to have been gone, because his phony salesman smile grew even larger, seeming to encompass his entire head rather than just his face. "I've got a bunch I can show you." He waved a hand dramatically toward a

virtual sea of recreational vehicles in the lot just to the
side of the office building.

Both Bryant's and Burton's eyes followed his hand.
There had to be at least six acres of motor homes sitting in the parking lot. Behind them, Bryant could see
the off-road vehicles the Lohman's sign had also advertised. Jeeps, three-wheelers, four-wheelers and other
rough-terrain means of transportation covered another
two acres. There were even several Jet Skis and other
personal watercraft ready to be sold.

Howard knew his business and had followed his cus-
tomers' line of sight. "I'm assuming you two are talking
about land vehicles?" he said.

"We are," Burton said. He looked to Bryant now as
if he was over the anger he'd experienced when Howard grabbed his elbow earlier. At least his voice was
smoother. Even friendly.

Yet again, Bryant was tempted to smile. Before yesterday, he had never met either Navy SEAL Raymond
"Shooter" Burton or Richard "Spike" Nash—the Delta
Force operative who had gone off to work with Matt
Cooper. But even during that brief time, he had learned
a lot of things about the other two men. The usual rival-
ries that existed between each man's respective group of
select warriors had vanished almost immediately due to
the blindfolds and other secretive aspects of their assignment. And while they knew in their hearts that Cooper
and whoever the rest of the people they were working
with were on the side of America, the Recon Marine,
Navy SEAL and Delta Force commando had bonded
almost as if they were already facing a common enemy.

Bryant had learned a few specific things about Burton and Nash, as well, and one of the things he'd learned about Shooter was that the man didn't like pushy people. And having his elbow grabbed to help him out of the Mercedes as if he was a ninety-year-old woman who couldn't get out herself undoubtedly fell under the SEAL's definition of "pushy."

"All right," Howard said. "How large a vehicle are you looking for?"

"We aren't sure yet," Burton said. "We need to take a look around."

Howard's smile was still glued to his face, making the corners of his mouth curl up at a most unnatural angle. "I can save you some time if I ask you a few questions first," he said in a forced-genial tone of voice. "Are you gentlemen planning to buy this together?"

"Yeah," Bryant said. "Thought we'd go half and half."

"Are you going to take turns using it, or do you plan to use it together?" Howard asked.

Bryant looked quickly to Burton. "We might take some individual trips sometimes," he said. "But we'll be going together most of the time, I suspect."

Howard's smile faded slightly for a moment, then flashed back into place. "Just the two of you?"

Both men exchanged glances, then smiled and chuckled softly.

"I think you might be getting the wrong idea," Burton finally said. "We're talking about our families taking trips together."

"Families that include *wives,*" Fireplug said. "Of the female kind."

Howard's phony smile disappeared altogether now and his face turned bright scarlet. "Oh…well…I didn't mean to imply—"

Bryant cut him off with a wave of the hand. "Forget it, Howard," he said. Then, turning back to Burton, he added, "Although he *is* kind of cute…"

Burton laughed, and Bryant joined him. Finally, a very confused Howard felt that joining in the laughter was the appropriate thing to do and wouldn't adversely affect his commission.

Forcing the smile back onto his face, he shook his head and said, "You guys are characters." Then, after a short pause during which he stared into both of the other men's eyes trying to read their reactions, he decided it was safe to go on. "But now we're getting someplace. Tell me, besides your wives, you have children who'll be going with you?"

"We do," Burton said while his partner nodded.

"How many kids do you have?"

Bryant thought a moment. He and Burton needed to see the largest motor homes the dealership had available. So he said, "Six kids—"

Even after the wristlock, Howard had been using his friendliest tone of voice in an attempt to create some kind of trust or bond; something warriors such as Bryant and Burton simply couldn't understand. Bonds for them came through risking their lives together and covering each other's backs.

But now the Recon Marine decided to return the favor and spoke again. "An even half-dozen children, Howard," he said softly.

"Big family," Howard said. Then he swung his eyes to Burton. He didn't have to ask.

"Just two," Burton said.

"That's still an even dozen people if both families travel together," the salesman stated. "I think we better look at the largest vehicles possible."

"I'd think so," Bryant said. "The kids are going to get on each other's nerves—and ours—any way you look at it."

"So why don't you follow me," Howard said, turning.

CHAPTER THREE

Mack Bolan and Spike Nash left the church and returned to the Enclave. As he slid behind the wheel, the soldier's mind was still focused on the unsnapped flap holster that hung from Captain Garcia's belt. It could mean only one of two things.

Garcia had either fired the shot that almost took off Bolan's head, or he had reacted to that shot, unsnapping the flap in order to access his firearm in response to the threat, then forgetting to resnap it.

Which was it? The soldier didn't know, but Garcia had already proved he could be bought when he'd ignored the marijuana Bolan supposedly had in the rear of the Enclave. Of course, it was a big step from cutting someone a break on a minor violation like that to attempted murder. And there was also the fact that the shot had to have come from the front of the church— close to where Garcia had been. It didn't seem likely that someone could have fired at them without Garcia pinpointing who it had been.

Which brought up another possibility: another would-be assassin could have fired the shot and Garcia could have ignored it, just as he had the imaginary marijuana that he'd thought was real.

Bolan wished he could have examined the gold-plated

.45 the captain had hidden beneath the leather flap. If Garcia had been the person trying to kill him, the gun would smell of burned gunpowder. But asking to look at the weapon would have been the very definition of awkward, and the soldier wasn't sure just how that could be done. It wasn't as if he could walk up to the man and say, "Excuse me, Captain, but would you let me smell your gun to see if you were the person who just tried to kill me?"

He started the Enclave's engine but left the vehicle in Park for the time being. In addition to brown hiking boots and faded blue jeans, he wore a white T-shirt beneath his now-damaged safari vest. From one of the garment's multiple pockets he produced a satellite phone, turned it on and tapped in the number to Barbara Price's direct line at Stony Man Farm. As always, he activated the built-in scrambling feature that would make it impossible for anyone to understand the conversation about to go up into space and then back again, even if they did happen to have located the correct frequency.

Bolan waited while the call bounced off several satellites and four cutouts to further cover its tracks. Then Price, Stony Man's mission controller, finally answered. "Hello, how can I help you?"

"Bring peace and harmony to the world," Bolan said with a slight chuckle.

"Hi, Striker. We keep trying," Price said. "But you've got a whole lot more bad guys to kill before we're even going to get close to achieving such nirvana."

"I'm doing my best," Bolan replied.

"You always do," Price said. "So what kind of *specific* help can I give you?"

"We've kind of run into a dead end for the moment. The church is one bloody mess, and I don't mean 'bloody' in the sense the Brits use the word. We also got shot at while we were in the church."

There was a moment of silence from the other end of the line, then Price said, "Do you know who the shooters were?"

"Shooter, singular. Just one shot. I've got my suspicions, but I can't be sure." He quickly told her about Captain Garcia.

"I can see how it could go either way," Price said.

"That's the problem. He either tried to kill me or he tried to stop someone from killing me."

"Big difference," Price said.

"As big as they get," Bolan replied. "In any case, ask Bear to hack into the *federale* files and see what he can come up with on Garcia."

"Our numero uno computer wizard is in the Annex right now," Price said. "Do you want to talk to him?"

"That won't be necessary," Bolan said. "Just tell him what happened. He'll know what to do."

"Affirmative, Striker," the mission controller said. "Anything else?"

"Yeah," Bolan said. Unconsciously, he reached up with his free hand and felt the mutilated epaulet on his shoulder. "Like I said, we've run into a dead end for the moment. Bear was also supposed to get me a list of addresses for the Morales family. That's as good a place as any to restart."

"I've got those addresses right here," Price said. "How many you want? It's a big family."

"Aaron was going to list them in order of probable priorities," he said. "In descending order of suspected drug activity. So just give me the first one for starters."

Another moment of silence came over the airwaves. Then Bolan heard Price tapping keys. A few seconds later, she gave him an address in one of the few wealthy neighborhoods in Juarez.

"Is there a specific name that goes with that address?" Bolan queried.

"Just Morales," Price replied. "You know how it goes when the Bear had to hack into the other agencies. Their intel isn't always as complete as we'd like. Anything else I can do for you?"

"Not for the moment. You heard anything from Burton and Bryant?"

"They're at the motor-home lot, Lohman's, looking at motor homes and dropping subtle hints that the story about their two families vacationing together is phony. So far they haven't come up with anything useful."

"Stay on them, Barb," Bolan said. "They're good men, but they don't fully understand the 'ropes' of the Farm yet."

"Will do, Striker."

"Striker out," Bolan said and disconnected the call. He entered data into the GPS, threw the Enclave into Drive and pulled away from the church.

Spike Nash had remained quiet during the phone conversation between Bolan and Price. He broke that silence by saying, "I take it we're going to the address you just entered."

"You take it right," Bolan replied.

"Any idea what we might be getting ready to face?"

Bolan turned to glance at the Delta Force veteran as the vehicle pulled in to traffic. He found himself behind a dilapidated pickup loaded with cages of live chickens.

"Well, Spike," the soldier said, "we're going to an address that belongs to a member of the biggest drug cartel in the world. What would you guess we'd be about to face?"

Nash nodded. "I guess I'd better double-check my weapons," he said.

"Yeah," Bolan agreed. "I guess you better had."

RAYMOND BURTON HAD BEGUN to think that if he had to look at one more motor home he'd scream and pull his hair out by the roots.

One of the things SEAL training had taught him was patience. But Howard's ongoing efforts to point out all the advantages of every single motor home on the Lohman's lot was straining the man to the max. What was particularly irritating to Burton was that the salesman stressed how secure the motor homes were.

Burton hadn't seen a lock on any of them that he didn't know he could open inside ten seconds using the plastic toothpick from a Swiss Army knife. He suspected Bryant possessed the same ability. He glanced to the wide-shouldered man who had become his new partner. And if Bryant couldn't pick the lock, Burton had no doubt he could just reach out and rip the door off its hinge.

The SEAL drew in a deep breath, letting it out slowly, careful not to let Howard see his impatience. The emphasis Howard was placing on security, however, was partially his and Bryant's own fault. They had been playing psychological games with Howard for almost an hour now. The minute they'd stepped aboard the first motor home, they'd started awkwardly asking questions about storage space. Then, gradually, it had been them who shifted the subject toward security, telling Howard that they were concerned with someone breaking in when they were camped somewhere but had gone off on a day hike or were otherwise away from the motor home itself.

"Like, what if we all want to go swimming at the lake or something?" Bryant had asked. "I'm worried about my watch, my wife's jewelry, stuff like that locked up inside."

Which had immediately launched Howard into his well-memorized and rehearsed—and monotonous—rambling about the locking systems and how secure the locks actually were. There were even loud sound alarms that could be added—for a price, of course—which would immediately alert anyone in the area that foul play was afoot.

Burton had been forced to bite his tongue to keep quiet. He wished he could count all the times he'd walked through a parking lot with a car alarm going off and watched the people walking past consider it little more than a nuisance. Truth be told, the only types of thieves from which these motor homes were even half-protected were the unskilled dope fiends who tended to kick in front doors, grab whatever they could and take off. And even they wouldn't be stopped by such rudimentary locks and alarms.

After a half hour or so of "security talk," Burton had, very subtly once again, turned the topic of conversation from outer locks and alarms to hidden storage inside the motor homes themselves. "I've never owned one of these things before," he'd told Howard. "But it seems to me that in addition to the locks and alarms, the safest way to protect valuables inside would be if they were hidden."

Howard had smiled so widely that Burton was certain the man's face would crack apart. Then he'd showed the men a false back to one of the overhead storage compartments.

Bryant had picked up on Burton's cue immediately, and finally spoken the words that convinced even a dullard like Howard that the two men were looking for a motor home for reasons other than the ones they'd stated.

"Is that the *only* hidden compartment on this thing?" he had asked. "I mean, I know I'd feel better if there was a lot of hidden storage space. For my wife's jewelry and stuff, of course."

Bryant had just turned the key to the lock all undercover operatives do their best to open. He had mentioned his wife's jewelry—an insignificant aspect to the conversation that honest men would never have thought necessary to bring up in the first place—one too many times. He was giving out more information than necessary, which made it look as if he was doing his best to cover up something. And that fact wasn't completely lost on Howard.

"Well, yes, sir," Howard had said with a slight stammer as his brain tried to shift into a different gear and mode of thought. "But there's more than enough room for watches, jewelry, a laptop or two and—"

Burton could see they would have to get even more blatant to complete the illusion that they were smugglers, so he cut the man off in midsentence. "Howard," he said, "can more such hidden places be built in if we wanted them? At an extra cost, of course."

Howard had finally caught on—the two men who had professed to want to take their families on vacation together were up to something illegal. Burton watched the salesman's face. He looked slightly surprised. But he was hardly shocked.

Finally, Howard nodded. "We can customize this baby just about any way you want," he said now, a bit uneasily. "But we're getting out of my field of expertise. Jobs like that have to go through the manager."

"But you've done this kind of work before, right?" Bryant said. "I mean, we don't want people customizing this thing who don't know what they're doing. We want the hidden compartments to be truly hidden." Suddenly, he looked down at the floor as if embarrassed and just realizing he was giving away too much information. When he spoke again, a slight stammer entered his speech. "What I mean is…my wife would have my ass for breakfast if her…jewelry got stolen."

Burton turned completely around, reaching out and turning on the faucet in the sink along the side of the motor home as if to test it. But the real reason he'd turned was to hide the smile he couldn't keep off his face. As far as he was concerned, Fireplug Bryant was turning in a performance worthy of an acting award.

"Why don't we go speak to the manager," Howard said. "I'm sure he can work out a retrofit for you."

Burton turned, forcing a serious expression onto his face. "That sounds like what we pretty much need to do," he said.

Howard, who looked more pale than he had before the conversation had turned to "hiding places" on the motor home and the insinuation of smuggling drugs, weapons or other contraband, reached out and grasped the door handle.

Bryant grabbed the salesman's forearm, which caused Howard to literally jump back.

"Just a minute," Bryant said, his eyebrows lowering on his forehead in concentration.

Howard looked as if he might scream. It was obvious by his behavior that he now knew he was in the presence of a couple of hard-core criminals, and he was scared to death of them. That, in turn, suggested that while Howard was probably not directly involved in the illegal activities for which Lohman's fronted, he at least knew they went on.

"One thing I gotta make clear," Bryant said.

Howard tried to nod, but his head appeared to be frozen atop his neck. He swallowed hard, and the lump that went down his throat looked like a boa constrictor eating a small pig. "Yes?" he finally managed to squeal out.

"I know you guys work on commission," Bryant said.

"And just because this job is getting turned over to your manager, I don't want you losing out on what you've got coming to you."

Burton smiled, reminding himself that Howard wouldn't be so nervous if he wasn't at least aware that the motor-home dealership included criminal activities. So with a slightly perverse pleasure at the knowledge that the salesman would read into his next words exactly what the SEAL wanted him to, he said, "We *always* believe in people getting what's coming to them. Especially those who do a good job and know when to keep their mouths shut about insignificant details that can get distorted and don't help anybody if people talk about them."

Howard nodded.

Burton could tell they'd finally gotten their point across, but Bryant seemed to think he needed to drive one more nail into Howard's psychological coffin.

"What he means here," he said in a voice that no longer held a hint of embarrassment, "is that if you mentioned our interest in hiding places on this thing to anyone, who knows who might get wind of it? Burglars, maybe. Burglars who might even chance to come across us while we're out and about and really steal my wife's jewelry." He paused for dramatic effect.

Howard's eyes had rolled slightly back in his head and he looked as if he might pass out.

"I can't tell you how angry that would make me, Howard," Bryant finally said. He let go of the salesman's arm. But Howard was in no condition to open the door, and Bryant had to reach down and pry the man's fingers off the handle before opening it himself.

The three men stepped down onto the retractable step outside the door, then onto the ground outside the motor home.

"Lead the way, Howard," Burton said to the salesman. Then he and Bryant fell in behind the man as he began the walk back to Lohman's office building on rubbery legs.

DUSK WAS FALLING over Cuidad Juarez. The Executioner steered the Enclave past the guarded gate to Twin Pines, one of Juarez's very few upscale housing communities. The homes that made up the subdivision would have stood out starkly from the poverty-stricken houses in which many of Juarez's citizens dwelled, had the developers not taken great pains to hide the residents' affluence from the common people.

Hence, the ten-foot-tall stucco wall that surrounded Twin Pines.

Bolan kept his eyes on the road, never looking directly toward the guardhouse just outside the entrance, but studying it intensely in his peripheral vision. Also out of the corner of his eye, he saw that Spike Nash was watching, too. But the man's eyes seemed to be fixed on some object farther down the street.

"We're going to have to find another way in," Bolan said as the Enclave drove away and out of sight of the guards and the front gate. We're going to have to run a clandestine recon before we attack—if we attack at all."

"What's the attack depend on?" Nash asked.

"It depends on what we find going on at the address," Bolan said. "According to the intel our computer man got from the DEA, CIA, BATFE and a few other sources, this is the major stopping point for dope going north before it's driven across the border. It's their intel that ours is based on. And they've been known to screw up on occasion."

"So," Nash said, "you're saying we can't trust the other federal law-enforcement agencies a hundred percent?"

Bolan turned to stare into the man's eyes. "Ever hear of Operation Fast and Furious?" he said bluntly.

"Point taken," Nash said. "Say no more."

"I want to check this place out and be certain myself," Bolan told him. "If it looks like it's just some innocent member of the Morales family living there, we're going to let things be and hightail it back out with no one the wiser as to us ever being there."

"But if we spot some criminal activity?" Nash prompted.

"Then we put a stop to it."

Nash nodded again. "Which brings us back to my earlier question. But I can answer that myself now. Whether we sneak in and attack, or just sneak in and then sneak back out, a couple of gringos like us are going to be remembered by the guards. So we've got to find another way in."

Now it was Bolan's turn to nod. He turned right when he came to the end of the stucco wall that hid the fancier homes from potential burglars and home invaders. Following more of the wall along the side of the addition, he glanced at the odometer, then looked back up at the streets that circled the property. The wall was of the common reddish-brown color that was found on most stucco structures. But a lip at the top—hanging a good two feet over the side to discourage anyone who might attempt to scale it—had been painted a light lime green.

Nash had to have been looking at the same thing because he said, "Not sure I've ever seen a more nauseating color combination."

Bolan chuckled. "Good thing we're not here to do a story for *Better Homes and Gardens*," he said.

"In more ways than one," Nash said. To his side, Bolan saw the Delta Force man turn slightly to face him. There was a big grin on Nash's face now. "I'm not sure they bought your journalist story back at the church. *Better Homes and Gardens* or not."

"Nothing ventured nothing gained," Bolan said as he continued to drive and watch the sun set along the horizon. "But you're right. Bad guys—whether they're cops or not—might not particularly like writers. But they rarely try to shoot them in the back."

The Enclave glided around another corner to the rear of Twin Pines and the same reddish-brown stucco wall with the light green overhang continued monotonously. The tedious color scheme of the ten-foot barrier was finally broken by another gate, and another guardhouse. Bolan and Nash kept their eyes straight ahead once more, doing their best not to draw any undue attention from the guards in the guard shack. Finally, the soldier in the driver's seat turned right again and rolled slowly along the last side of the housing addition.

By now, the final remnants of daylight were fading. Bolan glanced at his watch, then pulled the Enclave along the curb, threw it into Park and killed the engine. "We'll give it a few more minutes to get darker," he said. "Then we'll go. The two sides without the gates are our best bets, and this side's as good as the other. Any questions?"

"Affirmative," Nash said. "We going to change into those black stretchy things you showed us earlier? What'd you call them?"

"We just call them blacksuits," he said. "They're designed to fit close so you don't snag things during battle. And they're designed to stretch so you can move. But the answer is no, we're not going to wear them. At least not on this leg of the mission."

"Why not?" asked Nash.

"Because we're going to have to be going down the streets inside the community looking for the right address. And we're bound to get seen in the headlights of cars going down the same streets. I don't want to look like Spider-Man and have someone call the guards or the cops."

Nash unsnapped his seat belt. "So we go in what we have on?"

"Negative," Bolan said. "Like you said, a couple of gringos are going to be remembered and look suspicious on the streets as well as at the guard station." Twisting to reach between the seats to the back of the Enclave, he grasped a medium-size black ballistic nylon satchel and pulled it into the front. Unzipping the top, he pulled out two *guayabaras,* often referred to as "Mexican wedding shirts." One was pale blue in the moonlight. The other was a light yellow.

Bolan tossed the yellow one to Nash.

"I hope this color isn't a subtle reference to my courage," Nash said with a poker face.

Bolan shook his head. "More of a statement as to your size," he said. "It's a 2XL."

The soldier changed into his own shirt. As soon as he had buttoned the front of the ruffled garment, he reached back into the bag and withdrew two pieces of straw, rolled up and secured with a cloth band.

Nash recognized what they were immediately. "Panama hats," he said. "Made in Ecuador. Always wondered about why they got called Panamas." He began unrolling the hat.

"Because when Teddy Roosevelt came back from arranging the Panama Canal agreement he was wearing one," Bolan said as he lifted the band and spread his own hat out. As soon as he did, he slipped the band back over the crown to form the hatband.

"I've always heard these things spring back to their original shape," Nash said. "Is that true?"

"That's how they're advertised," Bolan replied. "I've found that they spring back into some kind of shape. But not always the same. Anyway, we aren't going to walk the runway in a fashion show. We're just going for a stroll through the streets of Twin Pines like a couple of residents out to get a little exercise."

"So," Nash said. "How do we get over the wall?"

"Let me show you." After looking carefully up and down the street to ensure there were no cars coming or eyes watching, Bolan got out of the Enclave and walked to the back. Reaching up and under the handle, he tapped a button and the back door began to rise on its own. As soon it was open, he searched through the conglomeration of equipment bags until he found the one he was looking for. As soon as he had it in his hands, he unzipped it and produced a coil of thick black rope with a grappling hook on the end.

Nash had followed him to the rear of the vehicle. When he saw the grappling hook, he said, "Now I *really* wish we were wearing those blacksuits. And a ninja hood and tabi boots."

Bolan chuckled softly. "The ninja were trained to blend in," he said. "And they did it so well they got the reputation for being invisible. Don't you think tabi boots and hoods might have pretty much the opposite effect in this situation?"

"Yeah," Nash said.

After another glance up and down the street, Bolan led the way to the wall. "Once this hook is set," he said, "we've got to get up and over as fast as we can. Every second we take makes the chances of getting spotted grow more likely." He turned toward Nash. The man had a good suntan, and with the Mexican shirt and straw hat would pass easily as a resident of Twin Pines. "The only hard part is going to be getting over that lime-green overhang you're so crazy about. Once we're at the top, we'll have to swing out on the rope, away from the wall, then grab the top and pull ourselves back and up. Got it?"

"Got it," Nash said. "It's better than if the wall had concertina wire on top of it."

Bolan didn't bother answering. He walked swiftly to the wall with the rope in his left hand then began looping the end with the grappling hook out from the coils. When he had enough line freed to reach the top, the Executioner swung the hook gently forward and backward. One. Two. And on three, he let go of the hook and watched it rise up over the wall and disappear out of sight on the other side.

As soon as he felt the weight of the hook pulling back on his grasp, the soldier began slowly pulling the hook back up the blind side of the wall.

Turning again to Nash, he whispered, "I'm going. When I get to the top, I'll signal you to follow."

Nash nodded.

A split second later Bolan's hiking boots were walking up the side of the wall while the rope strained against the muscles in his shoulders, arms and back. He reached the overhang in seconds. Letting loose of the rope with his right hand, his left shot up and over the lip.

Bolan's hand searched for anything he could grasp in order to pull himself over, but found nothing. The lip at the top of the wall was too wide, and his hand did nothing but slide over the flat top of the barrier.

The soldier pulled his left hand back and grabbed the rope again. The developers of Twin Pines had been serious about keeping the peons out. There was only one other possible way to traverse the wall with the limited equipment he had with him.

Taking a deep breath, Bolan ignored the searing pain

in his right shoulder and arm—the arm he had kept on the rope while he fruitlessly searched for a handhold with his other. What he was about to do would be dangerous. It would mean a second or so in the air, free of the rope or the wall. It would mean taking a tremendous chance of falling backward and landing on the concrete sidewalk ten feet below on his back.

Bolan knew there was nothing to be gained by overthinking the situation. Like all dangerous aspects of all dangerous missions, he calculated the risks, weighed them against the benefits, then made his decision and didn't look back. He either had to go for it or climb back down and try to find another way over, or through, the wall.

He made his decision.

With both boots against the wall, Bolan bent his knees, then, with all the strength in his quadriceps, he pushed off, swinging out as far from the lip as the rope would allow. When he reached the end of the line, he felt it pull him back toward the wall. And he helped it along with every ounce of power still left in his upper body.

Just before he reached the overhang, Bolan gave the rope one last tug, then let loose and dived up and over the green lip. He came down with his chest against the outer edge of the lip and, for a second, felt himself about to be pulled downward by the force of gravity.

But Bolan's arms had stretched out and over the overhang, and his fingers suddenly curled around the far edge of the lip. His feet had swung back under the overhang into the wall, but with one sudden pull he found them flying back outward. And then he had pulled himself up and onto the top of the wall.

For a moment, the soldier lay there, catching his breath. But the moment was brief. He knew the job wasn't even close to being over. The next thing he had to do was get Nash safely up and over the barrier.

Twisting to a kneeling position, Bolan looked down at the man below. Then, double-checking to make sure the grappling hook was securely positioned to the underside of the green overhang inside the wall, he waved to Nash.

Nash waved back, grabbed the rope and began scaling the wall.

A few seconds later, the Delta Force man had made it to the top, just under the lip. Bolan reached down and hauled him up and over the overhang in one swift simple motion.

"I could see what you had to do from the ground," Nash whispered as soon as Bolan let go of him. "It appears to be a lot easier once there's someone on top to help you." He paused, grinning. "You did such a good job, Cooper. I think you should get to go first when we leave here, too."

Bolan smiled but didn't speak. If he had his way, their exit was going to be in a completely different manner.

Switching the grappling hook to the other side of the wall was easy from where they were, and both men climbed down the rope with no trouble. When they'd both reached the grass at the edge of the wall, Nash said, "So what do we do now?"

"Go for an evening walk like any two wealthy Mexicans. Until we find the address we're looking for."

Without further discussion, the two men took off down the street.

CHAPTER FOUR

"I definitely get the feeling he's not part of the criminal end of this op," Shooter Burton whispered to Fireplug Bryant. The two elite warriors stood just outside Lohman's offices, in the showroom, at the tail end of an extra-large motor home.

Bryant watched Howard through the glass. The salesman was standing next to the manager, looking down at the man seated behind his desk, wringing his hands with anxiety as he spoke.

"I get the same feeling," the Marine said. "So I suppose we should try not to kill him when we take down the rest of this outfit."

"We can try," Burton said without emotion. "But I'm not making any promises. Our new buddy Howard may not be a direct part in this smuggling thing, but he knows about it. Otherwise he wouldn't have brought us in here to meet this guy."

"You've got a point," Bryant replied. "Fact is, Howard is actually a passive participant."

Burton turned to look at his new comrade in arms. "You learn that term in some advanced leatherneck school?" he said. "Passive participant?"

Bryant chuckled. "College class. Professors love to give things fancy names and titles." He paused a moment, then added, "Of course, I wouldn't expect a mere swabby to know anything about college."

Now Shooter Burton laughed.

"No matter what you call him," Bryant went on, "Howard knows what's going on, so he's an enemy combatant in my book. If we have to take him out, well then, we just have to take him out."

"Okay by me," Burton said. "Passive participation is as bad as being active. It doesn't even qualify as collateral damage in my book. But that's pretty much how I see it. Howard's at least a borderline enemy combatant. So we'll spare him if it's practical, but shoot him down if we have to."

The two warriors were simply making small talk now, doing their best to look like the motor-home-buying drug smugglers they were supposed to be for the benefit of the two men inside the office. In the meantime, they watched Howard, who was still talking to the man seated behind the desk on the other side of the glass. The man listened closely, glancing up now and then. Each time he did, he locked eyes with either Burton or Bryant, returning the stares they were casting through the glass at him. Finally, he nodded, said something that made Burton wish he could read lips, then sat back in his chair as Howard turned away and strode quickly out of the office, obviously relieved to finally be leaving.

The man behind the desk waved Burton and Bryant inside with a quick and impatient gesture of his hand, which made Howard's tensely spoken "He'd like to see you" unnecessary. But the salesman said it anyway then walked at a speed just short of running as he passed the giant motor home behind Burton and Bryant before disappearing out one of the glass doors to the outside lots.

"Come in, come in!" said the man behind the desk as the two men crossed the threshold into his office. He stood up behind his desk and extended his hand. "Tony Moreland," he said by way of introduction.

Burton and Bryant both shook his hand in turn but didn't speak.

A slight frown fell over Moreland's face. "You have names, I assume?"

The two men glanced at each other, doing their best to make it look as if they were trying to decide, without speaking, if they should give the man their real names. It was an obvious mark of amateur criminals; professionals would have made that decision and worked it out long before they went motor-home shopping.

Finally, Burton said, "Stanley. Just Stan for short."

Bryant shifted his feet in forced nervousness and, once again, Burton was impressed not only by the man's undercover-acting ability, but how quick he caught on, and responded to, the Navy SEAL's lead.

Little by little, one tiny subconscious insinuation at a time, the two undercover operatives were implanting in Moreland's brain exactly what they wanted to implant: that they were willing but inexperienced contraband smugglers, men who had the cojones to go it alone.

But also men who might be susceptible to an offer to become part of a much larger—and far more experienced—operation. After all, a small part of a big score was often more than all of a small one.

Only Burton and Bryant himself knew it was on

purpose when the Marine nervously stammered before grunting out, "My name's Oliver. But I go by Ollie."

Moreland frowned, then the frown turned to an expression of intense disgust. "I suppose your last name is Hardy, huh, Ollie?" he said. "And Stan is no doubt Stan Laurel."

The two warriors looked at each other again, forcing themselves to look embarrassed; the illusion they had created was that of two men, under stress, having to come up with fast false names and stupidly falling back on appellations that were familiar in the back of their minds.

It was a fine line they were attempting to walk. They needed to appear capable enough for Tony Moreland to take them seriously. But at the same time they had to look inexperienced so they'd have good reason to join his crew when, and if, he extended the invitation for which they were fishing.

Moreland closed his eyes for a moment and his facial expression screamed that he had been forced to grow used to dealing with immature men, and had developed the patience to do so. When he opened his eyes once more, he said, "Cute. Oliver and Hardy. Stan and Ollie. Okay, if that's how you want to play the game it's fine with me. For *now*."

"Have a seat," Moreland said, pointing to a pair of straight-backed wooden chairs directly in front of his desk. As Burton and Bryant moved toward the chairs, a sudden roar penetrated the walls and windows of the office building and seemed to shake the very foundation. Both men frowned and looked to Moreland.

"That's just the Wildmen," the Lohman's manager said. "Motorcycle gang whose clubhouse is a mile or so on down the access road. Filthy bunch. They race past here several times a day on their way to commit whatever petty crimes they're into." He shook his head and his lips curled down in disgust. "They don't bother us. We've got one of them working as a mechanic in the garage, but I won't let him wear his colors when he's at work."

"Yeah," Burton said. "We saw some of them earlier when we were driving in."

Moreland nodded and turned back to his own wheeled desk chair as Burton and Bryant dropped into their seats. After a few seconds of just looking at the men—further sizing them up, Burton knew—Moreland came to the point. "Howard tells me you're interested in some fairly unique modifications to a motor home."

"Well," Bryant said, "Howard seemed to think they were unique, although I don't see why. Wanting hidden compartments where valuables can be secreted on a motor home that's likely to be parked in remote areas, and left by itself for extended periods of time, doesn't seem unique to me. It just seems sensible."

Moreland nodded. "Howard mentioned your wife's jewelry. She must have a lot of valuable pieces."

Burton watched Bryant as the man let a frown cover his face. "That sounds a little bit like someone who might like to follow us and burglarize the vehicle first chance they got," he said. He sat back in his chair and crossed his legs, his right foot resting on top of his huge left thigh. "Or am I just being paranoid?"

"You're just being paranoid," Moreland said. "Unless she's got the queen of England's crown jewels, I can make a lot more money my own ways than I could hocking your wife's precious rings and necklaces. It'd be a waste of my time."

"No, he's being careful," Burton said. "He doesn't want his wife on his ass." He forced a chuckle. "She's the only person I know who he's afraid of."

Moreland looked back and forth between the two men across the desk from him, his face slightly puzzled.

"If you knew her," Burton went on, "you'd be afraid of her, too."

The joke broke the tension that had built up in the room and Moreland joined the other two men in low laughter. But Burton knew he had accomplished what he'd meant to accomplish. The story about the wife's jewelry had holes in it bigger than the largest cheese ball in Switzerland. So, in Shooter Burton's opinion, at least two things had gone well so far. First, their stammering around and giving Moreland the names of Oliver and Hardy had sounded exactly like something two men who weren't prepared to give out phony names might have done.

The second thing that appeared to have had the proper effect on Moreland was the ridiculous story about "Ollie's" wife's jewelry. Even if she did have valuable pieces, she wasn't likely to take them camping. It was another mark of men who might well have always had greed and larceny in their hearts but weren't used to criminal activity as a lifestyle.

The Lohman's office manager would have had to

have been a total idiot not to figure out that the two men who sat before him now were lying about why they wanted the hidden compartments built inside the motor home. And while Moreland might have been a low-life, scumbag drug dealer, Shooter Burton knew he wasn't anybody's idiot.

An uncomfortable silence followed. Then Moreland finally said, "Why don't we stop playing games." He leaned back in his chair, making it squeak. "You're planning to smuggle something, and the sooner I find out exactly what it is the better I can advise you on what modifications and secret compartments you're going to need."

Burton and Bryant looked to each other again. Then, turning back to Moreland, Burton said, "It occurs to me, Mr. Moreland, that as soon as we divulge that information, you've got a hammer to hold over our heads and we've got nothing on you. That wouldn't be good business on our part."

Slowly, still staring at the two undercover men and trying to size them up, Moreland nodded. "Would it help if I told you that we do a little 'secret transporting' around here ourselves?"

"Not unless you gave us some proof of it," Bryant said. "Until we see you doing something as illegal as we are, we'll have to just wonder if you aren't an undercover cop."

Moreland almost jumped at the accusation. "Gentlemen, I can assure you I'm not a law-enforcement agent of any—"

Burton held up a hand to cut the man off. "Save the

denials for the fools who think undercover cops have to admit to being what they are when they're asked directly. We happen to know that isn't the case."

For a few moments, Tony Moreland sat perfectly still. But Burton could almost see the wheels turning behind the man's wrinkled forehead. Moreland was trying to decide just how much he could trust these two men. He was interested in selling them a high-dollar motor home and making the expensive modifications they required, of course. But unless Burton was misreading of the signs, the Lohman's manager was even more interested in recruiting them to be part of the regular, ongoing smuggling operations that seemed to be centered around this legitimate motor-home and recreational-vehicle dealership.

Seconds went by. Finally, Moreland pulled open a drawer in his desk, lifted a set of keys on a thin wire ring attached to a small round pasteboard and stood up. "If you would, please, gentlemen," he said. "Follow me."

Burton and Bryant got up out of their chairs. Silently, they waited for Moreland to circle his desk and exit his office, then followed. The manager led them across the showroom past several more motor homes and recreational vehicles, then out a side door. He remained silent, his leather shoe soles slapping the black asphalt as he circled the building to the rear.

As soon as they turned the corner, Burton and Bryant saw a large Winnebago parked in a loading zone. A small man who looked to be Latino was just about to climb up into the cab area.

Moreland held up his hand. "Raul!" he called out as he quickened his pace toward the man. "Hold up."

Raul halted in his tracks, his feet on the ground, the Winnebago's driver's door open in his left hand.

As soon as the dealership manager reached Raul, his hand went into his right pants pocket and came up with a roll of bills. Shearing off several ones, he said, "Go get yourself a Coke and a candy bar out of the machine before you leave. I need to show these men something."

Raul took the money but looked at Moreland with concern in his eyes. He stared at Burton and Bryant the whole time as he headed back around the corner of the building and out of sight.

Moreland used the keys he'd taken from his desk to open the side door of the motor home, then held it open as Burton and Bryant stepped up and inside. Burton was slightly amused to see Bryant turn sideways in order to pass through the door; the big man appeared to do so without even thinking. More as a matter of habit, the way extremely tall men automatically ducked when they walked through a doorway.

As soon as they were on board, however, Burton's mind returned to the serious business at hand. He watched, doing his best to appear unimpressed and businesslike, as Moreland began to circle the inside of the vehicle, tapping here and there at just the right spots to make wall panels pop open.

And each time a panel came out, Burton and Bryant saw carefully banded stacks of money. Closer inspection revealed that the currency was all in twenty-, fifty- and hundred-dollar bills.

Burton had never been a math whiz by any means, and calculating scuba-diving decompression times during BUD/S training was about as technical as he got with numbers. But by the time Moreland had shown them the hidden panels in all the luggage compartments, beneath the carpet on the floor, inside the various seats and beds and other places, he had calculated that there had to be well over seven million dollars in cash aboard the vehicle.

"Does that satisfy you?" Moreland finally said as he straightened after showing the men a false bottom filled with bills under an extra propane tank inside a storage closet.

Bryant surprised both Moreland and Burton by saying a simple "No."

"What—" Moreland started to say.

"What you've shown us implies that you're doing some sort of business outside the law," the man said. "But it proves nothing." He stopped to take in a long breath and his barrel chest heaved in and out like a huge balloon being squeezed. "There's no law against having money. And no law against transporting it. For all we know, this could be an elaborate sting operation with this money being just part of the show. It might even be counterfeit."

Moreland let out a breath of disgust, his closed lips fluttering as the air passed between them. "Well," he said, and his voice was still exasperated, "what do I have to do to show you can trust me? Murder someone?"

Burton stepped in again now that he could see where Bryant was going with all this. "That'd probably do it," he said cheerfully. "Although we'd settle for something less dramatic. Anything illegal on its own. Or in conjunction with all this money."

Moreland stared at the two men for another few seconds, and now it was obvious that he was again trying to decide if he should trust *them*. But the momentum was with the two elite warriors now, and just as momentum during a football game could carry an inferior team's offense across the goal line of a better team's defense, Moreland was now set on a course of action that was difficult to stop.

"Come on," the manager said. He opened the door and this time led the way down the folding step back out onto the asphalt.

Circling the rear of the Winnebago, Burton was slightly surprised to see an almost identical vehicle a hundred feet down the line. Still parked in the loading area at the rear of the dealership building, it had been hidden by the motor home with the money secreted inside. Moreland walked briskly forward, and a few seconds later they were boarding yet another house on wheels.

And this time when Moreland opened the hidden compartments, there was no money to be seen. But what Burton and Bryant did see was stack after stack of white powder sealed inside large plastic envelopes.

"Each one's a kilo," Moreland said.

"Coke?" Bryant asked.

"Heroin," Moreland replied. "The new cocaine. It's at its height of popularity right now. Most cokeheads have gone to the crack pipe, and there's not as much profit in it anymore."

"You've convinced me," Burton said.

"Me, too," Bryant stated.

Moreland rolled his eyes as if it had all been a great imposition.

"It does appear you know what you're doing," Burton added. "Just for the record, where does all this smack go from here?"

Moreland frowned. "Now it's *you* who's beginning to sound like a cop," he said. "I've already shown you more than I should have."

"Just wondering," Burton replied. "Never mind." He studied Moreland's eyes carefully. He could tell the Lohman's manager still wanted to bring them on board.

And after a few more seconds, the man said, "We never off-load the dope until after dark when the dealership's closed. An added precaution. From here, it goes to all kinds of places in New York, Jersey and New England."

Bryant leaned in a little, then said, "Okay. I'm impressed. We've got our eye on the last motor home Howard showed us, and if we buy it we'll want the same modifications you've got in these two units. We're going to look around a little more, but we'll probably get back with you."

Moreland's face dropped suddenly. He had bared his smuggling operation as well as his soul to these two men and couldn't believe they were leaving without doing business. "What are you talking about?" he asked incredulously.

"We're saying we're going to try a few other dealerships before we make up our mind. Business is business, and we want to shop around for a better price."

Still somewhat confused, Moreland stammered out, "What do I have to do to put you into that motor home tonight?"

Burton and Bryant exchanged glances, then Bryant said, "I can't believe you guys really say that."

Tony Moreland knew he was being made fun of, but like any good salesman, he had composed himself again. "Look, guys, you're not going to find a better deal for what you're looking for anywhere else. And as I've shown you, we're all set up for exactly the kind of business you're wanting to get into." He paused a second, then said, "Tell me, Mr. Stan and Mr. Ollie. This is going to be your first run, isn't it?"

Burton and Bryant now became the hesitant ones, then Burton whispered, as if he was embarrassed, "Yeah."

Moreland nodded. "I thought so. I can tell. Well, let me tell you something. There are all kinds of traps you can fall into in this business that you don't know about yet. But they're traps of which I'm well aware." Leaning back against one of the overhead storage bins, he said, "My guess is you've got some small connection down south. Probably in Mexico. And you've got a buyer up here in New York. But they're both limited, aren't they? I mean, there's a limit as to how much dope your supplier can get you. And there's a limit as to how much your buyer can buy. Am I right?"

Bryant looked down at the ground. Then, finally, it was his turn to say "Yeah" in a soft tone.

Moreland believed that the momentum had changed, and that he had the advantage now. So he made the most of it. "Guys," he said, "how about you come to work for us, let me and my boys show you the ropes so you don't end up spending the rest of your lives in a New York or—God forbid—Mexican prison. And you make far more money than you'll ever make on your own."

These were the magic words for which Burton and Bryant had been working toward all afternoon. But rather than expose their sudden joy, they maintained their undercover personas and glanced at each other questioningly. Then, finally looking back to Moreland, Burton and Bryant both let smiles creep across their faces.

"Yeah," Burton said. "Sounds like it might be a good deal all around."

Bryant nodded his agreement.

Then they looked back at each other as their smiles grew from undercover put-on to genuine happiness. And those smiles were, perhaps, the only thing genuine that Tony Moreland had gotten from them since they'd set foot in his office almost an hour ago.

First with Howard, then with Tony Moreland, the whole afternoon had been one long, gigantic acting job. But it had finally paid off.

The two elite warriors had infiltrated the New York end of the Morales Cartel drug-smuggling operation.

CHAPTER FIVE

The streetlights illuminating the Twin Pines housing division were brighter than Bolan would have liked. But with the straw Panama hats pulled low over their faces, he and Nash didn't seem to attract undue attention from the passing cars as they strolled down the street like two wealthy residents getting a little fresh air after their evening meal. A few other men and women were on the streets as well—some walking dogs, others alone, and the two men even exchanged greetings with a few.

It was obvious that the people who lived within the neighborhood felt secure from the "unwashed masses" on the other sides of the walls.

Bolan hadn't known how large Twin Pines actually was before he and Nash had driven its circumference earlier, and by then it had been too late to find out the exact location of the Morales address. Until then, he had assumed they would stumble upon the correct street and go from there.

It was time for the alternate plan to which Bolan suspected they might have to resort. One of the many things he'd learned over the years was that nothing ever went exactly as planned. Sometimes it was just a small deviation from what had been expected. Other times, as the old adage went, "The best plans fall to pieces as soon as the first shot is fired." But this, Bolan suspected, was simply a minor bump in the road, and one that he'd be able to pass over with a little creativity.

Bolan reached behind him, lifting his shirttail slightly and running his fingers along the top of the stiff black leather case sticking up out of his back pocket. He had brought half of what he needed for plan B. But the other half would have to be acquired inside the compound.

The soldier frowned in thought as he walked on along the street. The guards at the gate would know how to find the right house, but asking them was out of the question. Neither he nor Nash could pass for Hispanic up close and, even if they presented some apparently legitimate reason for two gringos being inside the addition, the guards would wonder how they got in, why they didn't have visitors' passes, why they were on foot and—particularly—why they were dressed up, trying to look like Mexicans.

Bolan and Nash came to a small neighborhood park on the corner of a street and the soldier led the way to a concrete bench between a swing set and monkey bars. He took a seat on the concrete and Nash dropped down beside him.

"Any ideas?" the Delta Force commando asked.

Bolan glanced at Nash's face, then his eyes automatically fell to the baggy shirt he'd given his new partner, double-checking to make sure none of Nash's weapons were showing. He had watched the Delta Force operative arm himself while they were still in the car, before they'd scaled the wall, and was impressed with the man's weapons of choice. Nash's primary piece was a Kimber

Ultra+ CDP II .45 with a full-size grip. His backup gun was almost identical—an Ultra CDP II, which was the same weapon with a shorter grip. Known for both accuracy and reliability, the Kimbers came stock with most of the after-market features that were often added to .45s from other manufacturers. Both had three-inch barrels, which made them easy to conceal, and total concealment was what had been needed on this leg of the mission.

Like Bolan had done with his Beretta, Desert Eagle and gigantic Cold Steel folder, Nash had tucked both his pistols into his belt, then covered them with the tail of his *guayabara* shirt. But the Delta Force operative wasn't finished. His final firearm was a last-ditch hideout piece; an American Derringer DA38 double-action in .40 S&W. Bolan watched his partner stuff it into the back pocket of his jeans, noting that it was housed in a pocket holster that also carried an additional four rounds of .40s.

The sight had made Bolan smile. The DA38 served the same purpose that his .22 Magnum North American Arms Pug minirevolver served. The difference was that his NAA carried five rounds in its wheel, while the Derringer could be loaded with only two at a time. The derringer's rounds, of course, were far more powerful than the .22 Mag's. So it was like almost all aspects of combat—a trade-off.

You picked the weapons to which you were drawn, then worked within their limitations.

The last defense item Bolan had watched Nash add to his arsenal was a Columbia River Knife and Tool-produced Natural folding knife. Although the blade had been hidden inside the thick and sturdy black and bone-colored handle, the soldier knew it to be a modified clip point. The weapon utilized a spring-equipped-assisted opening device that kicked in as soon at the thumb stud was moved forward a fraction of an inch. All of which, in Bolan's opinion, made it more practical than an automatic or switchblade, which could accidentally be tripped while still clipped inside a pocket or waistband. The four-inch blade was a little short for Bolan's taste, but it was still plenty of steel to get the job done in the hand of a skilled knife wielder.

Nash cleared his throat. "I said, 'Any ideas on how we're going to find the Morales house in here?'"

Bolan nodded. "Yeah," he said then went silent again.

After a good thirty seconds, Nash spoke again. "Well? You care to share them with me? I mean, I appear to be in on this thing, too, you know."

Still, Bolan didn't speak. Then both men heard the sound of strangely erratic footsteps on the concrete street as someone passed the park. Looking that way, Bolan saw it was an old man hobbling by, half leaning on a wooden cane. Looking back to Nash, he finally spoke. "We're going to take a hostage," he whispered.

Nash's eyebrows rose. "Take a hostage?" he said. "For what?"

"To show us how to find the right street and house number."

The strategy sank into Nash's brain and he nodded his approval. "I only see one problem with that," he said. "What do we do with this hostage after we're finished with him?"

The soldier reached into the back pocket of his jeans and pulled out the leather case. "I brought this along just in case we had to resort to it," he said. Unzipping the zipper, he pulled out a hypodermic needle filled with clear liquid. "We'll get the intel we need from whoever we snatch, then leave him someplace safe and let him catch up on his sleep."

Nash looked back to the old man hobbling along the street. He still hadn't passed the small park where they sat. "Want to use that guy?" he asked. "He looks like he's been around awhile. Should be able to tell us where the street is."

Bolan stared at the old man for a second, then shook his head. "No," he said. "That guy is probably on every medication known to man. This is Valium here, and there's no telling what mixing it with his own meds would do to him. We need someone young who looks healthy." He stuck the syringe back into the leather case and returned it to his pocket.

The old man continued to tap his cane on the concrete, the sounds growing ever more faint as he slowly disappeared into the darkness down the street, never knowing just how close he had come to being temporarily kidnapped, then left somewhere to sleep the rest of the night away.

Ten minutes went by. After twenty, Bolan heard the sound of feet pitter-pattering along the street in the distance. The person making the noises was coming from the same direction the old man had, but at a faster pace. He had to be running, and that told the soldier two things: first, he was probably in good enough health that a little Valium wouldn't hurt him, and second—as a runner—he was likely to know the streets inside this exclusive neighborhood.

Bolan stood up from his bench and started toward the street. Nash didn't have to be told to follow him. A moment later, they got a surprise.

The jogger wore a pink-and-white workout suit and matching shoes. It wasn't a "he." The form nearing them at a rapid pace was definitely a "she."

As the runner got closer, the soldier could see that she was an attractive, thirtysomething woman with an olive complexion and long brown hair tied back in a ponytail that swished back and forth in perfect time to her footfalls. At almost the same time the two men saw her, she saw them, and for a brief second she slowed her stride. Then the fact that they looked as if they belonged in this exclusive area kicked in, her face relaxed once more and she sped back up to her original pace. As she passed under a streetlight, she even smiled at them.

"Buenas noches," the woman said when she was still ten feet away.

"Buenas noches," Bolan replied, then reached down and swept her up into his arms as she tried to pass.

The woman started to scream, but Bolan's big hand covered her mouth a split second before the sound could come out. Without further words, the soldier carried her back through the park toward a darkened area at the side of a large house just the other side of the swing set. She began to flail her arms and flutter-kick her feet in the air as if she might be trying to swim her way out of his grasp, so Nash moved in and grabbed her pink-and-white running shoes.

The flailing arms were left up to Bolan, who was too busy holding her with one hand and covering her mouth with the other to block the blows that landed on the sides of his head and neck. But the woman felt as if she weighed little more than a hundred pounds, and the big American barely felt her assault.

Bolan hated to scare the innocent woman, but he had little choice. Besides, the fear would only last a few seconds and would serve a much greater good.

As soon as they were in the shadows, Bolan stopped. He kept his hand over her mouth, and Nash continued to hold her feet. Looking down into the terrified eyes, he spoke in the calmest, most soothing voice he could muster. "Miss," he said in Spanish. "I know you're frightened. But you don't need to be—we aren't going to hurt you in any way." He paused a moment, then said, "If I take my hand off your mouth, can you keep from screaming?"

The woman still looked terrified, but she nodded.

Bolan removed his hand, and the woman immediately parted her lips to scream.

He had no choice but to cover her mouth again.

"Okay," Bolan said, continuing in Spanish. "I realize you thought that getting me to uncover your mouth was your way to scream for help, but that's not going to work. I can keep covering it all night if I have to. But please believe me this time when I tell you we have absolutely no intention of harming or molesting you in any way.

All we need is some simple information. Then we'll let you go." He waited again. Finally, the woman nodded.

This time when he removed his hand the woman didn't scream. Her eyes still betrayed her horror, but now they also looked angry. She answered Bolan in the same language in which he'd addressed her. "You say you will not hurt or molest me," she whispered in a trembling voice brought on by both emotions, "but you have already molested me."

"And I'm truly sorry we had to do that," Bolan said. "But I promise this is as bad as it gets. Now, I'm going to set you down. Don't try to run."

"All right," whispered the woman.

"Good," Bolan said. "Because believe me, if you do, I'm capable of catching you again." Removing his arm from beneath her legs, he set her on her feet as gently as he could.

"What is this information you need to know from me?" the woman asked.

Bolan looked down at her. Although they were in the shadows now, he had gotten a good look at her when he'd carried her there from the street. Under the light of the moon and the streetlights, he had seen that she was an attractive woman. Her complexion was a shade or two lighter than most Mexicans', which suggested that her lineage came more from Spain than the indigenous peoples of America. Her dark brown hair had looked almost black under the lights and now, in this darker area, was the color of coal.

"First of all," Bolan said, "do you have a name?"

"Most people do," the woman said, her voice still angry.

Bolan couldn't help but smile in the shadows. The woman had spunk. "Yes," he agreed in his most non-threatening voice, "you're right. Most people do, and mine's Matt." He glanced to his side. "My friend goes by Spike."

Nash reached up and grabbed the crown of his Panama hat, lifting it up over the hairs sticking up out of the top of his head.

"How *very* attractive," said the woman sarcastically, getting more angry and braver with each passing second during which she wasn't harmed. "That's the stupidest hair I've ever seen."

Bolan frowned. He was happy that the woman had relaxed, but if he let her become too comfortable with the situation, she was likely to quit obeying orders. "Okay," he said in a more stern voice. "You know our names. Would you care to share yours with us?"

"Anita," the woman said, and while the word didn't exactly sound friendly when it came out, it lacked both the fear and the surliness with which her earlier remarks had been singed.

"All right, Anita," Bolan said. "This is a big neighborhood, and the streets are confusing. We need you to show us how to get to Pelo Calle."

"Fur Street," Anita said, using English for the first time. "You look, and sound, like gringos. So I will use your language." She was still breathing hard from both her run and the adrenaline rush that had accompanied her fear, and she stopped speaking for a few seconds now to catch her breath. "I run down part of Pelo Calle every night. It's a long, winding street. What part of it are you looking for?"

Anita's English had been as fluent as her Spanish, so Bolan decided to switch languages, too. Before he spoke, he wondered briefly whether he should give her the actual address. She might recognize it, and might very well know the Morales family. And while he planned to use the Valium on her as soon as he had the directions he needed, this was only the recon part of the mission. If he decided it was necessary to actually attack the house, he had planned to first return to the Enclave with Nash so they could arm themselves with heavier weapons.

Bolan felt his eyebrows lowering in concentration. The problem now was that if he put Anita to sleep, then left to reequip, she was likely to be awake again before they returned. And as soon as she woke up, if she was of a mind to do so, she'd be able to warn whoever was at the Morales house that men had been asking for directions to their house.

Which would mean Bolan and Nash would be walking straight into an ambush.

Bolan made the decision in seconds, mulling over the facts and weighing the pros and cons of his decision at the speed of light.

He and Nash had their pistols and extra ammo with them. They would have to launch their attack—if it was needed—with what they had. Although he'd have preferred to be toting an M-16 A-2 or a H&K MP-5, he'd have to make do with his Desert Eagle, Beretta and NAA Pug—along with Nash's Kimbers and derringer. If they had to, they could probably pick up heavier armament—most likely AK-47s and Uzis from the Moraleses—as they went.

They would be undergunned, at least at first, but they would have surprise on their side while Anita was still sleeping off the syringe.

"We want 12313 Pelo Calle," Bolan said.

Even in the shadows, he could see the woman before him squint in thought. "That's in the very southern part of the neighborhood," she said. "I can take you there. You mentioned earlier that you could catch me if I tried to run away." She paused and lifted her face slightly to stare up at him. "It's about a mile and a half away. Think you can keep up with me?"

Bolan grinned at the feisty young woman. "We'll do our best," he said.

"Well, I've got two more questions before I help you," Anita said.

"Go ahead."

"Who are you looking for and what are you going to do to them? I could never live with myself if I learned that I had helped you rob, or even murder, some innocent neighbor of mine. If that is your intention, you may go ahead and kill me here and now." She stared up defiantly into Bolan's eyes.

The soldier couldn't help but admire her spirit of right and wrong, even in the face of death. But again, he wondered how much information he should give her. He reminded himself, however, that she'd be asleep during his recon and possible attack on the house.

The soldier stared down at Anita's shadowy silhouette. The woman was obviously the kind of person who responded more to truth and fairness than threats. So he decided to tell her the truth. "Their name's Morales," he said. "And what we do—or don't do to them—depends on what we find out after we get there and check things out."

Anita's body suddenly stiffened in the semidarkness. "You know about the Moraleses then?" she said.

"Some," Bolan replied.

"They're drug dealers, gunrunners and murderers," Anita said. Turning her head to the side, she spit on the ground in contempt. "We'd have run them out of this whole neighborhood if everyone wasn't so afraid of them. I hope you plan to kill them."

Bolan was slightly taken aback by Anita's frankness. "I'm not sure *all* the family fits that description," he said. "And we don't want to hurt any of them who were just unlucky enough to be born with that name. You don't happen to know any of their first names, do you?"

"Juan is one of the brothers," Anita said. "I think José is another." A sour look curled her lips downward. "I stay away from them as much as possible."

Bolan didn't answer. He remembered that José Morales had been the name on the title to the motor home the Texas Rangers had seized carrying what had to be drug money. But that hardly cinched the identities of the Moraleses in the house.

"Anyway," Anita said when Bolan hadn't responded, "I can assure you that everyone who lives in that house is dirty. It's three of the Morales brothers and one of their cousins. There are trucks and cars and motor homes coming and going at all times of the day and night. They don't even try to hide it. They've got the *federales* and *rurales* in their back pockets and the Twin Pines guards are as afraid of them as everyone else."

"You're sure about that?" Bolan asked.

"I'm a hundred percent sure of it," Anita said. "We built these walls to keep criminals out, but the worst ones are inside here with us." She stopped talking for another breath, and when her voice came back it had the angriest tone Bolan had heard yet out of the woman. "I hope you kill all of them."

Somewhere in the distance, a dog barked. It was answered by another dog, and then an entire chorus of canines joined in. Bolan had to raise his voice slightly so he could be heard. "Lead the way," he said.

Anita turned her back to Bolan and Nash and took off slowly, warming up again after the conversation, which appeared to have allowed her muscles to tighten up. But within a block or so, she sped up to what Bolan gauged to be a pace of roughly seven to seven and a half minutes per mile. They twisted through Twin Pines, down streets that wound around a golf course and several more small parks, crossing wooden and concrete bridges over streams and creeks, and finally turning onto Pelo Calle.

Suddenly, Anita stopped in her tracks. "The house you want is about two more blocks down," she said, slightly winded. "Do you want me to take you all the way there?"

Bolan shook his head. "No. I don't want them to see us coming. You've done your part. Thanks." His hand moved slowly behind his back. Then, as quietly as he could, he unzipped the black leather case in his back pocket.

"Well, then," Anita said. "What do you want me to—"

Before she could finish the sentence, the Executioner had swung the syringe around in front of him. Nash had seen what he was doing and stepped in behind Anita, bear-hugging her from the back to pin her arms at her sides.

"What!" Anita said, her voice muffled as Nash lifted a hand over her lips. "You promised—"

Bolan stepped in with the syringe. The top of her left arm was still exposed above where Nash grasped her and he jabbed the needle through the pink jogging suit and into her flesh. More mumbling came from behind the Delta Force operative's hand as Bolan pressed the plunger.

Looking straight into the once again confused and frightened eyes, Bolan said, "We promised not to hurt you and we won't. Don't worry. You'll have a nap in a safe place and wake up just fine and dandy."

But by the time he'd finished, Anita's eyes had closed and her body had gone limp in Nash's arms.

The two men carried the sleeping woman between two houses, then gently placed her behind a large square air-conditioning unit attached to one of the homes. Satisfied that Anita was out of sight from the street—and that she was in what was probably the most street-crime-free area in the entire city—they moved back to the grass in front of the house.

"You think we really needed to do that?" Nash whispered as he and Bolan made their way, slowly and cautiously, down the street toward the Morales house. "She sounded like she was on our side."

"Did you want to take the chance?" Bolan asked as he walked across the yard. "What were we supposed to do with her? Take her with us and get her killed? Or let her go and hope she wasn't just talking against the Moraleses in order to save her own hide?" He turned to glance at Nash as they continued on. "She might have run straight home and phoned these brothers and cousin she supposedly hates and tipped them off."

"Point taken," Nash said. "I guess there was no way to be sure."

"No," Bolan replied. "And she'll be just fine in a few hours when she wakes up."

They were only one house away from 12313 now, and Bolan moved up in the yard, almost in the flower beds along the front of the house they were passing. Reaching under the tail of his shirt, he drew the sound-suppressed Beretta, checking to make sure the chamber was loaded and flipping the safety to semiauto.

"You take this side," he whispered to Nash. "I'll circle the house and check the other. Look in every window you can. We'll meet back here, in front of this house, when we're done, to mull over what we've seen. You got it?"

"Affirmative," Nash said.

"Then let's do it." The soldier took off across the Moraleses' front yard.

REYNALDO MORALES LIFTED his square-toed boot from the gold Cadillac's brake pedal and let the idling engine inch the vehicle a few feet forward. His boot returned to the brake when the Toyota in front of him stopped again. It had been a case of roll, stop, roll, stop, roll for the past half hour. And the procedure had become almost maddening.

Pushing the button to lower the window, the man known to his friends—of whom there were very few—as Rey stuck his head out the window and into the heat. He strained his neck, trying to get a look past the long lines of cars in front of and in the lanes to his sides. Ahead, he could just catch a glimpse of the U.S. Customs checkpoints and the uniformed men working the booths.

He was still a good half hour away by his estimate.

Morales pulled his head back into the vehicle, rolled his window up and flipped the air-conditioner switch to the top notch. Even the short period of time, during which his head had been outside the car, had caused sweat to break out on his forehead. Now, as the cold air blew across his face, he felt the salty water roll down his cheeks onto his neck, which seemed to compound his poor mood.

Crossing the border hadn't always been so hard or tedious.

Morales settled back into his seat and did his best to calm his anger. It was those damn Arabs who were to blame for this inconvenience. Ever since al Qaeda had pulled their little stunts on September 11, 2001, entering the U.S. had become a royal pain in the ass. And it was taking even longer this day than usual.

He pulled the Havana cigar from between his clenched teeth. A long tubular ash had formed at the end and he began gingerly pushing it toward the ashtray in the dashboard. He almost made it.

Lost in serious thought now—as well as having to concentrate on the infuriating start-and-stop, stop-and-start traffic on the international bridge, Morales now saw the ash suddenly fall off the end of the cigar and land on his thigh, exploding like a frangible bullet and covering his old-fashioned black-and-white-striped slacks with gray powder. He cursed as he brushed at the mess on his pants, cursing even louder as his efforts succeeded only in turning the entire thigh area into a huge gray spot. Finally, seeing that the white stripes on his pants had darkened and the black stripes turned lighter, he gave in to the realization that they would have to be professionally dry cleaned.

He had other clothing with him in the Cadillac, and he would stop and change slacks as soon as he crossed the border from Mexico into the United States. With that irritating problem dealt with, his thoughts returned to their former subject, Don Pancho Morales—known better simply as Don Pancho. Don Pancho was the Don—or leader—of the Morales Cartel. At least in name.

He was also Reynaldo Morales's uncle.

Don Pancho still led the Morales Cartel. But, Morales knew, the old man did so in name only. For the last several years it had been Reynaldo who actually ran the day-to-day business and made the decisions for the organization. Don Pancho did little but sit around the swimming pool at his country mansion, drinking sangria and playing with women in bikinis young enough to be his granddaughters. He was never, however, remiss when it came to collecting his share of the money the cartel brought in; a share that was always the lion's.

And the lion received it for doing absolutely nothing.

The Toyota moved a few feet farther. The Cadillac followed.

Don Pancho had been out of the picture for so long now that the men within the cartel looked at Reynaldo Morales as the actual leader. But tradition was important in Mexico, and the other high-ranking men within the cartel were hesitant to completely retire Don Pancho. Besides, there was the family angle, as well. Most of those who ran the cartel were either Moraleses by name or by marriage. Different factions within the large family had inevitably been formed. But Don Pancho seemed a friend to all, and as long as he was in charge—even if in name only—the in-fighting and back-stabbing within the organization remained manageable.

Morales knew, and understood, all that. But he also knew that his cut of the cartel's money was hardly commensurate with his duties or position.

The infuriating line of cars moved again, then stopped. Morales looked down at the spot on his thigh, and with nothing better to do while he waited made another attempt to brush off the cigar ash. It was no more successful than his first try and only darkened the stain—and his mood—further. He had always been fastidious about his appearance, and regarded what he wore more as costumes than clothes. Clothes were costumes that projected an image. And the image he relied on to keep control of the cartel was one of power, success and individuality. Power and success were vital to gaining, and keeping, his men's loyalty and confidence; a confidence which—if not handled carefully—might well turn shaky after the massacre at the wedding. The individuality of the look he had chosen was designed to make sure he was remembered. And Morales believed he had found just the right mixture of eccentricity and sobriety to achieve those goals.

The Cadillac inched forward again as the lines continued their insanely slow pace. Morales attempted to relieve the mixture of anger and anxiety in his chest by using the time to further sort things out in his mind. He had, for all practical purposes, become the figurehead for Mexico's largest and most powerful cartel. At least he was the figurehead *within* the Morales family itself. Outside the organization, law enforcement on both sides of the border still thought his uncle ran the show. To them, Morales was known as a simple attorney who specialized in international law and who might, or might not, be somewhat involved in the less legal activities of his family.

There were certain advantages to being viewed that way; it allowed him to fly under the radar to a certain extent. But making the kind of money he deserved wasn't one of those advantages. Part of Reynaldo Morales—a part he did his best to keep in check—wanted the whole world to know his power.

Morales's anger dissipated suddenly as he realized that his days of anonymity were about to end. He grinned ear to ear as he reminded himself of what was in store for Don Pancho. But the smile on his face was short-lived as a car horn suddenly threatened to deafen him.

Looking up into the rearview mirror, the true leader of the Morales Cartel saw a ten-year-old Chevy. A white face with red hair sat behind the wheel. The driver was wildly waving him forward, and when Morales turned back to look through the windshield he saw that the Toyota had moved another car length farther toward the border. The man and his horn ruined his temporary good mood and infuriated him.

"We will get there when we get there, you stupid gringo," Morales mumbled as he allowed the Cadillac to roll forward again. "It makes no difference if I move now, or wait until another vehicle has passed through the customs booth." He shook his head in disgust, and while he quit talking aloud, his angry thoughts remained. The men driving the decrepit Chevrolet reminded him of airline passengers who fought and struggled to board planes the second their flights were announced over the loudspeaker. They seemed not to realize that no matter who found their seats first, all would arrive at their destination at the same time. The same principle held true for the automobiles atop this border-bridge.

Morales turned back to the Chevy. He started to give the man the finger, then stopped himself. Such would be the action of a wild and reckless teenager and he was no longer such a child. Whether he got credit for it or not, he led one of the most successful criminal cartels in Mexico's history, and his reaction to the irritating horn should reflect his status.

So Morales smiled into the rearview mirror and

waved. The Chevy was close enough for the driver to see his expression in the reflection, and he smiled and waved back. The drug cartel leader waited until the Toyota had moved again then followed quickly in order to get a look at the Chevy's front license plate. Pulling a ballpoint pen from an inside pocket of his black paisley vest and a small notebook from the side of his long black frock coat, he jotted down the numbers and letters. Just below the license he added the words *red hair* and *gringo* before turning in his seat to make certain the driver saw him smile again.

The man with the red hair returned the smile and waved once more.

Morales was still grinning—but for a different reason now—as he twisted forward in his seat again. He lifted the Cuban cigar from the ashtray, rolled it against the side of the receptacle to rid it of the new ash that had built up, then took in a mouthful of smoke. His thoughts returned to the important business he had to conduct within the next couple of days. Those thoughts, however, were broken once again.

As the smoke drifted back out of his mouth, Morales heard a tap on the window to his side. He turned to see a one-armed little girl who could have been no more than seven years old. In addition to the amputated arm, she wore a steel leg brace that started somewhere beneath her worn cotton dress and ended at the ankle. With her one hand, she extended a cardboard box filled with packages of chewing gum.

He shook his head at the little waif, waved her away, then turned back to the front. He pretended not to see the saddened look on her face. Beggars—almost all of them permanently injured or deformed in some way—repulsed him. They were as thick as flies and mosquitoes on this bridge, and of no more use than such insects. Had it been up to him, he would have machine-gunned down the worthless creatures and buried them in a mass grave somewhere out in the desert. Simply looking at them made him sick to his stomach.

Morales continued to wait, moving forward occasionally, then stopping, then repeating the procedure again and again. He waited for the next beggar to approach. But although he saw many mutilated people limping throughout the other cars around him, no one else bothered to tap on his window. He laughed softly. They had to have seen his reaction to the little girl and decided not to waste their time.

As the Cadillac neared the border, Reynaldo Morales glanced at the gray spot on his trousers again, noting this time that a small amount of ash had also stuck to his vest. He would have to change it, too. But it would be no problem. He had several changes of clothing in the trunk. That thought returned his mind to the style of clothing he wore as the true leader of the Morales Cartel. It was a sort of Old West look. He had gotten the idea from a painting of Jim Bowie that had hung in the Texas Rangers Hall of Fame in Waco for many years. It consisted of a cravat instead of a tie, a long frock coat, paisley vest and striped slacks. He knew such clothing was more than a century out of date, but he wore them anyway. The archaic mode of dress made him stand out.

People remembered him. And those who remembered him remembered his power.

Suddenly Reynaldo Morales saw that he was next in line at the border-crossing checkpoint. The customs official at the booth directly ahead had evidently checked all he planned to check on the Toyota and was waving it on into the United States. A second later, he turned to Morales and beckoned him forward. As he lifted his boot off the brake and pressed it gently onto the accelerator, the uniformed man suddenly recognized the Cadillac.

Morales pulled up to the side of the small guard booth and stepped on the brake again before shifting into Park. The U.S. Customs man was Gus Newton, one of the officers with whom he regularly dealt. Newton stepped up to his window carrying a clipboard. Just behind him was a younger man Morales didn't recognize.

"Morning, Rey," Newton said, leaning down and resting a forearm across the edge of Morales's open window. "How you doin' today?"

"Excellent," Morales said, smiling back. "If I was any better, I'd have to be twins."

It was part of their regular exchange and, as always, Newton treated it as if it was the first time he'd heard the line. Then he came back with what he always said next. "I see you still think you're living in the nineteenth instead of the twenty-first century." He eyed the man's coat, vest and cravat.

Morales finished their banter by saying, "You're just jealous of my exquisite taste in clothing." Then he laughed politely. "Looks to me like you've got a new rookie with you."

"Yep," Newton said, raising back up and gesturing for the young man to come forward. "Jack Stoops, meet Reynaldo Morales. Reynaldo's one of our regulars. A lawyer—but we don't hold that against him."

Both Newton and Morales laughed—again more out of courtesy than mirth.

"Rey here has law practices on both sides of the river," Newton went on. "Actually, a pretty darn good man."

Stoops shook Morales's hand.

"Rey," Newton said, "our supervisor's here today. I hate to put you out but I've got to at least make it look like I'm checking things."

Morales nodded, smiling. "No problem, Gus," he said.

Then, looking toward Stoops, he added, "Don't worry, kid. I never carry my dope in my car."

Stoops seemed slightly taken aback, but Gus Newton threw his head back and laughed out loud. "Get out and open your truck if you don't mind, Rey."

Morales slid out of the Cadillac and walked to the rear, inserting his key. A moment later, the trunk was up and Newton and Stoops were unzipping a suitcase and a long leather clothing bag. Inside was another long frock coat, but this one was brown instead of black.

"How many of these Wyatt Earp-lookin' coats you got, Rey?" Newton asked. "I half expect to find a double Buscadero rig and a pair of pearl-handled Colt Single Actions on you one of these days."

Morales chuckled. "That'd be illegal."

"Your *clothes* ought to be illegal," Newton said and

they both laughed again. By now the young Stoops had even loosened up and joined in.

Reynaldo Morales waited patiently as they continued to rummage through his suitcases. It was all for show—all for the supervisor's benefit—and the man in the long black coat knew they wouldn't look too closely. Actually, while he didn't have any Colts with him, Morales *did* have a pistol—a .40 S&W Glock to be exact—hidden under the spare tire. But the show Gus Newton was putting on for his boss wouldn't include going to all the trouble of unscrewing the tire and lifting it out of the trunk.

Finally satisfied that the supervisor—if he was watching—would be satisfied, Newton rezipped Morales's luggage and closed the trunk again.

"FYI," he said as he turned to Stoops, "Reynaldo here is good people. There's no need to put him through all this when the big man ain't around. Don't waste your time with him. Just pass him through and look for suspicious folks."

Stoops appeared to be learning the difference between what he'd been taught in the classroom and the way things actually operated in the field. He looked puzzled.

"You'll remember him," Newton said, clasping a hand on the younger man's shoulder and chuckling. "Just look for a guy dressed like an 1830s Mississippi riverboat gambler." He led the way back to the front of the car and picked up the clipboard he'd left on the Cadillac's hood.

Morales opened the door and the smoke from the still-burning cigar in the ashtray came streaming out in the vacuum. He slid back in behind the wheel and stuck it back in his mouth.

"Okay, Rey," Newton said. "Anything at all to declare?"

"Women are more trouble than they're worth?" Morales replied.

The customs man threw his head back and laughed again. Then, looking back down, he said, "You know what I mean." His gaze shifted to the cigar still smoking in the ashtray. "That's from Jamaica, I assume."

Morales laughed. "Uh-uh," he said. "Dominican Republic."

Newton closed his eyes and shook his head. When he opened them again, he said, "I guess we can overlook one half-smoked Havana. Take off, Rey. We've taken up enough of your time."

"No problem," Morales said as he threw the Caddie into Drive. "See you coming back, amigo."

"You coming back tonight?" Newton asked offhandedly.

"No," Morales said. "Probably be a few days this time."

"Well, take it easy," the U.S. Customs man said.

Morales glanced quickly into the rearview mirror and saw the redheaded man in the Chevrolet waiting. Pressing down lightly on the accelerator, he drove through the checkpoint, taking one final glance at Gus Newton. Soon, it would be common knowledge that he was the brains behind the Morales Cartel and he wondered if Newton—and other customs agents with whom he often joked—would still be friendly. He didn't know, but he didn't care.

The money would be worth it, and he'd no longer have need to pass through their booths anyway.

Reynaldo Morales was only three blocks into El Paso when he pulled his cell phone from the inside breast pocket of his long coat. Punching the button at the top to turn it on, he waited while it found service and then tapped the button for a frequently called number.

The number began to ring. A moment later, a sleepy-sounding voice said, *"Sí?"*

"Get something to write with," Morales ordered in Spanish.

"Just a minute," the voice said, sounding fully awake after recognizing who was on the other end. "Okay. Got it, sir."

Morales looked down at the small spiral notebook and read off the numbers and letters from the Chevrolet's license plate. "It's a Texas tag," he said. "Chevrolet. Couldn't tell the year but our inside man with the Department of Public Safety will have it when he runs the plate." He turned the Cadillac toward the highway. "Guy has red hair."

"Got it," the voice replied.

"I want him put down before sunset," Morales added.

"No problem. Can I ask what he did?"

"Sure," Morales said. "He honked his horn at me."

CHAPTER SIX

"Just our luck," Burton said under his breath as he twisted the key in the Winnebago's ignition and started the big engine. "Our first assignment is to deliver cash instead of H." To Bryant, sitting in the captain's chair that served as the front passenger's seat of the motor home, Burton's eyes appeared to be glued to the windshield in front of him. But the Recon Marine knew that his new Navy SEAL partner was actually watching a man a few feet in front of the vehicle. The man wore a jet-black shirt, a black leather Western-style vest and black slacks. He stood facing, and conversing with, Tony Moreland. "Julio," Moreland had called the man when he'd introduced them a few minutes earlier. He'd explained that anonymity was crucial to their business, and that the less they knew about each other the better. That way, if one of them got arrested they had little to give up to the authorities in exchange for a reduced sentence. For Moreland—who represented the link between the legitimate Lohman's Motor Homes and Recreational Vehicles business and the shadier side for which it fronted—that anonymity was impossible. But men like Julio didn't need a last name, and Bryant suspected that "Julio" wasn't even the man's real first name.

Moreland had made it clear that should they give in

to the temptation of trying to steal the money they were about to transport, he had police connections who could track them down. He'd forced the two men to leave their thumbprints on separate index cards, seeming to take true delight when he wrote "Laurel" on one and "Hardy" on the other. And "Laurel and Hardy" or sometimes "Stan and Ollie" was what the Lohman's manager had been calling them ever since.

How Moreland could track them down when both men didn't have their fingerprints on any database, Bryant had no idea.

He glanced at his watch as he continued to watch the two men in the front of the Winnebago. Julio had long hair which fell to his shoulders and matched the rest of his black outfit. He was clean-shaved except for a long, thick and well-trimmed imperial beard that fell from just below his bottom lip past his chin. It was as black as the rest of his hair and outfit. But the wrinkles in Julio's face made him look as if he might be a few years too old to have a total absence of gray in the hair on both his head and face. So the Recon Marine highly suspected the man made frequent trips to a drugstore for a little hair-and-beard dye.

Moreland and Julio continued to talk, occasionally glancing toward the windshield of the Winnebago.

Rephrasing his earlier statement, Burton said, "I'd feel better if we were hauling dope on this run instead of money."

"Why?" Bryant asked, swiveling in the captain's chair to face his new partner. "For one thing, it wouldn't make sense."

"I guess you're right," Burton said. "The drugs come from the South, which means the money has to go down from up here."

"Exactly," Bryant said. "Besides, Cooper strikes me as a fast worker. My guess is that if he and Nash haven't already found a way to infiltrate the Morales Cartel, they will shortly. The fact is, we might just be on our way to a drug deal where we'll find Cooper and Nash hauling the dope themselves." In his peripheral vision, he saw Burton frown.

"Now it's you who isn't making much sense," the SEAL said, but without any form of rancor or judgment in his tone of voice. "Cooper and Nash are already on the border, and I'd guess these deals—the exchanges themselves—take place shortly after the drugs cross into the U.S. We're several days away. So I suspect we're headed toward a different dope deal—one that won't cross over the line for another day or two."

"Well, let's hope so," Bryant said. "It wouldn't do much good to meet up with our brothers-in-arms and shoot each other, now, would it?"

Burton chuckled. "No, it wouldn't. And I don't know about our Delta Force friend, but there's something about Cooper—or whatever his real name is—that makes me suspect we might just come out on the losing side of such an encounter."

"I hear you, bro," Bryant agreed. "The man definitely has an air about him." The Recon Marine finished speaking and took advantage of the legroom at the front of the motor home to cross one leg over the other. It wasn't often that he had enough space to do that. For a moment, he eyed his new partner. Shooter Burton had one of those ectomorphic bodies that was the total antithesis of his. The SEAL was roughly six feet tall but probably weighed no more than 160 pounds. His arms exhibited the long, lean and wiry muscles that defined the ectomorph who trained hard. But Burton would never be able to build muscle past a certain point no matter what he did. Men like him could spend all day in the gym and eat the diet of a sumo wrestler and it would make no difference. They didn't gain muscle or fat.

Bryant knew he was different. He was the epitome of the mesomorph body type, and even took the word to new levels of definition. He was strong, and had yet to see the man who could outlift him in the gym.

Bryant squinted slightly. Matt Cooper was still on his mind. And the leader of this unusual "multiforce" mission might just be the first man he'd ever encountered who was actually as strong or stronger than himself. He wasn't sure. But he wouldn't want to bet his Marine retirement on himself.

The Recon Marine put those thoughts behind him. He had work to do, and now he noticed that Burton had grown silent for a few moments. The Navy SEAL grasped the steering wheel in front of him with both hands and tapped the hard plastic with the fingers of both hands as if playing a bongo accompaniment to some unheard song. His head swiveled to face Bryant.

"The part that I *really* don't like is this Julio character coming with us," he said. "For instance, we need to check in with the base and we aren't going to be able to do that with him along. Even now, with him outside the car but able to see in, we can't risk it." As he spoke his gaze was glued to the windshield and the two men just on the other side of it.

"Well," Bryant said, "what did you expect? I mean, Moreland's just met us, we've done our best to subtly let him know we're amateurs, and he only knows us by the fake names of a thirties and forties comedy team. The man doesn't know yet if he can trust either our loyalty or our competence. We made sure of that. So he's sending a babysitter." Then, feeling like that subject had been covered as well as it was going to get, he added, "You happen to see what our new best buddy is carrying? Weaponwise, I mean?"

Burton shook his head. "Not completely," he said. "But that vest looks like one of those that has holster compartments built into both sides. It's unzipped, and both sides of the front are hanging pretty evenly. But lower in the front than in the back. I'd guess there's a full-size handgun of some sort on both sides."

Bryant nodded. "I hadn't noticed, but you're probably right. I guess that means there's good news and bad news. The good news is that that carry mode makes for a slow draw. Depending on how the vest's designed, he'll either have to unsnap or unzip the holster pocket before he reaches inside."

"Yeah," Burton agreed, "but unsnapping is faster than unzipping. And I think that vest's made by Schaefer Outfitters, which means the holster pockets snap."

Bryant squinted toward the driver's seat. "How can you tell all that?"

"Because I've got a vest just like it," Burton said.

"But mine's brown." He cleared his throat, then went on. "But snap, zip, it doesn't matter much. The bad news is that he'll be riding *behind* us all the way from New York to Mexico. We can't watch him constantly, and he'll have more than enough time to get to one, or both, of his guns before we even know what he's doing."

Bryant chuckled. "That's okay for you," he said. "He won't shoot the driver. We'd wreck."

"He can still shoot you," said Burton. "What it really means is that he'll wait until we've stopped somewhere along the way, then kill us both. Besides, you're going to take your turn behind this wheel. I'm not guiding this tank all the way to Mexico."

"Truth be told," Bryant said, "I don't think he plans to shoot either one of us. He's just here to check us out as the new kids on the block. Moreland wants him to make sure we don't try to take the money and run."

"That means he'll be wondering if we plan to shoot *him,*" Burton said. "Which, in turn, means he'll be on high alert and have an itchy trigger finger for the next few thousand miles."

"And that, my swabby friend," Bryant said, "brings us back to square one. He'll be behind us, but we need to keep as close an eye on him as we can the whole time. Right up until we deliver the money to whoever we're taking it to." He reached up and pulled down the sun visor in front of him, smiling when he saw the mirror attached to the back. "This thing will help. At least some. See if you've got one."

Burton pulled his visor down far enough to see another mirror, then nodded. "These things come in handy for more things than putting on lipstick and eye shadow."

"You start putting on lipstick and eye shadow and you can find yourself a new partner," the Recon Marine said.

Burton flipped up his visor. "Sometimes I think I should have taken my mother's advice and gone to medical school," he said.

"You'd be bored out of your mind," Bryant said. Through the windshield, it looked as if Julio and Moreland's meeting was winding down. So he spoke quickly. "While we're still on the subject of guns, we don't even know what we're carrying or *where*. And if one of us does get shot, that could prove important."

"My Beretta 92 is in the back of my belt," the SEAL said. "Got the compact model in my left boot."

"You have 9 mm popguns?" Bryant said. "I thought they let you Team's boys carry anything you wanted to."

"They do," Burton said. "And that's what I wanted to."

"Okay, I'll try to make do if you get killed first. I've got a .40 S&W Browning Hi-Power stuck in my pants just behind my right hip and a featherweight S&W Scandium 5-shot in my right rear pocket."

"A little .38?" Shooter said. "And you're making fun of my 9 mms?"

"It's a .357 Mag," Bryant answered. "Considerable difference."

"What's it weigh?"

"Around fourteen ounces, loaded."

"Must have some kind of recoil," Burton said.

"Kicks like a six-legged mule." Bryant laughed. "But

having a sore hand the next day isn't something I worry much about when my life's on the line."

That subject exhausted, Burton turned his gaze back to Moreland and Julio and shook his head in disgust. "Are they ever going to stop talking?"

Bryant was getting impatient, as well. The discussion between the two men was dragging on. "I don't know," he said. "You're right. We do need to contact base and get them up to speed when we can. But it can wait until we know more about where we're going. Right now, we're just going to be following Julio's directions. And he won't tell us any more than we need to know during each step of the way. I think—"

"Wait a minute, Jarhead," Burton cut in. "The meeting's breaking up. Here comes our new friend who dresses like Zorro."

Moreland suddenly stuck out his hand, Julio shook it, then turned quickly and started toward the side of the Winnebago.

As Julio neared, Burton shook his head. "If you were casting the part of a Mexican cartel drug dealer for a movie," he said under his breath, "you couldn't do any better than Julio." A second later the door opened, Julio stepped up and into the motor home, taking the seat directly behind Burton.

"Let's go," he said with a thick northern Mexico accent.

"Your wish is our command, Julio," Bryant said.

Seconds later the Winnebago pulled out from behind the office and showroom building on the Lohman's lot and was heading south through Brooklyn.

Toward Texas, and maybe Mexico.

SEVERAL OF THE LIGHTS were on inside the house along the side Nash had been assigned to recon. The trouble was, the window shades were down on most of them. Those without shades had curtains that limited any view from the outside.

Still, Nash hoped to at least be able to see tiny bits of the rooms behind the visual barriers by peering into the corner and the sides. He had taken off his Panama hat, rolled it up and stuck it into the back pocket of his faded jeans.

His hat out of the way, Nash was able to press his face against the screen covering the first window near the front of the house. By looking through a tiny space where the shade had begun to curl outward in the bottom right-hand corner, he could see the end of a gaudy, burgundy-colored piece of furniture. It was either a couch or a stuffed easy chair, but too little of it was visible to determine which. Not that it mattered much. He assumed he was looking at a living room.

Nash moved on to the next window. The view there was completely blocked so he wasted no time, moving on along the side of the house. The next glass-covered aperture was smaller, and higher up on the brick that covered the outside wall. But it didn't look as if it was blocked by either shade or curtain. The problem was that it was too high up for him to see through.

Looking around quickly for anything he might stand on, Nash saw nothing, then turned back to the house. He hadn't drawn a weapon yet, so he bent his knees, then propelled himself upward, catching the row of bricks just below the glass with both hands and pulling himself up.

When he looked through the window from this chin-up position, he saw exactly what he'd expected to see—a bathroom, light on, but vacant. It told him nothing about what kind of people lived inside.

Dropping back to the grass once more, Spike Nash shook his head in mild frustration. He wasn't sure they were going to learn anything from this clandestine recon of the house, and they were taking a chance of getting caught with each second they spent skulking around the yard. But if there was one thing he'd learned about Matt Cooper, it was that the guy knew what he was doing. He wasn't just big and fast and tough. He was smart, too. So if Cooper felt that this was an aspect of the mission worth doing, that was enough for the Delta Force operative.

There was one more window on his side of the house, near the back corner, and while it wasn't illuminated, it looked as if there was a soft glow somewhere behind it. Moving stealthily, Nash crouched beneath the glass and saw that while the curtains were closed, they didn't quite come together in the middle of the window.

It reminded him of a thousand hotel and motel rooms he'd stayed in over the years where the same flaw always irritated him. It was one of Nash's pet peeves. As unlikely as it usually was, he still hated knowing that someone might sneak up and be able to peer inside through the crack and see him.

And *shoot* through the crack if the notion to do so struck them.

But this was one instance where that flaw in security was working in his favor. Drawing his Kimber Ultra+, he squatted just below the window. Then, pressing his face against the glass, he stared between the curtains. Across the room, lit only by a small lamp next to a reclining chair, he could see a man from the waist down to the floor. An open book was in the person's lap. Nash waited until the man turned a page, then moved to the side of the window again before standing back up.

All he knew now was that there was a man inside the house, reading. Again, hardly evidence either way to the man's criminal activity or lack thereof.

Rounding the corner of the house, the Delta Force man suddenly heard the loud barks of a dog. In the middle of the backyard he saw a Doberman pinscher straining against a chain. He wondered briefly if this might be one of the dogs they'd heard earlier.

Not that it mattered. The dog's sudden activity was likely to alert anyone in the house that something was going on outside, which meant he needed to finish his recon as fast as possible before the back door opened and one of the Morales clan shoved the barrel of a shotgun through the opening and cut him in two with a load of buckshot.

In addition to the glass in the door, Nash saw three more windows in the back of the house. All four openings were covered, and there weren't any cracks between the shades or curtains through which he could gain partial vision of the rooms inside. So, without further ado, as the dog continued to bark and growl, he turned and hustled back to the arranged meeting place in the front yard of the house next door.

Bolan was already waiting for him.

"See anything?" Nash asked the big man.

Bolan shook his head. "Nothing conclusive," he said. "You?"

"Same problem. Just a guy reading a book in what was probably a back bedroom."

"That dog isn't there just by chance," Bolan said.

Nash nodded. "He's their first line of defense. Their warning. Their low-tech alarm system."

"Which means," Bolan said, "that unless he's the kind of dog that barks all the time for no good reason, they're inside the house right now wondering if something is going on outside. At this point, they won't be sure."

"No," Nash said. "But they'll have stepped up to the next alert level."

Bolan nodded. "Neither of us wants to kill innocent people who just happen to be part of the Morales family," he said. "But we've got Anita's word that the four men who live here are dirty."

"You think that's enough?" Nash asked.

"Not by itself," Bolan said. "There could be all kinds of reasons she might say such things, and the fact that it's the truth is only one possibility."

"I'm not following you," Nash stated. He could feel himself frowning.

Bolan looked at the Delta Force man and, even in the semidarkness, Nash felt as if the big man's eyes were penetrating his own. "The Morales family is a big name around here—and all over Mexico and the U.S. border states, for that matter. That means that anyone related to them—dirty or clean—is suspect. That's how rumors get started and rumors are like snowballs rolling downhill. They just get bigger and bigger as they go whether they were originally based in fact or not."

Nash nodded.

"Or Anita might just be mad at one or all of them," Bolan went on. "Maybe they don't keep their lawn up the way she'd like. Or maybe she just flat out doesn't like them for whatever reason and sees a chance to cause them trouble. That doesn't mean they're actively involved with the part of the family who smuggles drugs, runs guns, kidnaps people and mows them down with AK-47s."

"You're right," Nash said. "So, what do we do from here?"

Bolan smiled in the moonlight. "We confirm what Anita told us from another source," he said.

While Nash waited, Bolan pulled a satellite phone from a pocket of his jeans and lifted it to his face. Tapping in a number, he pressed it against his ear, and then waited for the scrambler to kick in. After the call was routed through a series of cutouts, he was connected to Barbara Price's line.

"Barb, I need the Bear." he said after she'd picked up.

Whatever *that* meant, Nash thought.

A moment later, still speaking in hushed tones, Bolan said, "Bear, I need an immediate check on an address in Juarez—12313 Pello Calle. There should be four men living there. The name is Morales. See what you can find out about them and call me back." He hung up.

Nash and Bolan stood silently for two minutes or so, waiting. Then the sat phone in the big warrior's hand began to vibrate, and he pressed it against his ear once more. "Yeah, Bear," he said softly into the phone. Several more seconds went by. "Okay, Bear. Exactly what we needed. Thanks." The phone went back into his black jeans.

Bolan looked at Nash and said, "My contact found some DEA intel on the house. It's suspected of being the primary transfer location for drugs heading north across the border. It confirms what Anita said, including the fact that three of the four are brothers and the fourth's their cousin."

"Then I'd say it's time to go inside and take them out," Nash said.

"My thoughts exactly," Bolan replied. "But if possible, I'd like to take one of them alive." He paused, looked over his shoulder for a second, then turned back. "You want the front or back door?"

"Makes no difference to me," Nash said.

"Then you've got the back," Bolan told him. "Since the front is closer, I'll give you ten seconds. Ready?"

"Born that way."

"Then let's go."

Nash started to sprint toward the rear of the Morales house as the man he knew as Matt Cooper took off for the front door.

BOLAN JOGGED across the grass, drawing his big .44 Magnum Desert Eagle as he ran. When he reached the front porch of 12313, he leaped up from the grass, vaulting over the two steps that led to the door. Then, counting off ten seconds in his head, he lifted a foot to knee level before sending it shooting straight out in what was known as a thrust kick within karate circles.

The sole of Bolan's shoe struck just below the keyhole, forcing the door inward and splintering the wooden frame around the bolt. The door not only swung open, it came off its hinges and sailed inside.

A split second later, Bolan heard a dull moan, then the door fell to the floor on top of a man dressed in khaki slacks. The man's head and shoulders were hidden beneath the door.

As he reached down to jerk the door away from the man's head, Bolan heard a crash at the rear of the house. And as he caught his first glimpse of the Morales man who'd been struck by the flying door, he heard two shots ring out.

Bolan looked down to see an abrasion on the forehead of the man beneath the door. A knot was already swelling where the door had made contact, but the man—whether one of the brothers or the cousin—was still conscious. One of his hands was fumbling around on the floor, trying to grab a Walther P-38 that he'd dropped when the door crashed down on him.

The Executioner had told Nash that he wanted to take one of the men alive in order to gain intel. That desire hadn't changed, and he doubted he'd have a better chance than this one during their raid on the house.

So, as the man's hand finally found the grip of the P-38, Bolan rapped the Desert Eagle against his prey's temple, sending him off to dreamland. A second later he'd pulled several plastic cuffs from his pocket and bound the man's hands and feet. With a sweep of his foot, he sent the Walther sliding under the fallen door, out of sight.

Straightening, the Executioner found himself in a short foyer. To his left stood an opening that he suspected led to a living room. Taking two quick steps, he turned the corner into the room and saw a man with an Uzi submachine gun grasped with both hands. The man had heard the shots from the rear of the house just as Bolan had, and had turned that way.

That was a bad move on the gunner's part. Before he could turn back around to face the Executioner, Bolan had fired two .44 Magnum hollowpoint rounds from the Eagle, which all but destroyed his adversary's head.

More shots rang out from the back. They sounded like pistol rounds, too loud to be 9 mm rounds, not loud enough to be .44 Magnums.

They were .45s. Nash and his three-inch-barreled Kimbers were in the game.

The Executioner rushed forward, prying the Uzi out of the nearly headless man whose brain and skull fragments covered the living room carpet. Holstering his Desert Eagle Bolan looked down at the weapon. The safety was already off. He lifted the barrel to his nose.

The absence of gunpowder odor told him the weapon hadn't yet been fired. So, unless the Uzi hadn't been completely loaded to begin with, he had a full magazine with which to work as he made his way through the house to meet up with Nash.

Bolan could see the entry to another hallway in the

far wall and he moved that way, treading softly across the carpet, determined not to give his exact location away until he absolutely had to. When he reached the hall, he stood just to one side of the opening, listening. More shots came from the back of the house. Some, he pegged as more from Nash's pistols, but mixed in with those were rifle rounds. They sounded like 5.56 mms, which meant somebody probably had an M-16 set in semiauto mode or the civilian version of the rifle, the AR-15, which fired semiauto only. Not that it mattered.

Even in semiauto, the weapon was fast enough to cut a man in two with enough well-placed shots.

Leaning slightly around the corner, Bolan caught a quick glimpse of an eye at the other end of the hall. It jerked back as soon as Bolan's head made its appearance. The man at the other end was using the same tactic that Bolan was employing.

Unfortunately for him, he wasn't as good at it as the Executioner was.

Bolan dropped to one knee, then lowered himself to a prone position. Twisting the Uzi slightly in his hand, he again peered into the hall. Whoever was at the other end was still in hiding.

A moment later, the same head he'd seen seconds before appeared again. In the same standing position. In the same spot. Firing the Uzi one-handed, Bolan sent a trio of 9 mm rounds down the hall. The first struck the corner of the drywall in front of the man's face, drilling through the eye, throwing the man backward.

Bolan corrected his aim instinctively and the second and third rounds struck the man in the other eye and chin. His rearward progress toward the wall sped up, and his back slammed against a closed door before he slid down the wall into a sitting position, dead.

Jumping back to his feet, Bolan stepped into the hall. With the Uzi held down at a forty-five-degree angle, he passed a closed door across from him as he slid his back along the wall toward another opening halfway down the corridor. It was through this wide opening that he heard the gun battle raging, and he suspected that Nash and whichever of the Morales clan he had encountered were pinned down in a stalemate.

Utilizing the same strategy as he had before, but leaning around the corner from a kneeling position this time, Bolan made sure his head didn't appear at either of the other heights it had before. What he saw made him shake his head in amazement.

His back fully exposed to the Executioner, a man wearing a black T-shirt and blue jeans knelt behind a sofa that looked to have been pulled away from the wall. That wasn't so amazing. What was, was the fact that the entire rear of the sofa had been fortified with a steel plate to stop bullets.

If there had been any doubt still in Bolan that these men were among the family's criminal element, it left his mind now. He knew of no law-abiding citizens who turned their household furniture into forts just in case they came under attack.

Just to the side of the sofa, an end table had been overturned and it lay on its side along with a broken lamp and a book that had fallen to the floor.

Bolan watched as the man in the black T-shirt and

jeans raised up slightly over the couch and repeatedly pulled the trigger on his AR-15. But he was hurrying his shots, worried that he might get hit, and most of them went high or wide of their intended target.

And that target was, as Bolan had suspected, Spike Nash. Nash had come into this back room after kicking in the door. Now he found himself pinned down behind a reclining chair. Bolan had heard at least two of the 5.56 mm rounds strike steel with a zinging sound that meant Nash had been lucky. The reclining chair behind which he'd taken cover was lined with steel just like the sofa.

The solution to this problem was simple.

Bolan raised the Uzi a split second before the man behind the sofa rose again. The bolt slid closed and three more 9 mm rounds flew from the Israeli subgun, stitching up the man's spine from his waist to the back of his neck.

The Morales gunner fell forward against the steel on the couch, then rebounded to fall on his side. His eyes stared back at Bolan as if asking the question "Where did *you* come from?"

Nash's eyes appeared over the back of the reclining chair. "I guess a thank-you is in order," the Delta Force man said.

Bolan couldn't help but grin at the man's coolness under pressure. "Don't mention it," he said. Then his smile faded. "We've taken out three so far. There's at least one more guy here. Maybe more if they had any guests or business associates." Taking a short step backward, he looked down both ends of the hall again. Down near the wall where the dead gunner sat, he could see

two doors and a T-turn in the hall. He guessed that
both doors and the turn led to bedrooms. The fourth
Morales—or maybe he and an unknown number of ac-
complices—might be hiding in those rooms. But what
interested the Executioner more was the first door he'd
passed in the hallway when he'd left the living room.
The bottom of the door hadn't quite reached the carpet,
and he'd seen a line of light in the narrow space. He
couldn't quite explain it, but his instincts told him he
needed to check it out. And Bolan's instincts had never
failed him over the years.

Nash walked toward the Executioner, the Kimber
Ultra+ in his right hand, the slightly smaller Ultra in his
left. Bolan looked down at the AR-15 on the floor next
to the man with the 9 mm rounds in his spine.

"I'd upgrade if I was you," he told Nash, and waited
while the Delta Force warrior slid his pistols back into
his pants and picked up the fallen rifle. "There's another
mag sticking out of this guy's back pocket."

Nash leaned down and retrieved the extra 30-round
magazine, dropping the nearly empty box from the carriage and replacing it with the full load.

"Take the back of the house," Bolan said, pointing the
Uzi down the hall. "Check all these bedrooms."

"Where are you going?" Nash asked.

"I'm not sure. I'll tell you when I get back."

Nash shrugged, then nodded.

Bolan spun on the balls of his feet toward the mysterious door near the living room. With the Uzi leading
the way, he stopped to one side, then pressed his ear
against the hollow core and listened. Nothing. Reach-

ing out with his left hand, he gently twisted the knob and inched the door open.

His eyes fell on the top three carpeted steps of a staircase leading downward.

A basement of some sort. As good a place as any for a coward who didn't want to take part in the fight to hide and hope for the best.

Bolan inched an eye around the door. The steps led straight down to the bottom floor. It appeared that the staircase then opened to the left into whatever kind of room had been built beneath the main floor.

Slowly, the Uzi's folding stock against his shoulder and the barrel pointed down, the soldier began to descend the steps.

A million thoughts raced through the Executioner's brain as he took in every tiny bit of information about the steps and subterranean opening he reached. Among them was the fact that not only were the steps carpeted with the same covering he and Nash had encountered on the main floor, what he could see of the room to the left was carpeted as well. That meant he was likely to find a finished basement below the rest of the house rather than a more crude area filled with central air-conditioning units, water heaters and other such utilitarian objects.

A den of sorts, perhaps. Maybe a game room with a poker table or other amusements.

And, his gut told him, the elusive fourth Morales.

When he reached the bottom of the steps, Bolan turned to his left. The first thing that caught his eye was a divan against the far wall. Peering inside, he saw no one, so he stepped on in, the Uzi still aimed ahead of him.

There was no poker table.

But a full-size pool table stood in the center of the room, the balls racked and ready and the cue ball resting at the other end of the green felt-covered slate. On one wall was a cue-stick rack filled with sticks of various lengths. Tiny blue squares of chalk rested on top of the table's rails.

The rest of the walls were taken up with full-size, arcade-style video games, their brightly colored lights flashing on and off. None of that interested the Executioner.

But the door in the corner on the side of the room where he still stood caught his eye.

Slowly, Bolan walked across the carpet toward the door. It looked to be directly below the one that had led him from the upper hall down the steps, which meant that it had to open into an area beneath the stairs. The distinct smell of freshly cut marijuana hit his sinuses when he was still several feet from the door. Shifting the weight of the Uzi so he could hold it in his right hand, the Executioner's left reached out and twisted the knob.

He opened the door to see a man sitting cross-legged on the floor, his hands clasped together as if in prayer and his eyes closed.

Crying.

Bolan kept the Uzi aimed at the man, watching him in his peripheral vision as he took in the rest of the small room. As he had guessed, the ceiling followed the contour of the stairs above it, angling sharply downward toward the spot where the steps reached the floor. Shelves were built into the room on both sides, and what appeared to be one-pound plastic bags filled with the green leafy substance were stacked along the wall.

The soldier had expected to find heroin, but marijuana didn't really surprise him. In this day of carefully cultivated, bred and crossbred "specialty grass," the price of top-grade marijuana was rivaling cocaine, which meant the profit margin was just as good for the Morales family and other drug dealers. Quickly, the soldier glanced up and down the shelves, then across. The amount of money represented here depended a lot on the quality. But if what he saw before him was top-of-the-line grass—as the Morales Cartel was known to cultivate and sell—there was roughly ten million dollars' worth of the weed here in the basement of the house.

When he'd seen all he needed to see, the Executioner bent, grabbed the sitting man by the hair and hauled him up and out of the storage area into the game room. The man's eyes opened briefly and more tears flowed down his face. Then his eyelids closed as if trying to block out the man holding the submachine gun and the reality of the situation.

Bolan shook his head in disgust as he twisted the man around and shoved him toward the stairs. He had hoped to take one of the Moraleses alive. It appeared he had two, and he intended to make good use of them.

As the crying man shuffled toward the steps, the barrel of the Uzi poking him in the back, Bolan couldn't resist saying, "I've always heard how tough you Morales men were. Now it's confirmed. You've got to be really tough to do business when you're crying like a baby who had his pacifier taken away."

CHAPTER SEVEN

It had begun to rain as they left Brooklyn and turned into a downpour by the time they reached the Pennsylvania state line. Julio's English had left something to be desired, and a misunderstanding had caused Shooter Burton to make a wrong turn. The mistake had forced them to drive down a long-neglected access road in order to return to the highway, and the Winnebago's shocks had been tested to their limit as the vehicle bounced over deep chug holes in the asphalt, splashing dirty water and mud into the air like a fat man doing cannon balls off a swimming pool's high dive.

But they had survived, and were only a few miles outside of Pittsburg when Burton first saw the flashing red lights appear in his rearview mirror. A nauseous feeling suddenly started in his throat, then dropped to the pit of his stomach. He turned to Fireplug Bryant next to him, who had already swiveled toward Julio in the seat behind him.

"You're the old veteran here," Bryant said to the man with the long stringy imperial beard beneath his bottom lip. "What do we do now?"

Julio licked his lips, leaving them wet and shiny in the scant light of the moon that drifted into the Winnebago. His eyes darted left and right, then he turned to look over his shoulder.

Which was an exercise in futility, Burton thought. They weren't in a car with a rear windshield right behind the backseat. The whole of the living area was behind Julio, and the back window of the rear bedroom was blocked by the closed door.

Turning back, Julio said, "*Alto,* I guess."

"Stop, you *guess?*" Burton said. "This doesn't seem like a good time to be guessing about things. I mean, if you guys are such pros at all this like Moreland led us to believe, I'd think you'd have already had a contingency plan worked out for just this sort of occasion."

"Just stop!" Julio yelled. "If we have to, we will kill him!"

"Oh, that's a *great* idea," Bryant said from the passenger's seat. "You know anything at all about how cops work?" He drew in a long and angry breath. "He'll have already called in the fact that he's stopping us, and he'll have given the dispatcher the license tag and a description of this vehicle."

Burton glanced into the mirror attached to the back of his sun visor and saw Julio glancing nervously around, his brain obviously trying to process all the information it was taking in and come up with a solution to the problem. But if the face of the Mexican man in the backseat was any indication, that brain wasn't doing a very satisfactory job.

"My partner's right, you know," Burton told the man to his rear. "And how long do you think it'll be after we kill him before they figure out something's gone wrong?

My guess is that he has a specific time period during which he has to contact them again before they assume he's in trouble. That time'll be short, my friend. But probably not as short as the time it takes them to get a couple dozen other Pennsylvania state cop cars heading this way, and a plane or two in the air."

"And this cruise ship on wheels is going to be easy to spot from the air," Bryant chimed back in.

The lights had been flashing for almost a full minute now, and the Winnebago had shown no signs of pulling over. A short staccato-like buzz from the siren being turned briefly on then off again sounded behind them.

Burton heard a clicking sound and looked back into the mirror to see that Julio had unsnapped the left-inside holster pocket of his vest. "Stop!" he said. "If you don't, he'll call in backup anyway. There may still be a way to get out of this."

"Much better thinking," Burton said as he twirled the wheel toward the shoulder at the side of the highway. A moment later, he brought the motor home to a halt, rolled down his window and turned off the ignition, wondering exactly what he was going to do if the man in the marked unit who was even now pulling in behind them decided he wanted to search the vehicle.

Without turning that way, Burton whispered, "Fireplug, open the glove compartment and find the registration and proof of insurance. Hurry." He heard a click as the compartment opened.

The truth was, Burton didn't know what he was going to do if this cop decided he had probable cause to search them. He'd have to play every step of the way by ear. All he was sure of was that he had no intention of letting Julio kill an officer of the law. Shifting slightly in his seat, he made sure his Beretta 92 was still secure in the waistband of his pants. If he had to, he'd shoot Julio. And hope, somehow, that he and Bryant could get it across to the uniformed man that they were on the right side of the law before he shot *them*.

In the side mirror, Burton saw the state cop get out of his vehicle and put on his hat. A moment later, he strolled toward the Winnebago. The "stroll" was intended to make the driver believe this was no more than a routine stop for speeding or some other minor offense. If the occupants inside the motor home were truly bad guys, it afforded the officer some semblance of safety. The state cop wanted to put their minds at ease—at least during this part of the operation during which he was particularly vulnerable.

Burton's father had been a Maryland state trooper and the SEAL had grown up learning little cop tricks like that. But what meant even more to him was that the officer's right hand was resting casually on the butt of the pistol holstered on his Sam Browne belt.

The man was ready for anything, but he was trying as hard as he could not to look like it.

A moment later, the uniformed man stopped just to the rear of the driver's open window. He leaned forward, and with a well-practiced movement looked past Burton to Bryant and all around the front of the motor home.

"Evening, Trooper," Burton said. "I'd ask you if I did something wrong, but that would be kind of a dumb question. If I hadn't, you wouldn't have stopped me."

The trooper ignored the comment and said, "License, registration and proof of insurance, please." With his left hand he braced himself on the top of the door beneath Burton's open window. His right was still on the grip of his pistol.

It all still looked casual. Unless, as Burton did, you noticed that the trooper's holster was just as unsnapped as Julio's vest pocket.

"Here you go, sir," Bryant said, leaning across Burton with the proper papers and a big smile.

Burton had retrieved his billfold from his jacket pocket before the trooper had walked up to the motor home and set it in plain view on the dashboard. Now he slowly picked it up again, opened it and fished out his driver's license.

The state cop took the registration and insurance papers from Bryant's hand and glanced down at them.

The trooper's name tag read Tanner. Burton could see it in the moonlight as the man looked at the papers in his hand. Then, looking back up, Tanner said, "Just the two of you on board here?"

Burton repressed a frown. From where the trooper stood now, he should have been able to see Julio behind him and Bryant. But before he could respond, Bryant leaned over and said, "That's correct, sir. Just me and my buddy here."

Without turning, Burton knew Julio had to have disappeared into the back bedroom of the Winnebago. Just another nail in their coffin if Tanner decided to search.

The trooper glanced down at his hand again. "This vehicle belongs to Lohman's in Brooklyn?" he said.

"Yes, sir," the Navy SEAL said. "We just rented it."

"You have the rental papers with you?"

Burton's mind raced. He'd painted himself into a corner. But he made the decision to say what he said next just as fast as he'd decided upon all the other lines in this impromptu undercover interrogation.

"Well, no, sir," he said, glancing to his hands, which were in the ten and two position on the steering wheel. "My brother-in-law works for Lohman's. So they just trusted us."

A long silence ensued during which Tanner did his best to stare the SEAL down again. Burton let him, returning his eyes to his hands on the steering wheel. He knew what was going through the trooper's mind: Tanner would assume his brother-in-law had snuck the Winnebago out without Lohman's knowing about it, and had either loaned it to Burton free or was pocketing the rental money himself. But either way, it was a minor offense in another state, and Tanner didn't look as if he cared to go through all the paperwork and other annoyances it would take to make such a trivial case.

So far, Burton knew he and Bryant had been doing everything right.

Tanner glanced at Burton's hands on the steering wheel, then over to Bryant. The Navy SEAL followed the man's eyes and saw that the Recon Marine had his own hands in his lap.

"You two certainly know the drill," the trooper said. "You had your papers ready, you keep your hands in plain sight all the time, you're polite and you've got an answer for everything." He paused for a breath. "If I didn't know better, I'd say you're old hands at getting questioned by police officers."

Bryant surprised both Burton and the trooper by bursting out laughing.

"Did I say something funny?" Tanner asked.

"Sort of," Bryant said, leaning over again. "You see, we know the drill because we used to be cops."

Burton let his breath out again.

"Where?" Tanner asked.

"Enid, Oklahoma," Bryant replied without hesitating.

"You're not anymore?" Tanner asked. "You don't look old enough to be retired." His face took on a slightly suspicious frown. It appeared to Burton that the man suspected some kind of malfeasance on their parts that would have gotten them fired or, at least, forced to resign.

Bryant picked up on the trooper's expression, too, and, as his next words left his mouth, Burton decided the Recon Marine had to be one of the best undercover operatives he'd ever worked with. The man could not only think on his feet, he seemed to do so at the speed of light. As Trooper Tanner had said only seconds earlier, Bryant had an answer for everything. What made the man remarkable was that—even though his answers were all bold-faced lies made up on the spur of the moment—they all made perfect sense and sounded a hundred percent sincere.

"Well," Bryant began, "there were these two sisters from Brooklyn who were visiting their relatives in Oklahoma. Their uncle, actually. He'd been Air Force, you see, and was stationed there at Vance AFB. Anyway, we stopped them one night for failure to signal a turn at a stoplight—"

"Okay," Tanner said. "That's—"

"Wait," Bryant said, "I'm just getting to the good part. We ended up taking them out for a later dinner and—"

"That's enough," the trooper said.

"Okay, I'll shorten it a little. Their father had this rec-vehicle dealership in Brooklyn, you see, and offered us—"

"That's enough!" Tanner said again. "I don't need to hear your entire life history."

His eyes fell back on Burton again. "Please step out of the vehicle, sir," he said.

Here it comes, Burton thought. Slowly, he moved his left hand to the door handle, opened the door and slid down from his seat. He was waiting for Tanner to order him to turn and put his hands on the Winnebago. Maybe if he started to turn, then whirled back unexpectedly, he could disarm the trooper before—

But those orders never came.

"Please follow me, sir," Tanner said then turned his back to Burton and walked to the rear of the Winnebago.

And that one simple act—turning his back to Burton—told the SEAL all he needed to know. They weren't going to be searched, let alone arrested. Tanner had bought their story about being ex-cops and trusted them.

Burton followed the man back to his patrol car.

Three steps past the rear of the motor home, Tanner turned and pointed toward the rear bumper. "The reason I stopped you, is that your license tag is unreadable. You've evidently driven through some serious mud somewhere."

The SEAL felt as if a thousand pounds had been lifted from his chest. "Well, I'll be darned," he said. "Yeah, we got off the highway back in—"

"Like I told your friend," Tanner said, "I don't need your life story. Just get it cleaned off. You got a rag or something?"

"Sure do," Burton stated. "Er, am I getting a ticket for this?"

"Not this time," Tanner said. "But I'm warning you. I'm headed down the highway to set up a speed stop somewhere—I won't tell you where. But if you pass me and I still can't read it, I'll ticket you for everything I can find wrong with this buggy. Ex-cops or no ex-cops."

"Thank you," Burton said. "You're a professional and a gentleman and—" He didn't finish the sentence because Tanner had already turned and headed back toward his car. The trooper had evidently listened to all the blather out of the two former Oklahoma cops he could stand.

Burton started back toward the front of the motor home, waving at the man as he passed in his patrol car. The trooper didn't bother waving back.

Two minutes later, Burton had scrubbed the mud off the license plate with a towel from the Winnebago's bathroom and was looking up at the night sky as he returned to the vehicle. "Thank you, God," he whispered under his breath, still wondering what he would have done if the honest—sarcastic, maybe, but honest—state trooper had demanded to search the motor home. He couldn't kill a cop, but he couldn't have afforded to allow Tanner to arrest them and interrupt their mission, either.

Sliding behind the Winnebago's wheel again, Burton started the engine and pulled back onto the highway. By now, Julio had emerged from the rear bedroom and returned to his seat behind Burton and Bryant. The SEAL kept the vehicle five miles below the speed limit, and wasn't surprised a few miles later when he passed Trooper Tanner's marked unit on the shoulder of the road. The state cop held a radar gun out of his open window, aiming it across the median at oncoming traffic but swinging it toward the Winnebago as soon as the motor home passed.

Burton smiled to himself. Evidently, Tanner was satisfied that he had cleaned off the tag and was driving slowly enough. The Navy SEAL felt his shoulders relax again as he drove on.

Time passed as he forgot the trooper and drove through the night. Silence fell over the Winnebago and he glanced to his side to see Bryant reading a Western paperback. Behind him he could hear Julio snoring softly in his chair, and he wondered why the man didn't just get up and go back to the bedroom.

A green road sign with white letters hit the Winnebago's front lights and Burton saw that he was only forty-seven miles from Columbus, Ohio. A quick glance to both sides of the road told him they were in an isolated rural area. The half-moon was high in the sky and, although he knew it was impossible above the sound of the motor home's engine, Burton imagined he could even hear crickets chirping alongside the highway in the ditches.

The Navy SEAL drove on, the only break in the near silence being when a pair of pickups—one an off-white Chevy F-150 and the other a dark red Toyota Tundra—passed, one behind the other and far exceeding the speed limit. They caused Burton to glance down at his speedometer. He was paying careful attention to his own speed, doing his best to avoid another traffic stop that could lead to a search. Satisfied that he was just under the limit, he relaxed again.

Then, suddenly, far louder than the imagined crickets and easily breaking the hum of the Winnebago's motor, a familiar roar penetrated the vehicle. It took Burton a moment to recognize the sound. But at the same time he identified it, a Harley-Davidson Fat Boy motorcycle passed on his left, the man grasping the handlebars wearing a black leather vest with Wildmen, M.C. on the top rocker.

Burton stared at the logo beneath the rocker as the rider pulled back into the right-hand lane just ahead of him. It featured a cartoon Tasmanian devil staring back at him with angry eyes. The Taz held a bowie knife in his left hand and aimed what looked like an oversize Colt Single Action army revolver with his right. The Navy SEAL remembered the motorcycle outlaws who had driven past Lohman's back in New York, and for a split second thought it had to be another chapter of the gang. But as the Fat Boy pulled into the beam of the Winnebago's headlights, he was able to read the bottom rocker on the back of the black leather colors.

Brooklyn, New York.

It wasn't another chapter of the Wildmen. It was the same guys who'd ridden past them back at the lot. Tony Moreland had told them that the Wildmen did so a couple times a day, and that one member of their club even worked as a mechanic for Lohman's.

All the pieces of the picture suddenly fell into place for Burton. The Wildmen hadn't driven past the motorhome lot just to intimidate people, or for fun. They were scouting the place out, using their own form of recon. And when that was added to the information that the outlaw-biker mechanic had undoubtedly picked up by working in the garage, it figured that the Wildmen knew the motor homes that left the lot were loaded with money.

Money that they wanted.

Burton felt his fingers tighten around the steering wheel. The man on the Harley Fat Boy had grinned up at him as he passed, almost as evilly as the Tasmanian devil on the back of his vest. His dirty beard had been so encrusted with food and who knew what other substances that it had barely waved in the wind. But his cleanly shaved head had gleamed in the moonlight. Now, as the Navy SEAL guided the motor home on, another equally filthy biker drew up alongside the Winnebago on a Harley Super Glide, then passed. Then another. And another. And another.

The SEAL looked into both the rear and side mirrors, and saw what looked like an endless sea of Wildmen behind them.

Another thing Tony Moreland had said when Burton

and Bryant had still been in his office now came back to the SEAL: they don't bother us.

Burton's lips were pressed tightly together, then he blew out a lungful of air. It appeared to him that the Wildmen had ridden their Harleys one heck of a long way from Brooklyn. And he didn't think they'd have done so if "bothering" them in some way—like killing them and taking the money they obviously knew was on board the vehicle—wasn't on their minds.

More and more outlaw bikers, riding a wide variety of Harley-Davidson motorcycles, passed the Winnebago. When Burton glanced into the mirror again, he still couldn't see the end of the pack.

Bryant hadn't missed what was going on, either. His book was still open in his lap, but now the man let it fall to the floor at his feet and turned in his seat. "Julio," he said, "if you've got any heavy artillery on board this crate, I think it's about time you break it out."

Julio had been nervously staring into the side mirror next to Burton, then moving to Bryant's mirror, then back again. All the while he'd been wringing his hands, but he hadn't spoken a word. And now, again without speaking, he jumped up out of his seat and almost ran toward the bedroom at the rear of the motor home.

THE SURVIVING BROTHER was José Morales. Fredrico Guzman—the man who had been knocked cold by the door when the Executioner kicked it off its hinges—was the cousin Anita had told Bolan and Nash also lived in the house.

Now, both men were tied hand and foot with plastic

cuffs and sitting on the floor of the living room, their backs against the wall. So far, none of the uniformed security stationed at the entrances to the elite housing addition, their roaming brother-guards who patrolled in cars or Mexican police of any kind had shown their faces or even telephoned the house at 12313 Pelo Calle.

As he looked down at the men seated on the carpet, Bolan suspected things would stay that way. There were obvious advantages in scaring your neighbors half out of their wits when you were in the drug-running business; such fear kept the people in the surrounding houses from bothering you. But there were more latent disadvantages to creating such terror, as well. It meant that the neighbors who ignored you when you were committing crimes also ignored you when you needed help.

Bolan stared at Guzman. The red lump on his forehead had grown to the size of a baseball and turned bright red. The bump sported an abrasion not unlike that of a skinned knee and a tiny trickle of blood had run down the man's forehead, stopping just above the eyebrow where it had clotted and looked like a dark black mole. Guzman stared back at the Executioner, his dark eyes revealing a mixture of anger, pain, fear and anxiety.

José Morales, on the other hand, showed no signs of injury whatsoever. But even though Bolan had barely touched him, Morales's eyes reflected only one pure and unadulterated emotion: terror.

José knew something had gone terribly wrong. He just didn't know exactly what it was yet. If the Executioner had been guessing, he'd have had to assume that José suspected the men who had just attacked the house were with the same group responsible for the massacre at the wedding.

Nash caught Bolan's eye, nodded sideways toward the kitchen door leading off the living room, then turned and walked that way. The Executioner followed. As soon as they were out of hearing range from their two captives, the Delta Force warrior whispered, "I don't see how we're going to get these guys back out with us. They can't climb over the wall with their hands bound behind their backs. If we try to push or pull them over, it's going to create a ruckus that draws attention to us that we don't want." He paused and glanced back at the two men through the doorway, then finished with "And if we cut their hands loose, they're likely to run on us."

Bolan nodded. "That's why we aren't going over the wall with them."

Nash frowned. "Well, then," he said. "How—"

"We're going to take them straight through the front gate." Bolan watched his partner's face for signs of understanding. It took a few seconds, but finally his strategy set into the Delta Force man's features and Nash smiled.

"We're going to drive this load of dope out ourselves," the Executioner whispered. "Using their faces—and the fact that the guards know them and are too afraid to stop or search them—as our cover. Then we're going to smuggle their dope across the border into the U.S. ourselves."

Now Nash's smile turned back into another frown, but this frown reflected more concern than misunderstanding. "Across the border?" he asked. "What do we do if the customs folks decide to search the vehicle?"

Bolan had drawn the Desert Eagle as they spoke, and now he dropped the partially spent magazine from the grip and replaced it with a full load from one of the carriers under his right arm. "We'll cross that bridge when we come to it," he said, thinking about the bridge over the Rio Grande that led from Mexico to the United States. "Pun intended."

Nash shook his head in wonderment, finally saying, "You're the boss. I just hope you know what we're risking."

"Everything's a risk, Spike," Bolan said. "Each step of the way on a mission like this. You know that. You just have to calculate the chances of running into trouble and then weigh them against what you stand to gain."

"And what do we stand to gain?"

"The Morales connection on the other side of the border, and maybe a direct connection to the top dogs on both ends of this smuggling ring."

The Delta Force commando finally nodded. "Okay." Then, with another shake of his head, he said, "I just don't want to get into a gunfight with fellow Americans."

"Neither do I. And we won't." It was his turn to glance back through the doorway now, and he did so as much to check on whether the two captives were trying to get out of their plastic cuffs as to formulate the best way to say what he had to say next. "These guys will be familiar faces at the checkpoints. One way or another, they've been getting across the border for years.

They've either got some of our customs people on their payroll, or they've created some illusion that they're honest Mexicans who cross frequently for legitimate purposes. What we've got to do is find out what ruse they're using, and inject ourselves into it."

"How do we do that?" Nash wanted to know.

"We ask them."

"And if they lie?"

"We make it so they don't want to lie," Bolan said, then stepped back through the doorway and walked to the seated men.

José Morales appeared to be the easiest man to break, so Bolan stopped in front of him, squatting in order to be more level with the man. He drew the freshly stoked Desert Eagle again while staring into José's horrified eyes. Depressing the button to eject the magazine he'd just inserted moments before, Bolan used his thumb to flick the top round of .44 Magnum hollowpoints from the box mag.

The sniveling man had watched each and every movement the soldier had made with the giant pistol, his eyes skirting back and forth like an anxious ferret. Now Bolan held the lone .44 round in front of José's face. "Are you familiar with .44 Magnums?" he asked in a polite tone.

For several seconds, the seated and bound José didn't respond. It was as if he was trying to decide whether the man who had dragged him out of the marijuana stash room wanted him to say yes or no and he wanted to make sure he gave the right answer. Finally, he said,

"I know what they are. I've never used them before myself."

The Executioner smiled.

"Well, José," Bolan said, "you ever see any Dirty Harry movies?"

"Clint Eastwood," José stated. "I've seen them all...I think."

"Well," Bolan said, still holding up the semijacketed cartridge and letting the ceiling light shine off the brass casing. "In the first one, Harry states that the .44 Magnum is the most powerful handgun in the world. But that movie's pretty old. There's a 500 Magnum now, a .50 caliber, and a whole lot of what they call 'wildcat' cartridges between the .44 and .50." He paused to take a breath, a smile on his face. "What we could say now, however, is that the .44 Magnum is the most powerful caliber that is still practical for combat. The others are great for hunting, silhouette shooting and specialized conflict situations. But the .44 is still my favorite all-around choice. That is, if a man can handle the recoil."

"And you can handle it?" José rasped out through dry trembling lips.

"Take a look around you," Bolan answered. "Two of your brothers seem to have thought so."

A lump almost as big as the one on Guzman's forehead slid slowly down José Morales's throat.

"But we're wasting time here," the Executioner said. "I want you to look at this cartridge and imagine what it would do to your head. Or, if your imagination is limited, I could take you through the rest of the house and show you what they've already done to your brothers. Should I do that?"

Tears were forming again in the corners of José's eyes. They might have come from sorrow over his brothers. But Bolan suspected that in the eyes of a selfish drug dealer like Morales the tears were more from anticipation of what might be about to happen to *him*.

"You don't…need to do that," José said hoarsely.

"Then let's move on. Picture a pumpkin being dropped off a ten-story building onto the sidewalk. That's kind of what your head is going to look like if I decide I need to shoot it with one of these." He twisted the .44 Magnum round in his fingers so that the light glimmered off the brass even more.

"I don't…want that," José whispered.

Next to Morales, Fredrico Guzman had been watching the entire minidrama. Bolan could tell from the man's face that while he knew he had fallen into a precarious position, he lacked the level of intimidation that gripped José's heart and soul.

Guzman had heard enough and he looked down at the floor and spit. "You are a weak little prick," he told his cousin in Spanish. "Don't let this—"

That was as far as he got. Nash had been standing next to the Executioner, and now the Delta Force commando took a half step forward with his left leg, then brought his right hiking boot up in a fast snap-kick that caught Guzman just below the chin. The man's head jerked back, striking the wall. Then his eyes closed and he fell unconscious.

"Thanks," Bolan said over his shoulder. "José and I hate interruptions, don't we, José?"

José nodded vigorously, glancing to his side where Guzman slumped, and looking as if he was afraid that in a second or two he'd fall victim to a kick—or a .44 Magnum round.

Turning his attention back to José, Bolan said, "Okay, here's the plan. We're going to load up all the dope you've got in the basement, and the four of us are going to deliver it to your contacts across the border. When were you planning to do that before we came calling?" As he spoke, the Executioner had thumbed the .44 back into the magazine and inserted it into the Desert Eagle. But he kept the mammoth weapon in his hand.

"Tomorrow night," José said.

Bolan twisted the pistol slightly and rested the barrel on the bridge of José's nose. "You know where the hollowpoint I just showed you is going if I think you've lied to me, don't you, José?"

"Yes! Of course!" The cowardly Morales brother had found his voice again and the words came out almost as screams. "I am telling you the truth!"

"Well," said Bolan, leaving the Desert Eagle where it was. "Tomorrow's not good enough. We don't plan to hang around here and play video games in your basement for the next twenty-four hours. You have a cell phone?"

"Of course," José said.

"And you've got a number for your contact, I assume?"

"Yes."

"Then I want you to call him—or them—and tell them something's come up. Tell them you've got to make the border crossing tonight and that your brothers can't make it, so you're bringing two other men with you."

"But why wouldn't my brothers not come?" José asked. "They always—"

The Executioner was growing weary of dealing with this cowardly, passive-aggressive cartel man. He pressed the barrel of the Desert Eagle hard against the spot between José's eyes and said in an exasperated tone of voice, "I don't care what excuse you give them for the fact that we're crossing a day early, or that your brothers aren't coming along. Just make sure it works. Because if it doesn't, your head is going to look like that pumpkin we talked about."

Slowly, José nodded.

"One more thing," the soldier said. "There are going to be several steps in this operation during which you're most likely to take a .44 to the brain. First, if I even suspect you've lied to me, here and now. Second, when we cross the border, at the security checkpoint, if you do *anything* that gets us searched and I'll have plenty of time to kill you before we—" he indicated Nash with a sideways nod of his head "—get taken into custody. Third, if you sound like you're trying to give your contact a heads-up during the phone call you're about to make. And fourth, if you try to tip them off when we meet to do the deal on the other side of the border." He waited a moment to let it all sink in, then finished with, "You got all that, José?"

José nodded. By now, tears were streaming down

his face. "You *know* that the other members of the cartel—even though it is run by my family—will kill me for this."

Bolan shrugged as he stood back up. "Maybe," he said. "But what you've got to decide is whether you want to take the chance of that happening later, or die by my hand first. And if you decide the latter, keep in mind that there's not just a chance of that happening. It's one of life's few absolutes."

José closed his eyes tightly, but not tightly enough to prevent new tears from leaking out beneath the lids. He opened them again just in time to see the Executioner draw the Cold Steel Espada Knife, hook the opener on the edge of his pocket and snap the huge blade into position. The flashing steel caused the cartel coward to take in a quick but deep breath. He didn't exhale until Bolan had reached around behind him and it became obvious that he had produced the Spanish-designed knife simply to cut the restraints that bound José's feet and hands.

Nash followed Bolan's lead, pulling out his folding knife and letting the assisted opening device spring the blade like a switchblade. The Delta Force operative cut the plastic cuffs off Guzman, who was still unconscious.

"You have your cell phone on you?" Bolan asked Morales.

José nodded.

"Then get it out and make the call. Put it on speakerphone so we can hear both ends. And remember, if you screw up it'll be the last mistake of your life."

José had been rubbing his wrists ever since Bolan cut him loose. Now he leaned slightly to his side so he could reach into the front pocket of his pants. When his hand came out again it held a cell phone. The cartel man pressed a button at the top to turn it on, then pressed more buttons until he'd reached the speed-dial page. A moment later, he was talking to someone in the Morales Cartel on the other side of the border.

"Reynaldo," José said, before advising the man they'd be crossing over a day early and bringing new faces.

"The situation is not ideal," the voice on the other end of the call said. "But adjustments can be made." Bolan listened carefully. The man called Reynaldo occasionally switched from Spanish to English and back again, but he voiced little problem in either language in regard to taking the shipment a day early. "I will contact our U.S. connection," he said. "I am sure they can be at the ranch house in time."

As soon as the call had ended, Nash began slapping the unconscious Guzman back to wakefulness. When the Morales cousin finally opened his eyes, he saw the Desert Eagle and a Kimber Ultra+ CDP II .45 pistol staring him in the face.

"Get up on your feet," the Executioner ordered the two men. "You've got some loading to do."

Guzman's eyes skirted back and forth from gun to gun, his face confused since he'd missed both the last part of the conversation between Bolan and José and the phone call to Texas. "What loading—"

"The herb," José told him. "We're delivering it tonight. With these guys."

"Like hell we—"

Nash stepped forward and slashed his pistol across

the man's face. The drug runner stayed conscious this time, but a welt on his cheek joined the one on his forehead. "Just do as you're told," the Delta Force man said, "and you might even live through this night." He aimed his .45 at Guzman's head again, then added, "Although I'm not making any promises."

"Neither am I," Bolan added, "but at least there's a chance." Without waiting for a further response, he said, "What kind of vehicle do you use for transport across the border?"

Guzman had missed out on a lot of the drama that had taken place while he was unconscious, but by now José was used to cooperating, and speaking when spoken to. "We've got a fleet of several different types of motor homes," he said quickly. "We were planning to use a Winnebago on this one. It's not parked here, but I can call and have it delivered."

The Executioner nodded. "My guess is that it has New York license plates on it," he said.

José looked slightly surprised. Of course, Bolan thought, the man had no idea that they had another part of this operation going on out of Brooklyn.

"How'd you know that?" José asked.

"Because that's where your motor homes come from," Bolan said. "A place called Lohman's. Now, enough questions. Call and tell your man to deliver it. And keep in mind that this is another period of time when your chances of getting your head blown off are high as well."

José made the call. On speakerphone again. Bolan and Nash learned that the motor home would arrive within thirty minutes.

Bolan jammed the barrel of the Desert Eagle into José's ribs, using his other hand to grab the man's shoulder and whirl him around. With the big .44 now pressed against the cartel man's spine, he said, "Get moving. You and your cousin have a lot of grass to bring up from downstairs before the Winnebago gets here."

Then, Bolan and the Delta Force operative pushed the two drug runners down the hallway toward the basement door.

CHAPTER EIGHT

Ever since Fireplug Bryant had been in grade school, he'd loved a good fight. The first thing he'd learned about fighting was that he was just naturally good at it. At least most of the time. The second thing he'd learned explained why he hadn't been victorious during some of the punch-ups he'd gotten into on the school's playground.

Early on, Bryant had discovered that he had to be on the side of right if he expected to come out on top. If he wasn't—like during the very few fights he'd started himself—his arms and legs suddenly felt as if they'd been dipped in concrete that had hardened. And his balance and timing were atrocious. It was almost as if he *wanted* to get beaten, as if he deserved a good beating for starting the fight himself.

That lesson hadn't taken long to sink in, even to a grade-school brain. So as soon as it had, the boy who was already getting far wider than his classmates but had yet to acquire the nickname Fireplug, had specialized in being a "defender of the innocent." From third grade on, he more or less patrolled the playground during recess, and before and after school, waiting for some older kid to start picking on a smaller one. Then, the broad-shouldered "antibully" went to work.

With gusto.

Now, as Fireplug Bryant watched the Wildmen bikers throttle their Harleys and pull, one by one, around the front of the Winnebago, his mind traveled briefly back to his third-grade year. Even though he no longer fought unless he knew he was right, he had lost a few of those battles to fifth and sixth graders. After all, he had been only eight years old, and he had been facing kids who were eleven or twelve. After those few losses he had gone home with a black eye and bloody nose. But such incidents had never killed his spirit, or his belief that God had put him on this earth to look after weaker people. By the time he was in the fourth grade, he wasn't losing to anyone anymore, regardless of their age or size.

And a strange change had occurred on the playground: the older kids rarely picked on the younger ones anymore. They knew if they did, they'd have this crazy, broad-shouldered boy to contend with. And older bullies had no upside to such a fight. If a sixth grader beat a fourth grader, there was no great honor attached to it—it was expected. And if the older bully lost the fight against an opponent two years younger than him, it produced nothing but shame and ridicule, even from his friends.

Over the years, Fireplug Bryant—the name had finally been tagged to him by a drill sergeant in Marine boot camp—had continued to follow that same philosophy, just on a much larger scale. He fought now for his country, and had proved he was on the side of right in both Iraq and Afghanistan. He had ten times the combat experience of even the most gung-ho Recon Ma-

rine, and he continued to use what he'd learned from it
to fight on the side of right.

The truth was, Fireplug Bryant couldn't remember
the last time his arms and legs felt like concrete. It had
to have been when he was still in grade school.

And they certainly didn't feel heavy or slow now.

As Shooter Burton drove on, staying right at the
speed limit, Julio returned to the front of the Winnebago
with three AR-15s. Bryant took one and looked down
at the selector switch. The weapon he held in his hands
was the semiauto civilian version of the U.S. military's
M-16. And no one had seemed to have seen fit to con-
vert it to full-auto capacity. That meant that he would
have to pull the trigger each time he wanted a round to
fire. There would be no squeezing and letting the rifle
go "rock and roll." Bryant squinted in the dim light, but
he grinned, too. Semiauto was fine with him. Truth be
known, if he'd had his choice he'd have preferred the old
M-1 Garand, which fired a much harder-hitting round—
on semi only. The 3-round burst of the M-16 A-2 might
have been nice, but he could live without it. The bottom line was, as always in combat of any sort, a person
made do with what he or she had.

Julio had leaned another of the AR-15s against the
side of Burton's seat, then laid the third across the arm-
rests of the seat he'd been occupying. He'd hurried back
into the rear of the Winnebago again and now returned
dragging a gunnysack stuffed with items that caused
the rough-hewn material to jut in sharp corners up and
down its length. When he finally set it down between
Burton and Bryant, the open top drooped forward and

a 30-round AR-15/M-16 magazine fell partially out of the opening.

Bryant smiled. He had just pulled back the bolt to make sure that his rifle was already loaded and to chamber the first round. It was good to know that extra 30-round mags—at least twenty, if his guess was close—were available to him and Burton. And Julio.

Now the Recon Marine glanced at the Latino just behind him. He had no doubt that Julio was on his and Burton's side—they had a common enemy and such circumstances dictated it. So the two undercover operatives weren't going to get shot in the back by the Lohman's-Morales man. At least not here and now.

But how good was Julio? How much experience did he have? He was obviously trusted enough by the Morales end of this drug-smuggling operation to be their representative in New York. But that didn't mean he was an experienced combat soldier like they'd need to fight the battle with the Wildmen bikers, which was about to commence. Most cartel gunners were killers, but they were the kind of murderers who lined up, then shot, defenseless, unarmed men and women.

That kind of experience was a lot different than firing at men zipping past on motorcycles who were trying just as hard to blow your heads off as you were theirs.

He caught Burton's eyes briefly, and although he had known the Navy SEAL only a short period of time, he could see that Burton was wondering the same thing he was about Julio. He could also see that neither of them were worried about each other. There might be a tremendous amount of competition—even jealousy—between the SEALs and Recon Marines at times, but when it came down to the wire, both knew that the other had top-notch training and skills, and could be depended on during any kind of altercation they might face.

"Take the wheel for a second, will you?" Burton said.

Without bothering with words, Bryant reached across the Winnebago and grabbed the side of the steering wheel closest to him. As he steadied the motor home on its path down the deserted highway, Burton snatched up the assault rifle Julio had leaned against the back of his seat and laid it across his lap. Ejecting the magazine into his left hand, he checked to ensure that there was a round at the top, then slammed the palm of that hand against the mag to seat the cartridges. A moment later the magazine was in the carriage, and Burton had pulled the bolt back to chamber a round. Bryant watched as the man flipped the selector to safe then nodded to him as he took control of the steering wheel again.

"What'd'ya think their plan is?" Bryant asked Burton.

The SEAL shrugged. "Your guess is as good as mine. But we're only forty-some miles outside Columbus. I'd guess they're going to try to take us down long before that."

Bryant nodded. "The closer we get to the city, the more traffic there'll be. Meaning more witnesses. And they aren't doing anything to disguise who they are." In his mind, he pictured the Tasmanian devil with the knife and revolver. "The closer we get'll mean a faster response time from cops and Ohio state patrolmen, too."

He reached up and rubbed his chin, feeling the two-day growth of sandpaper-like beard he had on it. "Julio, you got any ideas?"

The Morales man behind them shook his head. "I know nothing about these Wildmen," he said. "We had no idea that they suspected anything was going on."

"Well," Bryant said, twisting in his seat just enough to stare at Julio over his shoulder, "you should have because it's pretty obvious that *they did*. That's the problem with big operations like yours. You get to thinking you're so clever that you don't give anybody else credit for having any smarts at all."

Julio didn't respond. To Bryant, he looked too frightened and frozen to react.

Burton continued to drive.

Bikers continued to pass.

"You got any ideas on how to handle things?" the SEAL asked his partner.

"Just keep driving for now," Bryant said. "Pulling over certainly isn't on the agenda."

By now, many of the bikers who had passed them had sped up, disappearing completely beyond the highway's undulating terrain in the distance. The others, who could still be seen, were increasing speed as soon as they passed the Winnebago. Bryant guessed that at least thirty of them had passed the motor home and gone on. Another dozen or so were quickly speeding off to join them.

But what caught his attention even more was that the bikers behind the Winnebago had slowed, and no more of them were attempting to pass.

The Wildmen's strategy hit Bryant and Burton simultaneously, but the SEAL was the first to put it into words. "They're setting up an ambush ahead of us," he said, his hands tightening again on the wheel so hard that Bryant saw the knuckles turn white. "Think it's a roadblock?"

"Uh-uh," Bryant said. "They know we could run right through their bikes with this thing. They'll be on both sides of the road. Firing at us as we come. Probably with rifles."

Julio suddenly came out of his frightened stupor. "I saw no rifles on the motorcycles that passed us," he said, his voice trembling slightly.

To Bryant, it sounded like wishful thinking on Julio's part. The Recon Marine snorted through his nose. "That doesn't mean anything. There are all kinds of ways to camouflage a long gun on a bike. And if you were riding from Brooklyn to Ohio, would you carry weapons out in the open where every Tom, Dick and trooper could see them?"

Julio retreated back into himself and didn't answer.

They drove on for several miles, with no more Wildmen bothering to pass them. If anything, the outlaw bikers slowed even more, putting more space between them and the rear of the Winnebago.

Burton glanced into the side mirror. "They're backing off. They don't want to get hit by stray bullets from the front."

"And they don't want to kill their brothers up ahead with the fire they'll be putting into our back," Bryant added. He turned in his seat again. "Didn't think to ask you before, Julio, but this thing have any kind of armor built into it?"

Julio smiled for the first time since the two warriors had picked him up. It was a faint and nervous smile, but a smile nonetheless. It told Bryant that the thought had suddenly given the man at least an inkling of hope in what had heretofore seemed to be a no-win situation that would quickly lead to his last few moments of life. "The windshield is bullet resistant," the Morales man said. "As are the tires."

"The operative word there is *resistant,*" Bryant said. "And bullet resistant doesn't mean bulletproof, which translates into the windshield and tires will take a certain amount of fire—more than regular—but eventually the glass will break and the rubber will go flat."

"I believe that is correct," Julio said.

"I happen to know it's correct," Bryant replied, noting the irritation in his own voice. He didn't like Julio, he hadn't liked taking the man with them, and he didn't like the fact that the man knew so little about the motor home in which they were about to live or die. But getting mad at Julio would do nothing but take his mind off the life-or-death matter at hand. "So we don't exactly have an Abrams tank with us here," he said, more to Burton than to Julio. "But we don't have a half-rotten old country school bus, either. My guess is that they'll have set up several ambush sites. They probably know about the bullet-resistant thing from their mechanic, so they won't expect the first site to take us down. But they won't want to space themselves out too thin, either. It can't be more than twenty-five more miles before we hit Columbus."

Burton nodded. "I'm going to have to fire one-handed out the window while I drive with the other hand." He glanced over his shoulder. "Are the side windows reinforced, Julio?"

"Not that I'm aware of."

"Didn't figure they would be," Burton commented. "That means they won't stop anything—especially rifle rounds—so you might as well just move behind me and roll down your window like I'm gonna do. Help me fire at the shooters on my side."

He turned his head back to Bryant. "You'll have both hands available, so you'll be expected to take out everybody on your side on your own."

"Can't wait," Bryant said as he pushed the button to lower his window. "Sort of like running a college-fraternity gauntlet line."

"Uh-huh," Burton said. "Except that instead of getting hit with belts or wooden paddles by a bunch of spoiled rich kids, we'll be getting shot at by a gang of heartless sociopaths with rifles." He paused a moment, then added, "A bit of a difference."

The Winnebago topped a hill and suddenly, a hundred yards or so in the distance, Bryant could make out the shadowy forms of men and motorcycles on both sides of the highway. Burton hit the bright headlights and a second or so later, the details of what they were about to face became clear.

Four Wildmen knelt behind their motorcycles on both sides of the road. Rifles—it was impossible to identify what kind each man held—rested on the gas tanks or padded seats of their bikes.

The muzzles were all aimed at the oncoming motor home.

Burton floored the accelerator. "Hold on to your chewin' gum," the Navy SEAL said.

A second later, the first round from the Wildmen struck the bullet-resistant glass, which shattered like a crystal punch bowl being dropped from a thirty-story building.

"So much for this thing even being *resistant*," Bryant said as he pulled the trigger back on his AR-15 and sent his first round of fire toward the men and motorcycles on the right side of the road.

As shards of glass continued to rain down all around Bryant, he heard the other two semiauto AR-15s open up on the other side of the Winnebago.

The rifle rounds from the men behind their Harley-Davidsons kept coming, too.

MACK BOLAN COULDN'T remember how man times he had crossed the bridge between Juarez and El Paso over the years. Or all of the other bridges leading from Mexico to the United States and vice versa. All he knew was that he had entered both countries illegally far more times than he had in this conventional manner.

That was more dangerous in some ways but safer in others. Whether he took one of the little-known back roads that linked the two nations, waded the shallow parts of the Rio Grande, swam deeper waters or dropped in via parachute in either a HALO or LALO jump, he'd been at risk of being killed by drug runners, kidnappers, murderers, revolutionaries and terrorists. But this was the first time in Bolan's career that he was taking the chance of getting busted for bringing illegal drugs across the border.

Seated in the shotgun seat of the Winnebago, the soldier watched the people on the bridge. They were a pathetic lot, and his heart went out to them. Disease, deformation, amputations and every other physical and mental problem imaginable was represented on the men, women and children who sold chewing gum and other near-worthless trinkets, doing their best to rely on the pity of Americans tourists for a few last-minute pesos before the gringos returned home.

Bolan's heart went out to the unfortunates. He thought about the poor and homeless people in the United States for a moment. Except for those who, through mental illness, pride or other self-destructive personality traits refused help, they had shelters and other charitable organizations to which they could turn. Mexico offered few such services, leaving their sick and indigent to their own devices and survival. Not only were the poor in America better off than the indigent in Mexico, their lifestyle would probably have been considered middle class south of the river.

Bolan's attention turned toward José Morales, behind the wheel of the motor home. The man looked nervous, not a good sign when they were about to try to pass through customs with a ton of marijuana. Bolan had originally planned to drive the motor home himself, but José had convinced him that it was better that the border guards see a familiar face in the driver's seat.

The soldier frowned at the slightly shaking man. A familiar face made sense, at least on the surface, but he suspected that the obvious stress seen on José's face and in his jerky body language more than negated any advantage of him driving.

"José," Bolan said, breaking the uneasy silence that permeated the Winnebago.

The drug cartel man's head jerked toward Bolan as if he'd suddenly had a cattle prod jammed into his backside.

"You either loosen up and act normal," Bolan said, "or I'm going to switch places with you and drive this thing myself."

"But if you do that—" José started to say.

"Shut up," Bolan told the cowardly drug runner. "I've already heard your arguments. Relax and act cool or you're going to be replaced."

Seated directly behind José, his cousin, Fredrico Guzman, spoke up. "I have something that could help him."

Bolan turned slightly to see Guzman holding up a small prescription bottle. He glanced at Nash, next to the man, and frowned. Nash had searched both men, but he'd obviously missed the bottle.

Nash's face reflected both embarrassment and a little self-anger. He shrugged, the movement practically shouting out, "Okay, I screwed up, but it won't happen again."

Turning back to Guzman, Bolan said, "What is it?"

"Alprazolam," the man replied. "Generic Xanax. One milligram. He nodded toward the back of José's seat. "He should take one."

Bolan wasn't in the habit of advising a man to take prescription drugs assigned to another, but unique problems sometimes demanded unorthodox solutions. "Give him two," he said, "and be fast about it. We're getting close to the moment of truth."

As if fate wanted to emphasize the soldier's last words, the procession of vehicles—which had stalled while someone at the crossing booth got a thorough search—began to inch forward again.

Guzman shook a pair of pills from the bottle and handed them around the seat to his cousin. José popped them into his mouth, but instead of swallowing them, he began chewing, the pills making loud crunching sounds as they began to dissolve through the membranes inside his mouth.

By the time it was the Winnebago's turn to cross the border, José was feeling no more anxiety—and very little pain. He pulled up and stopped as a khaki-sleeved arm extended from the booth, palm out. A moment later, the rest of the khaki uniform stepped out of the booth and leaned down just outside José Morales's open window.

Bolan twisted slightly in his seat to look past José. What happened next could determine the entire fate of the mission. If they were waved through, they would continue into the United States to meet the Morales Cartel's connection somewhere in south Texas. But if they were searched, even a rookie U.S. Customs agent would be able to find the marijuana hidden under and behind the false bottoms of the benches, beds, closets and luggage compartments inside the motor home.

The soldier's breathing was as relaxed as if he'd taken the Xanax himself. He wasn't afraid for what might happen to him. Even if they were busted, he could contact Hal Brognola, and the Stony Man Farm director—who doubled as a high-ranking Department of Justice official—would get him and Nash out of whatever jail they were put into. But that didn't mean Bolan wasn't worried. It might take the big Fed to wade through several hours of bureaucratic red tape to get them released, and the marijuana would be seized by customs authorities.

A bust this big would make the news, and that news would scare away their buyer in Texas. The end result would be that the whole mission would be thrown off. After all the time and work they'd put into infiltrating the Morales family and their associates, they'd be back to square one with little-to-nothing to show for their efforts.

"Ah, Mr. Morales," the customs agent said in a friendly voice. "Haven't seen you for a while. How have you been?"

Bolan watched José carefully as the man answered. It was a narrow path they were walking now, and the soldier could only hope that this cowardly member of the Morales clan had gotten over his nerves but not slipped into the slow slurring speech that could be brought on by the drug he had taken.

"Doing fine, Carl," José said, and Bolan could see

enough of his face to tell he was smiling. "Just been busy."

"Who are your friends?" Carl asked, looking past the driver toward Bolan, then glancing around the man to see into the backseat.

"You know my cousin Fredrico, I think," José said. "These two gringos are good friends."

"Careful now, José," Carl said in a teasing way. "I'm a gringo myself, you know."

José laughed softly. "I meant the term in the most endearing way," he said. So far, the pills hadn't kicked in enough to affect his speech, but Bolan noted that José's eyelids had fallen slightly lower over his eyes. He just hoped they could get this border interview over with before it became apparent that the cartel man was well on his way to a prescription high.

Carl looked at Bolan. "You've got a name, I suppose, my fellow gringo?" He was still smiling.

"Cooper," Bolan said. "Matt Cooper. My buddy in the back's name is Nash. But we usually call him Spike—for reasons that are pretty obvious."

Carl glanced into the back again, undoubtedly taking in the hair sticking straight up from the top of the undercover Delta Force man's head. "Can't imagine why," he said, still grinning.

Bolan was still looking at the U.S. Customs man, but in his peripheral vision, he suddenly saw another man in a khaki uniform walking past the front of the Winnebago. The man held a leather leash in his left hand. A German shepherd walked a pace of two ahead of him on the other end of the leash, which was attached to a steel choke chain.

As Bolan watched out of the corner of his eye, the dog suddenly stopped in his tracks and turned toward the Winnebago. Then, showing an eagerness he had not demonstrated before, the dog jerked forward, causing the choke chain to tighten around his neck as he tried to move closer to the motor home.

The movement caught Carl's attention and he stood up.

The dog handler was holding his animal back with the leash. "Hey, Carl," Bolan heard the man call out. "I think—"

Carl waved him away. "Don't worry about it," he said to the man. "I know these guys."

By now, Bolan had felt it safe to turn his attention toward the dog and his handler. He watched through the windshield as the second customs man looked suspiciously at them for a moment, then shrugged and moved on.

The dog wasn't as easily dissuaded. He kept straining against his choke chain until he'd been half dragged out of sight toward another booth in the next crossing lane.

Carl looked back inside the Winnebago. "Happens all the time," he said. "Every one of us probably has money in our pockets with drug residue of some kind on it. The dogs get a lot of false hits."

Bolan watched Carl's face, and he didn't miss the quick wink Carl shot at José Morales at the end of his speech.

Their crossing was going to go smoothly no matter

what happened, the Executioner suddenly realized. All of his second-guessing had been for nothing. No matter how nervous or guilty any of them looked or acted, Carl was going to pass them through without any searches, which could only mean one thing.

The Morales Cartel had Carl in its pocket.

A righteous anger rose in Bolan's chest as he realized exactly what was going on. It might be working out for the best for him and Nash at the moment, but, overall, it was a travesty of justice. It meant that the U.S. agents—long known for being more honest than their Mexican counterparts—were no better than the men who worked the south side of the Rio Grande.

Bolan made a mental note to inform Hal Brognola of that fact. If Carl was dirty—and he obviously was—there had to be other customs men who were on the Moraleses' payroll, as well. The fact was, there was no way of knowing how many others might be getting regular payoffs to ignore the drug shipments.

"Okay," Carl said. "José, I know you and Fredrico have your green cards. But you two gringos," he went on, using the term again with a smile on his face, "just need to give me a verbal statement that you're American citizens."

"I'm an American citizen," Bolan said.

"I'm an American citizen, too," Nash added from the backseat.

"Then I'll quit taking up your time," Carl said.

Then, in a much lower, whispering voice, he leaned back into the window and addressed José. "Same drill as before?"

"Bus station in El Paso," José said in his own hushed voice. "Locker 307."

Jose's voice was starting to slur and it wasn't missed by the customs man. Carl frowned slightly. "You aren't using your own products these days, are you?" he whispered again.

Bolan leaned across the front seat. "José had a rough night," he told the man outside the Winnebago. "Wife trouble. He took a muscle relaxer a few minutes ago." It sounded plausible, and Carl nodded.

"Maybe you'd better drive," he told Bolan.

The soldier had no intention of arguing; he just wanted to get through the border crossing and get on with the mission. "I'll switch places with him as soon as we cross over," he said. "No use delaying traffic any longer than we already have." He glanced toward the rear of the motor home where the vehicles were backed up, more for effect than to confirm his last statement.

Carl nodded, then stepped back and waved them on. "Have a nice time, gentlemen," he said. "And remember, don't mess with Texas."

Bolan let the man drive for three blocks before he ordered him to pull over to the curb.

"What's wrong?" José asked, his words slurred.

"You're stoned," Bolan told him. "And we've got a good chance of getting killed when we meet your contact here." As José pulled to the side of the street, Bolan grasped the Winnebago's door handle. "I don't see any reason to up the odds by letting you drive any longer."

A moment later, the soldier had walked around the front of the Winnebago and climbed up behind the wheel. By the time he was back inside the motor home, Nash had evidently made Guzman take the shotgun seat. The Delta Force man still sat in the back. José was next to him, snoring like a freight train.

Bolan turned to Guzman. "You know where we're going?" he asked the man.

Guzman nodded.

"Good," Bolan said as he threw the motor home into drive. "Because I'd sure hate to disturb your cousin's beauty sleep."

CHAPTER NINE

Wind whipped through the huge gap where the Winnebago's windshield had once been. Shooter Burton could have stood that. It was the gunfire that kept whizzing past his head and shoulders that made him realize that he, Fireplug Bryant and Julio came another inch closer to death with every new foot the Winnebago traveled.

Burton steered the motor home with his right hand, firing somewhat clumsily out of the driver's window with his left. Limited to semiautomatic, the Navy SEAL was unable to reliably send the 3-round bursts he preferred toward the men behind the Harleys on the left side of the road. Once he got the *feel* of the trigger, Burton knew he could quickly press the tiny lever three consecutive times and achieve the same results, shooting trios of 5.56 mm ammo from the AR's barrel.

But he wasn't going to have much time to get that *feel*. Not before they passed this roadside ambush.

On the other side of the Winnebago, Burton could see that his partner had taken advantage of the shattered windshield and now rested his own AR-15 on the dash. Bryant had angled the sights toward the right side of the road, and was cutting loose with fast semiauto blasts of fire. In his peripheral vision, he noted that Bryant's first few rounds hit the grass in front of the motorcycles. But the savvy Recon Marine used them as a base from which to walk his next rounds up onto the bikes and the men behind them.

The sudden stench of gasoline blew into the Winnebago on the wind, and Burton realized that either he, or Bryant, had ruptured at least one of the Harley-Davidson's gas tanks. Behind the Navy SEAL, Julio was firing his own rifle, but Burton doubted that it was the Morales man who'd shot into a tank. The fact was, the SEAL was more worried that the man in the rear seat would accidentally shoot *him* than whether or not Julio could hit any of the Wildmen.

His fears weren't unfounded.

A searing-hot pain suddenly shot up Burton's left arm and he felt the cloth of his jacket rip open. "Julio!" he shouted out in anger. "If you can't keep from hitting me, quit shooting altogether!" He was tempted to pull his arm back inside to see if the Morales man's round had cut through his arm or just his jacket. But he didn't want to take the time. They were almost on top of the ambushers now, his arm and hand were still working and in another few seconds they'd be past the ambush site. He could check for injuries then.

Burton angled his assault rifle again and pressed the trigger, over and over. Muzzle-flashes burst from the end of the barrel, lighting up the dark night, and the SEAL noted that one of his rounds cut through the spokes of a Harley Forty-Eight with its front wheel facing the highway. Taking a cue from the Recon Marine at his side, Burton adjusted his aim accordingly and did his own bullet walk. The fourth round to leave the barrel of his weapon struck the forehead of the Wildman kneeling behind the Forty-Eight, cutting the top of the man's head off almost as cleanly as if he'd been scalped with a knife.

The rifle in the man's hands flew into the air, visible in the muzzle-flashes from the other Wildmen who continued to send barrages of rounds through the space where the motor home's windshield had once been. The weapon was silhouetted against the moon for a brief second, and Burton saw why the bullet-resistant glass hadn't performed.

The rifle the biker had used was a large-framed lever-action, probably a 45-70 Marlin. That caliber was an "elephant gun," and if the outlaw biker had been shooting solids, it was far more likely to have penetrated the windshield than the less powerful rounds from an M-16 or AK-47. Especially if the bullet had found a weak spot in the glass.

By now, the Winnebago was almost even with the men on the sides of the road. Burton noted that Bryant had switched magazines and was now emptying his new one as quickly as he had the first. He wasn't just "spraying and praying." As the AR-15 in the man's hands continued to bounce and roar, both men and motorcycles fell like dominoes on the highway's shoulder and in the ditch on his side of the road.

Behind him, Julio was firing his own AR-15. The man had taken Burton's earlier remark to heart, and none of his 5.56 mm rounds were skimming across the SEAL's arm. Whether the cartel man was hitting any of the bikers, however, was anybody's guess.

Burton cut loose with another blast of fast semiauto fire as they finally drew alongside the ambushers, and watched a biker with an AK-47—wearing a black eye patch over his left eye—take a round in his other eye. The man slumped over the bike in front of him, causing the motorcycle to sway back and forth for a moment then topple forward. The man who'd now lost both eyes lost his life.

The SEAL continued to fire. His next several rounds struck a biker squarely in the chest, sending blood out of both the man's front and back as the 5.56 mms entered, then exited. The members of the Wildmen had been aiming another AK-47—this one with a folding stock—at the Winnebago, but now the weapon fell from his hands, skidded off his motorcycle and landed in the grass.

Only one more biker still stood, firing, from the ditch. Burton raised his aim slightly and pulled the AR's trigger again. His round disappeared in the darkness, hitting somewhere out of sight and not affording him any suggestion of how to correct his aim. Operating on instinct alone, the Navy SEAL swung his weapon hard to the left and fired again.

A final muzzle-blast and a lonely-sounding *pop* came from the last biker's rifle. Then he crumpled behind a highly customized Harley-Davidson Cross Bones to be seen no more. Burton tried to fire one final time to make sure he'd gotten the man, but the bolt on his rifle had locked open, empty.

The Winnebago sped past the ambush site and on into the night.

"One down," Bryant shouted through the wind blowing in around the broken glass. "But who knows how many more to go?"

Burton pulled his arm back into the motor home and laid his rifle across his lap as the wind continued to whiz into the vehicle with near-gale force. For the first time since the shooting had begun, Burton realized that the cold air had caused his eyes to tear up, and now he wiped them with the back of his sleeve. Moving the AR-15 from his lap to the top of the gunnysack filled with magazines, he shouted over his shoulder, "Julio! Load me up! I'm empty!"

Julio didn't respond.

Finally finding time to check his arm, Burton shrugged out of his jacket and took his right hand off the steering wheel long enough to run it up and down his left forearm. The skin was still burning, but when he took his hand away, there was no blood on it. There was, however, a long rip through the sleeve that had covered that arm, and the scent of burned fabric now mixed with the smell of burned gunpowder and gasoline that still permeated the Winnebago in spite of the constant wind blowing through the shattered windshield.

Burton slid his arm back into the ragged sleeve.

"You're okay?" Bryant asked. He had evidently watched Burton slide out of his jacket sleeve.

"I'm fine," Burton retorted. Then, over his shoulder again, he yelled, "Julio! I told you to get another magazine into my weapon!"

Julio still didn't respond. Bryant, who Burton had just seen turn to look into the backseat of the Winnebago's cab area, said, "I don't think Julio's going to do that, my swabby friend. Or much of anything else anymore."

Burton glanced up into the mirror, but he couldn't see the cartel man who had been sitting behind him.

Without speaking, Bryant reached over and took the wheel. "Take a look," the Recon Marine said.

Burton twisted in his seat and saw Julio lying on his side on the Winnebago's floor. Blood surrounded him, soaking the carpet. In the semidarkness inside the motor home it was impossible to see where Julio had been shot. But it was more than obvious that he wasn't breathing.

The SEAL turned back and took the wheel again.

Bryant had evidently noticed Burton checking his arm and tattered sleeve. "At least that explains why he didn't shoot the rest of your arm off," he said.

Burton nodded. "This isn't over," he said. "Not by a long shot."

"You're right there, amigo."

"Have you checked behind us?" the SEAL said. "I can't believe the Wildmen trailing us are going to stand by and do nothing while we shoot their bros up front."

"I can't, either," Bryant agreed. "They've got to have some kind of contingency plan in case we don't get killed in one of these ambushes."

"How many of these sites do you suppose they've set up?" Burton asked.

Bryant shrugged his massive shoulders. "Your guess is as good as mine," he said. "But if we're dividing the number of bikers who passed us by the number who were back at the first site, I'd say roughly three."

"That's assuming that they've staked out the same number of men at each one."

"Right." Bryant nodded. "But there's no guarantee that that's what they've done. They might very well just have one more massive roadside attack planned. Their thinking may have been that if we get through their first line of defense—or, I guess, offence in this case—they need more men to stop us at the second site."

Burton could feel himself frowning in thought. "That's what I'd do," he finally said.

"Me, too," Bryant stated. "But there's no telling how these guys will look at it. They aren't SEALs or Marines."

"No, but lots of outlaw bikers have military service in their backgrounds," Burton reasoned. "And some of them, I'm sorry to say, were even in special units like us. They're the ones who couldn't deal with the real world when they left the service."

"Yeah," Bryant said. "Too bad. Gives the rest of us a black eye when the subject of their military service comes up. And besides toting a gun for Uncle Sam, they've undoubtedly got a lot of crank, and probably cocaine, in their backgrounds. And currently in their systems, too. That alone makes them unpredictable."

The Winnebago raced onward, the rural countryside so quiet again that it was hard for Burton to believe they had been involved in a full-scale gun battle only minutes before. He glanced over his shoulder again to where Julio lay.

Hard to believe, maybe. But the dead cartel man was proof.

"We'll just have to take things as we find them, then," Burton said.

Bryant reached behind him, grabbed the AR-15 the SEAL had used, then fished a new magazine out of the gunnysack. A moment later, it had clicked into the rifle and the Recon Marine dropped it back down next to his new partner. Without further words, he pulled his wide frame out of the captain's chair and stood up. "I'm going to go back to the rear and see what I can see behind us," he said.

Burton nodded. "Try to get back before we start the next gunfight, will you?" Burton said.

"Wouldn't miss it for the world."

"Before you go," Burton said, "better check in with whoever it is Cooper has us checking in with. The guys back at that top-secret whatever-it-is site. We need to give them an update, and we haven't had a chance to talk to them since before we got to Lohman's."

"Right," Bryant said. Still standing between the captain's chairs, the air coming in through the windshield hole in the front of the Winnebago rushing past him, he pulled a cell phone from his pocket. "The number's on speed dial, didn't they say?"

Burton was slightly amazed that the man could stand perfectly still against the rush of wind. He suspected it would have blown a slighter man—like himself—completely off his feet. But this guy so aptly nicknamed Fireplug just stood there like the trunk of a giant redwood tree. "Yeah," Burton said. "Speed dial—that's what they told us. And they said it was the *only* number on speed dial on the phone, so even an old devil dog like you should be able to figure it out." He could feel himself grinning in spite of the danger in which they still found themselves, and the grunt he heard come out of Bryant's mouth sounded amused as well.

The Recon Marine tapped a couple places on the phone before raising it to his ear. "I'll fill them in. Who knows when we'll come to another ambush site."

Burton drove on while Bryant made the call, advising the good-looking honey-blonde they'd met and been introduced to back at whatever that place had been of all the things that had happened since they'd left Lohman's.

During the aftermath of the gunfight, with the adrenaline pumping like a freshly tapped oil well, it hadn't occurred to Burton that with Julio now out of the picture, they had no idea where they were going. Now, it did, and he was about to tell Bryant to obtain advice on that subject when Bryant suddenly ended the call.

The Navy SEAL's eyes had turned toward his partner as they topped a hill. Bryant's face suddenly grew hard as he stared out through the broken windshield.

Burton followed the other man's gaze and, in the Winnebago's headlights, suddenly saw two more impromptu fortresses on both sides of the highway. Two hundred yards or so ahead, he could make out more of the Wildmen's motorcycles balanced on kickstands to the sides of the road. Their angry faces, tattooed arms, long dirty hair and the black-but-shiny-metallic surfaces of rifles also appeared in the motor home's lights. "Nice timing on the phone call," he said as he reached down for the rifle Bryant had just reloaded for him.

"I'm famous for such things," Bryant said. Returning

the phone back to a pocket, he grabbed his own weapon. "Looks like it's showtime again. Guess I'll just sit down and enjoy the ride."

"I think we must have different definitions of the word *enjoyment*," Burton said as they quickly neared the men on both sides of the road. "I think I'd *enjoy* things a lot more if the odds weren't stacked so heavily against us." He raised his AR-15, extended it out the window with his left hand again and squinted into the darkness. He could just make out one of the Wildmen—sporting a long ZZ Top–style white-and-brown beard, speaking into a walkie-talkie. "They've got radio com, which means there's at least one more blockade set up somewhere after this one. His finger prepared to pull the trigger back on his AR-15. "So you should have all of the enjoyment you want before this is over."

Bryant had lifted the barrel of his weapon and rested it on the dashboard again. He grunted out a low laugh. "Don't tell me you don't enjoy a challenge, swabby," he said.

"No wonder they call you guys jarheads," Burton said as he finally pulled back on the trigger and sent his first semiauto 5.56 mm round of this second encounter with the Wildmen out the window.

As soon as they'd crossed out of the El Paso city limits, Bolan pulled the Winnebago to the shoulder of the highway. Twisting in his seat, he saw Spike Nash in one of the seats behind him. José Morales was still sleeping off his Xanax, but Guzman was wide-awake in the seat directly across from the soldier.

Bolan reached into an inside pocket of his jacket and pulled out his sat phone. Looking at Nash, he said, "I've got to make a call. Keep your eye on our friend here."

"I'll keep my eye on him," Spike said. "But I can assure you he's no friend of mine."

The Executioner chuckled. A half-moon lit the sky as he dropped out of the driver's side of the vehicle and walked to the back. The sky was unusually clear considering how close they still were to the city, and above he could make out the constellations. Satisfied that the sound of the motor home's idling engine, the wind and the intermittent roar of passing traffic would drown out his words from Guzman's ears, he leaned his back against the chromed aluminum ladder that led to the top of the motor home and tapped in the Stony Man Farm number.

Eventually Barbara Price answered with her usual use of Bolan's mission name. "Hello, Striker."

"Hello, Barb. How're my new teammates up north getting along?"

"They've encountered a little unexpected resistance," the Stony Man mission controller said.

"Explain?"

"Some outlaw bikers—Brooklyn chapter of the Wildmen," said Price. "They followed Burton and Bryant all the way from New York to just outside Columbus, Ohio, with the intention of robbing them."

"Outlaw bikers?" Bolan repeated. "We know we've got the Morales Cartel on one end of this thing, these new mysterious mercenaries who are trying to take over their business along the border, as well, and the

Lohman's connection in New York. Are you telling me these Wildmen fit into the picture somewhere, too?" A roaring semi passed the Winnebago, drowning out Price's next words.

"Hang on a second," Bolan said as he walked to the other side of the motor home, away from the traffic, and leaned back against the side of the vehicle. Pressing the sat phone harder against his ear, he stared out at the open prairie of south Texas. The noise from the highway still wasn't low, but it was better.

"Sorry, Barb," Bolan said when he thought he might be able to hear her again. "You were cut out by an eighteen-wheeler."

"I said that I asked Bryant that very same question. Are the bikers in league with the rest of these murderous miscreants? Fireplug doesn't think so. He said he had it on good authority that a full-patch member of the Wildmen worked at Lohman's as a mechanic, where he could pick up info on the drug and money runs. He thinks it's totally independent of the Morales-Lohman connection. The bikers have figured out that there are millions of dollars on board the motor homes when they leave heading south, and they decided to rob one."

"That seems like the most likely explanation to me," he said. "How are Burton and Bryant faring?"

"They've gotten through the first of what they think are several ambush sites," Price said, "but they've still got a whole herd of Wildmen on their tail, and they expect more trouble farther up the highway." The mission controller paused for a moment, and Bolan heard her take in a soft breath. "And while it's still operating okay—at least for the time being—their Winnebago's shot to hell. Windshield's gone, bullet holes peppering the sides. Even if they don't get killed, there's no way they can drive it all the way to Texas without drawing the attention of a highway patrolman who sees them."

Bolan felt his eyebrows lower toward his nose in concentration. He didn't answer.

"And there's one more problem," Price finally said.

"What's that?"

"Tony Moreland, the manager of Lohman's who seems to be in charge of that end of the operation, sent a Mexican named Julio with them. Burton and Bryant got the feeling, and I think they're right, that Julio represents the Morales interests on that end. The problem is that Julio got killed in the last roadside gunfight, and he was the only one who knew where they were headed with all the money."

Bolan went silent again, thinking, his mind racing with thoughts, ideas and strategies. As each new possibility of how to handle the Navy SEAL's and Recon Marine's situation popped into his head, he analyzed it, weighed it, then rejected it as impractical.

One of those thoughts concerned the possibility that the cash Burton and Bryant were driving south might be for the purchase of the marijuana he, Nash and the two cartel men had just smuggled across the border, but that didn't seem likely. The SEAL and Recon Marine were still hundreds of miles away, and even though the Winnebago in which Bolan and Nash now found themselves had crossed the river a day or so earlier than José Morales had planned, the timing still seemed off. According to Guzman, they were only a few miles from the exchange point. But Burton and Bryant were still over twenty-four hours away, even if they drove straight through.

It seemed far more likely that the money Burton and Bryant were escorting was meant to go straight into the Morales family bank accounts in Mexico. Or that it would be used to pay for a different shipment of illegal drugs.

A soft crackle of static was the only sound over the sat phone as the silence imposed by Bolan's thoughts continued.

Price knew Bolan as well as any other person alive, knew that his warrior's mind was preoccupied and waited patiently. But, finally, after a good two minutes had gone by, even the Stony Man Farm mission controller's patience had begun to wear thin. "Any ideas, Striker?" she finally asked.

"Yeah," Bolan said. "Too many." Then, as so often happened, as soon as he quit focusing directly on the situation—distracted by Price's voice—his unconscious mind took over and the perfect answer popped into the front of his brain. "But I think I just had one good one, Barb."

Now it was Price's turn to remain silent.

"As far as our guys up north are concerned," he said, "tell them that as soon as they're clear of the Wildmen, they should call back to Lohman's and talk to this Moreland character. Just have them tell him the truth, at least part of it—the Wildmen attacked, Julio got killed and now they don't know where to take the money."

Price cut in. "You think that money's on its way down to you?" she asked. "It might be the buy money for the—"

"I thought of that," Bolan interrupted. "It might be, but I don't think so. The timing's off. With Julio dead, Moreland will either have to send another man out to guide them toward their destination or trust them with that information themselves. Considering the time it would take to get a replacement for Julio to Columbus— even if he flew out—and the fact that their vehicle is shot up to the point of being a law-enforcement magnet, my guess is he'll just tell them where to go."

"That still doesn't solve the problem you mentioned there at the end, Striker," Price said. "Their Winnebago really is an attention-getter, and they've still got a half-dozen states to pass through before they even get to Texas."

Bolan had already thought of that, too, and said, "Tell them not to mention the condition of the motor home when they talk to this Moreland character. I've got an idea for that, too. We might as well make use of all the Stony Man resources." He went on to explain, in detail, what he had in mind.

"I'd better get started if we're going to get all that set up and in place," Price said when he'd finished. "I see one other problem."

"So do I," Bolan replied. "But you go ahead and put it into words."

Price said, "A replacement Winnebago won't have all the hidden compartments to hide the money built into it."

"No, Barb. It won't. They'll just have to come up with some story to cover that discrepancy. My guess is that as long as all the money is still with them it won't be that big a deal." He stopped talking long enough to let Price catch up on the notes he knew she'd be taking as they talked, then went on. "Get them some suitcases or trunks or both, and tell them to stash the money inside. They're both supposed to be top operatives, which means they should be able to solve the unexpected problems that come up during any mission on their own. So tell them to be creative, particularly if they find out from Moreland that they'll be crossing the border into Mexico."

"Affirmative," said Price. "Now, what's your situation?"

"Nash and I are just north of El Paso," he said. "We've got one Morales brother and a Morales cousin—who's part of the cartel—with us. In a way, we're in somewhat the same situation as Burton and Bryant. The bad guys are directing us to the meeting place."

"You don't know where it is yet?" Price asked.

"We know the general area is close by, but not the precise location yet."

"Okay," Price said. "Let me know when you do."

"You've got it. Anything else?"

"Jack's on standby, right?" the mission controller replied. "I might need him."

"No problem. Keep me informed, then, on what's happening in Columbus," Bolan said. "And if I'm vague with my answers to you over the phone, just figure I'm inside the Winnebago or somewhere else where I can be overheard." Without further ado, he tapped the button, ending the call.

He walked back to the driver's door and climbed behind the steering wheel. He looked first to Nash, who was still covering Guzman with his Kimber Ultra+ .45, then to José Morales, and finally to Guzman. "All right, Freddie," he said to the man, "time to meet your connection. Which way?"

Guzman wasn't happy, but the look on his face told Bolan that the man knew he'd be killed if he didn't cooperate. He had sensed from the beginning that he wasn't dealing with normal American law-enforcement personnel whose hands were tied by the rules and regulations that savvy drug runners and other criminals could manipulate.

"Straight ahead," Guzman said. "I'll tell you when to turn."

Bolan threw the motor home's transmission into Drive. "I'll be looking forward to it," he said with only a trace of sarcasm in his voice.

CHAPTER TEN

Reuben Ortiz was the name the man had chosen to use when he'd first decided to organize what he thought of as his dream team. The idea hadn't come to him in a dream, but he had been in that mystical, magical period halfway between sleep and wakefulness, having laid in bed after an extremely stressful day. He had just begun to drift off when the thought had suddenly struck him and jerked him upright in bed into a sitting position.

His unconscious mind had screamed at him to recruit mercenaries, well-trained men who can shut down the Morales Cartel and threaten their very livelihood!

Now, as Ortiz rolled back the sliding door to the clothes closet in his Springfield, Missouri, motel suite, he remembered the event as if it had happened only minutes before. He couldn't recall which early-American statesman—perhaps Benjamin Franklin, perhaps not—had once said, "Nothing is invented and perfected at the same time." But regardless of who had uttered those words, Reuben Ortiz had to take exception with such a conclusion. Granted, great ideas and their improved-upon finalities seldom came hand in hand. But once in a while, as had happened to him when he bolted out of his own personal twilight zone, a man experienced the grand idea of his lifetime, and the future that lay ahead of him, all at once.

Standing before the row of suits that he had carefully hung in the closet, Ortiz let his eyes roam from hanger to hanger. As they did, he congratulated himself on the fact that he wouldn't be needing the ski mask he'd worn when he led his mercs on the massacre in the Mexican church. That thing had been hot, and had itched like crazy in the heat. But it had been necessary. Now it wouldn't be.

Ortiz continued to search the hangers. While all the suits were quality garments, a few were *extra* special, and it was one of these that was called for now in the meeting over which he was about to preside.

Ortiz smiled to himself as his eyes continued to run back and forth along the silver bar inside the closet. He had read a book many years ago entitled *Dress for Success.* He couldn't remember the author's name but that didn't matter. Authors were never important—only the information they presented was—and Ortiz remembered one particular theme that had run through the book. Navy blue and gray suits—with or without pinstripes but if striped very *subtly* so—emanated seriousness, confidence and power from the man who wore them. Khaki and other lighter colors subconsciously relegated their wearers to a more subservient role. But black—not black pinstripes or even subtle checks—just flat black, was what he needed now.

The plain black suit represented one thing and one thing only: intimidation.

The suit Ortiz finally pulled down from the closet

was not only black, it was unique in other ways. It had
been tailored by an Italian company whose name—
scrolled in such fancy script just above the inside left
breast pocket that he couldn't read, let alone pronounce
it—even had the expensive striped lining in the sleeves
that marked it as truly top quality. Ortiz remembered
waiting patiently while the company's representative
had carefully measured him for the suit in a room at
the Anatole Hotel, just off Dallas's market center. He
had waited even more patiently during the six months it
took—even for a man of Ortiz's money and influence—
to receive the suit from Milan. He remembered the man
with the measuring tape, and how that man had winced
when Ortiz had first asked, then finally *demanded,* that
this suit be cut and styled a little differently than most
Italian garments.

Ortiz was from the Texas-Mexico border area, he had
explained to the measurer. And he wanted his clothing
to reflect that heritage. The suit was to be constructed
in the "Western" style, with a yoke in the back and front
that dipped into subtle-but-noticeable arrowhead points
just above the pocket on the left side of the jacket, as
well as the front of the right side. The pant was to have
slash pockets, and the legs had to be cut slimmer than
would be found on a more traditionally styled custom-
made suit. With an ever-so-slight "bell" from the knee
down to accommodate cowboy boots.

Ortiz had been afraid the man with the yellow tape
measure might burst out in tears upon hearing these de-
mands and, indeed, the Italian tailor's eyes had become
somewhat watery. His voice had even trembled slightly

when he'd said, "But *signor,* sir, you are paying close to ten thousand dollars for this suit. Surely you do not want to—"

"I want exactly what I just told you I wanted," Ortiz had interrupted him. "Nothing more and nothing less. And since I am the one who will be paying for it, I expect you to follow my orders."

The man from Italy had finally shrugged in resignation and continued his measurements, taking notes.

Now, Reuben Ortiz, clad only in plain white boxers, a handcrafted white silk dress shirt and black socks, carried the suit to the bed and placed it carefully on the bedspread. Tearing away the transparent plastic that had protected the garment since its last dry cleaning, he unbuttoned the jacket and set it to the side, careful not to place it in a position that might cause it to wrinkle. Again, careful not to disturb the sharp crease that had been steam-pressed into the fabric, Ortiz stuck first his left, then his right foot into the legs. He smoothed his heavily starched white shirt over his abdomen and upper thighs, then pulled the slacks up over the tail of the shirt, zipped the zipper and buttoned the waist.

At the foot of the bed stood a crocodile boot bag, and Ortiz bent and unzipped the protective cover. Being as careful as he had with the suit, he removed a pair of black Old Gringo cowboy boots and slipped his feet into them. The boots—like the rest of the clothing— were unique unto themselves, Ortiz having commissioned the company directly to construct them out of full-quill ostrich skin that had been carefully dyed a specific tone of black.

Next came the suit jacket before he flipped up the collar of his white shirt and walked around the bed. His suitcase already lay open on top of the short metal and canvas luggage table next to the sliding glass door. He looked down to see an assortment of bolo ties, bracelets, belt buckles and rings—all in turquoise and silver or silver alone. His eyes roamed the collection, his brain trying to come up with the most impressive combination to go with the clothing he had chosen. Finally, he reached down and pulled out a huge silver bracelet featuring a buffalo head, and a gigantic bolo with the same design. The set had come from a noted Navajo jewelry-maker, and together were worth over three thousand dollars. Ortiz frowned. He needed a buffalo-designed ring to go with it but hadn't yet located one. In the meantime, he settled for a bold silver ring that featured an Indian pueblo and slipped it onto the middle finger of his right hand. The bolo went around his neck, the bracelet onto his wrist.

Ortiz knew that the impression he made on the men with whom he was about to meet was important. They had to see him as tough but elegant; scrappy but successful. And it was the subtle little touches, he knew, that separated the true leader from the wannabes.

Frowning slightly, the man with silver on his right side chose turquoise for his left. Two nearly identical rings—both sporting semicoiled snake designs that featured turquoise eyes inlaid into the serpents' heads had been soldered onto the blue-stone background. The larger of the pair went onto the middle finger of his left hand. The smaller on the finger where a married man might wear a wedding band.

Walking back to the bed, Ortiz shrugged into his black coat, opened a leather hatbox and pulled out a black handmade cowboy hat. Glancing at the inside band, he saw the words Custom Made Especially for Reuben Ortiz. The sight made him grin. He had covered all the bases in creating the mythical identity he was using in his position as leader of the mercenaries. No one—even if they checked his hat—would ever think to wonder if that was his true name.

With the hat now sitting on his head, Ortiz strode purposefully to the full-length mirror just off the room's bathroom. He turned, facing full front into his image, then tipped the hat slightly down and to the right. Then, squinting slightly, he scrutinized the overall picture. He liked the way the shiny jewelry played off the flat black of his suit and hat. The sharp contrast seemed to make both more distinct, and carried with it the message that he was a man of both power and imagination.

And a man not to be messed with.

Working quickly now, Ortiz closed his suitcase, stuffed it into the closet and shut the door. He glanced at the face of his watch and saw that he had a few minutes to spare before his mercs arrived. He used the time to straighten the suite's bedroom on the off chance that one or more of his men might need to leave the living area to use the restroom. He wanted nothing in the room to appear permanent; the entire suite should look as if he had rented it solely for the meeting about to commence, not that he had spent the previous night there.

Ortiz walked into the living room and took a seat on one of the small divans facing the door. A few minutes later, the men began to arrive. Some came singly, others in pairs, but by the time the last one was let into the room there were twenty.

He and the men remained silent until the last man had arrived, but during that interval, the man wearing the black suit and custom cowboy hat surveyed them. Some were *norteamericanos* who were former Green Berets, Army Rangers or elite warriors from other branches of the U.S. armed forces. Others had been police officers who, for one reason or another, had been fired or pressured into resigning. But others came from south of the Rio Grande. Before him, Reuben Ortiz saw men who had once been *federales, rurales,* or Mexican soldiers of one variety or another.

But, American or Mexican, all the men in the motel suite had at least two things in common: they knew their way around weapons and combat, and they had all been let go from their previous positions for less-than-honorable reasons.

The divans and chairs in the living room had been taken quickly, and now half the mercenaries stood, leaning against the walls. But as soon as the last man had entered, Reuben Ortiz stood, moved to the far back of the room so he cold face them all and cleared his throat.

"Gentlemen," Ortiz said with a trace of a smile, "we are gathered here today for two reasons. First, we are about to make a great deal of money. Once again, we are going to kill as many members of the Morales Cartel as we can." He forced a smile onto his face, a very special smile that he'd been told instilled fear in those who saw it rather than reflecting the mirth most smiles conveyed. "And be on the lookout for an older, grey-haired man who looks more like he should be sitting on a beach drinking something with a little umbrella sticking up out of the glass instead of still overseeing drug transactions. That would be Don Pancho Morales, who has been called out of retirement due to the fatalities we inflicted on his family during the raid at the church."

"You think the old man will actually be on this drug run?" one of the mercenaries, a black man, originally from Jamaica who had served in the British army, asked.

"I doubt it," Ortiz replied. "But we should be ready for the possibility in order to take advantage of it should the opportunity present itself."

All around the room, everyone nodded their understanding.

"I want all the Morales Cartel men who have brought the marijuana across the border dead," Ortiz said, "but I want Don Pancho in his grave most of all."

The men already knew their assignments. There was nothing more to discuss.

So without further discussion, the meeting broke up and Ortiz and his band of hired killers headed out into the parking lot toward their vehicles.

THE ARRANGED MEETING place was an abandoned ranch house less than twenty miles north of the border. It wasn't easy to find. It was one of the many geographical areas of Texas that had never been divided into quarter sections for farming, but rather left as prairie on which cattle could graze.

Bolan said little as José Morales guided him first along one twisting ranch road, then another. The roads—dry from a lack of rain for several months—seemed to curve and turn for no particular reason. At least none that the soldier could discern. Bolan glanced occasionally to the map that José had opened and placed on the console between them. The cartel man had opened it to the area that displayed the ranch on which they now found themselves, folding it awkwardly and pressing it down hard to keep the sides from closing back over the appropriate section.

José was resorting to the map almost as frequently as Bolan and, even though the soldier knew the Moraleses had used this site many times in the past, he couldn't help but wonder if José could have found the house without it.

The roads seemed as if they would never end as the Winnebago passed oil wells pumping at various speeds—all resembling some prehistoric bird leaning forward to grab a drink of water, then straightening again before repeating the process. An occasional herd of cattle grazed within the fences on both sides of the hard-packed dirt. Most of the animals ignored the Winnebago, but occasionally, one of the bovines looked up as they passed, chewing its cud as its dull eyes tried to focus on the strange vehicle.

Overall, the atmosphere was one of pastoral peace and tranquility, which the Executioner knew stood in direct contrast to what would inevitably occur on this isolated ranch land before the day was over.

Finally, José directed Bolan to turn left. A hundred yards later, the road curved sharply back right as it started up a hill. By the time they had reached the top, the soldier could see a run-down house in the distance. Perhaps another hundred yards farther on—beyond a cattle guard beneath a padlocked gate—stood not only the house but a large, dilapidated barn and several other sheds and outhouses. All the structures looked as if they had been abandoned for years, and according to both Morales and Guzman, they *had*.

Bolan's eyes fell on the chain wrapped around the gateposts. "You've got a key, I'm guessing," he said to the man next to him without bothering to look that way.

"It is a combination lock," José replied.

"Then I'm guessing you have the combination."

Out of the corner of his eye, he saw José nod.

"Then let's get to it," Bolan said. "By the way, can you tell if the moneymen are here yet?"

José shook his head. "It is impossible to know. They would be in another motor home. I think it will be a Thor or a Daybreak rather than a Winnebago. But either will have been hidden in the barn. If they are here."

"Well, I guess we'll know soon enough, won't we?" Bolan said. "Get out, open the gate and let me drive through." He patted the Desert Eagle stuck into his pants beneath his shirt. "And do I have to remind you that if I even suspect you're trying to signal them, or doing anything else even slightly funny, I'll blow your head off before you can even get three steps away from the cattle guard?"

José shook his head. Then, his eyes closing for a moment—probably in terror, less likely in prayer—he opened the Winnebago's door and dropped down to the dusty ranch road.

A few seconds later, the cartel man had spun the combination lock and pulled the chain off the wooden fence post. Bolan saw him lift the gate slightly to keep it from dragging, then walk forward, opening the wooden barrier and allowing the soldier to drive through.

As soon as the rear of the motor home had cleared the cattle guard, Bolan tapped the brake. In the rearview mirror, he watched carefully, looking for any sign that José was trying to signal his contacts in the house, barn or any of the other ramshackle structures dotting the area. He saw nothing of the sort, but his gaze stayed glued to José as the man walked the gate back into place, rewrapped the chain around the posts, then returned to the passenger's side of the vehicle.

As soon as José had taken his seat again, Bolan said, "What's usually next in the procedure?"

José took a deep breath. "We go to the house," he said. "If they're already here, their motor home will be in the barn. But the house is where they'll have gone to wait."

"And if they haven't arrived yet?"

"Then it is *we* who wait."

Bolan nodded his understanding, but he kept his foot on the brake for a moment, doing his best to think two to three moves ahead again. He and Nash—who still sat behind him keeping an eye on Guzman now—still had no heavier weapons than their pistols, having been forced to leave their long guns back in their vehicle before climbing over the wall into the Twin Pines neighborhood compound. The men who were about to buy the marijuana would be more heavily armed—of that Bolan was certain. That meant that when gunfire erupted—and he had no doubt that it would—he didn't want it to begin or end out in the open. The difference in firepower outside the house would be tremendous. But inside, within the confines of the walls, that advantage would seriously diminish.

Bolan guided the Winnebago slowly up the dirt-and-gravel road that led to the front porch. For a second, he thought he saw movement through the splintered glass that still covered part of one window, but he couldn't be sure. It would have been nothing more than shifting shadows as the south Texas sun moved in and out of the clouds.

"I take it you already know the men we're about to do business with," Bolan said to Morales.

"For years," the man in the shotgun seat replied.

"So how are you going to explain my friend and me being with you instead of your brothers?"

José didn't answer, but his face contorted into what looked like a very pained frown.

"I'll tell you how," Bolan said. "You tell them that your two brothers were killed at the wedding at the church when it was attacked. So you've been forced to go outside the family and hired us in their place."

The frown stayed on José's face. "I suppose that's

as good as anything," he said, but he sounded far from certain.

"Something wrong with that story?" Bolan asked.

José hesitated again, then finally said, "There is something wrong with *any* story that deviates from the norm. Men in our business do not like changes or surprises of any type. They make us nervous. We much prefer things go the same way they always have."

"Well," Bolan said as he slowed the motor home. "Change is the only constant there is in life, and drug dealing isn't an exception to that rule. Life changes, so transactions like this one bring about certain modifications from time to time." Now he removed his foot from the accelerator altogether and tapped the brake. "You'd just better make sure you make this little wrinkle in the procedure sound plausible. Because if you don't, you're going to be the first one dead."

José's expression didn't change. He was already as frightened as a person could get.

Bolan pulled the Winnebago to a halt in front of the house. When he looked through the broken glass in the front windows, he was certain he saw movement toward the broken window he'd seen before. Something red—a shirt perhaps—stuck out slightly from one side of the window frame. "Get out," he told the other men in the car. "And let's get all the intel about these guys we can before everything goes south. And, again, if possible, I'd like to take at least one of these guys alive."

"Gotcha," Nash said. He was the only one who spoke. José and Guzman just opened their doors and stepped down to the ground onto the scattered gravel.

Bolan rounded the Winnebago and fell in next to José. "You lead the way," he whispered, dropping a step behind the man. "And remember what I said about shooting you first." As they neared the rickety, weather-worn wooden steps leading to the front porch of the old ranch house, the soldier was tempted to place his right hand beneath the tail of his shirt. But the position in which he'd been forced to carry the Desert Eagle was hardly conducive to a fast draw—he'd have to snake his hand up under the shirt, then try to keep the light, bunched-up material high enough with his wrist to pull the .44 almost straight up out of his belt. A thousand things could go wrong utilizing such a draw, several points during which the sights could snag or the gun could otherwise get caught on his pants or shirt. The Desert Eagle's position required a two-handed draw, with his left hand crossing his body to lift the shirt while his right produced the weapon. Positioning his hands for such a procedure would telegraph his intentions to even the least experienced gunman.

José reached the stairs a step ahead of Bolan, just as the soldier mentally discarded the whole idea of going to the Desert Eagle first. The Beretta 93-R was stuck in his belt under the *guayabara* shirt on his other side, grip toward the front, in a cross-draw position. This wasn't exactly a quick-draw method of carry, either. But it would be easier to access the Beretta than his Desert Eagle hand cannon.

The rotting wooden steps creaked loudly, threatening to snap as Bolan mounted them behind José. Near the top, an ancient, termite-infested wooden platform gave way beneath one of the cartel man's shoes and his foot started to fall down through the staircase. Bolan's hand shot out reflexively, catching the man by the arm and hauling him on up to the porch before his foot could get stuck. A split second later, both men found themselves on the porch.

José had been terrified ever since Bolan and Nash had attacked his house back in Juarez, and now the tiny, unexpected surprise of almost falling through the steps threatened to be the straw that broke the camel's back and turn him into an out-of-control, babbling, useless fool. Bolan had dealt with informants for years and knew there was a time when they needed to be scared out of their wits in order to be motivated. Fear that took a person to the edge went too far and was counterproductive. Now Bolan sensed how near José Morales was to losing the composure he needed to be convincing in the role Bolan was forcing him to play.

It was time to give the drug runner back at least a sliver of confidence.

"Keep it together, José," Bolan whispered into the man's ear. "You're doing great so far. Keep it up and you'll get out of this alive."

José's nod was all but imperceptible as Bolan released his arm and they started toward the front door.

Behind them, the soldier could hear the footfalls of Nash and Guzman. The two men had seen the wood give way a second before, and their steps sounded slow and cautious.

As soon as he reached the front door, José Morales grabbed for the knob. Before he could twist it, the door opened. A bright red shirt—the same red Bolan had seen through the window—suddenly filled the opening. The shirt was of the Old West style, double-breasted with two rows of buttons running down the bib in the front. Above it, Bolan looked up to see a face with high cheekbones, but the light skin made the cheekbones appear to have come from Slavic ancestry rather than Native American heritage. And the blue eyes of the man in the gunfighter shirt seemed to confirm that suspicion.

The penetrating blue eyes flickered from José to Bolan, then back to José before finally settling on Bolan again. A head of thick unkempt brown hair shot out at all angles from the drug contact's head above thick, equally unruly eyebrows. The grimace around the ragged mustache and goatee conveyed the suspicion about Bolan and Nash that José had predicted would come from the men in the house.

"Who is this?" asked the man in the red shirt. "And why were we not informed that you were bringing new men?" His voice was high-pitched but still commanded authority.

Considering José's mental state, Bolan was surprised at how genuine the man now sounded. "There was no time to contact you, Norman. Surely you've heard about what happened at the wedding?"

"Of course," Norman replied. "You lost both your brothers?"

José looked down at the splintery porch next to his feet and nodded.

"I am sorry," Norman said. "But that was two days

ago. You had no time to pick up a phone and alert me to a change in personnel during that time?"

José looked up again, and once more Bolan was slightly surprised at the show of confidence the terrified man was able to muster. "You will excuse me," he said in a sarcastic tone, "but I was somewhat busy with funeral arrangements. Not to mention the grief of suddenly finding myself an only child."

The words temporarily stumped Norman, and it was obvious to Bolan that this man in the red shirt wasn't used to José taking the alpha role in their relationship. But the Slavic-looking man evidently bought the story.

"Then it is only logical that you had to replace your brothers with new men," said the man with the goatee. "I am somewhat surprised, however, that you chose gringos such as myself."

José straightened, gaining more confidence as the conversation went on. "It is hard to find good help these days," he said with a straight face.

Norman couldn't help but laugh at the clichéd words. "Come inside," he said. "All of you." He stepped back and held the door as José, then Bolan, and finally Nash and Guzman walked into the old house.

As he passed through the opening, Bolan noted that Norman's hands were free of any weapon. But stuck into the front of his blue jeans, contrasting sharply with the bright red color of his shirt, was a dark gray, large-framed Glock, either a .45 or a 10 mm.

The Executioner found himself in a large living room. Hardwood floors that had probably once shone with wax were now dull with neglect and dust. Several threadbare couches and chairs stood around the room, and on them sat hard-looking men, some with AK-47s and M-16s across their laps, others holding Uzi submachine guns or pistols. Next to the seats where the men had positioned themselves, crumpled on the floor, were brown-streaked bedsheets. Other pieces of furniture, which the men had obviously not needed, were still covered by the dirty sheets.

The Executioner counted eight men, including Norman. They all looked Caucasian rather than Latino, which made Bolan suspect they represented the Brooklyn-Lohman end of this drug-running connection. He wondered if there were more in the barn with the cash. Probably.

"Have a seat," Norman told the new arrivals.

Bolan took this opportunity to speak up. "No, thanks," he said, reaching out toward the nearest sheet-covered chair, running a finger down the arm, then raising his hand to his face for inspection. "I washed my clothes a few years back. Hate to get them dirty again."

Norman's penetrating eyes tried to bore through the soldier's. When Bolan just stared back, the man in the red shirt smiled. "The cleaning lady called in sick this millennium," he said. "But we use this house very little."

Bolan nodded. "Then why don't we get on with our business."

Now Norman turned to face Bolan, head-on. "The way you take charge," he said, "you seem to have risen quite high in the ranks for a new employee."

He turned to José. "Does this man work for you, or do you work for him?"

Bolan didn't give José a chance to answer. "I work for him," he said, "but he didn't hire me to be some lackey butt-kisser who never expresses an opinion or adds anything to business." He paused for a moment to make sure he had Norman's attention again, then said in a more friendly voice, "Look, I didn't mean to offend you, but it's always been my policy that the less time you spend doing a deal, the less time you have of something going wrong."

Norman had turned to Bolan while he spoke. "Words of wisdom," he said. "Words to contemplate that I cannot dispute."

He looked back at José once more. "Please accept my apology, old amigo. It appears you have recruited a good man here after all."

José shrugged. "I believe so," he said. "Replacing my brothers, who, as you know, were highly skilled and knowledgeable, wasn't easy. But this man, as well as the other gringo you see before you now, are new *only* to us. Both have had extensive experience in our line of work with other organizations."

Norman glanced back to Bolan. There was still a trace of suspicion on his face, but he shrugged. "I suppose if you trust them…" he said, letting his words trail off in midsentence.

"I do," José said. "Now, if we might continue. May I assume that you have brought the money?"

"You may. And may I assume you have brought our product?"

"Of course." José nodded. "Your marijuana is all hidden within the Winnebago."

"And your money," Norman came back, "is in our Thor motor coach in the barn."

Bolan had continued to watch Norman—and the other armed men inside the old ranch house—as José and the man in the red shirt spoke, his mind racing a million miles an hour. He had originally hoped to get the inevitable gunfight over with here, but he and Nash were not only outnumbered four to one within a smaller living room than the Executioner had guessed the ranch house would have had, the superior firepower that Norman's gunmen possessed was also far and above what he'd hoped to find. But there was another reason that Bolan was about to change his initial strategy in mid-plan, and that was the fact that he highly suspected there were even more drug-buying gunmen—in one way or another connected to Lohman's in Brooklyn—in the barn with the money. He, Nash, José and Guzman had ten million dollars' worth of marijuana in their motor home. Bolan seriously doubted that this man Norman would leave that much money unattended, even with his small-but-well-heeled army only fifty yards away.

Bolan needed to know if there were other men guarding the money, because the sound of gunfire within the house couldn't help but be heard in the barn. As soon as he and Nash had finished off Norman and his men—assuming they could surmount such odds and actually do so—they would have to cross that half-a-football-field span of open area.

In doing so, they would become like ducks in a shooting gallery for the men in the barn.

The problem was, Bolan had no idea how he could

broach the subject of men in the barn without alerting Norman that something was amiss. So he would just have to play things by ear and handle the situation as it unfolded.

Once again, however, José's newfound confidence surprised him. But this time, it was hardly a good surprise.

"Yes, the Thor," José said. "I could not remember which brand of motor home you were using. Do you like it?"

"It gets the job done," Norman said. "I have no other feelings about it one way of another. But our people who modify these things—who construct the hiding places—did a good job as always."

José smiled. "Your men in New York do, indeed, do good work. But even considering their expertise in constructing secret storage places, you have not left the money alone in the Thor in the barn, have you?"

Almost instantly the atmosphere in the living room changed from one of mild suspicion to arctic distrust that hung in the room like some vicious, wild-and-carnivorous entity. Bolan wanted to slap José.

The man's question had been completely out of context within the conversation and even a fool, which Norman wasn't, would have snapped to the fact that José was probing for information concerning armed guards in the barn.

José had tried to cross the bridge that Bolan had recognized as uncrossable; he'd tried to find out how many other men they'd be facing, and the only reason he would have wanted to know that was if there was some kind of double-cross about to take place.

The second the words had left José's mouth, Norman's face had reflected his suspicion. A moment later the look of suspicion became a furious mask of certainty. Something was wrong. Two new faces plus the out-of-place question added up to a swindle of some kind, and the man in the red shirt knew it.

Bolan grabbed his Beretta 93-R and set the selector switched to semiauto.

The only problem was that the rest of the men around the room were readying their rifles and submachine guns as well.

The gunfight was on.

CHAPTER ELEVEN

A split second after Burton pulled the trigger of his freshly loaded AR-15, the Wildmen on both sides of the highway opened up with their own weapons.

M-16s, AK-47s, Uzis and a wide variety of pistols exploded almost in unison like some strange, choreographed ballet of violence. Round after round of all calibers flew at the oncoming Winnebago, many of them striking the motor home in the grille or skimming along the sides. Many others sailed past Burton's and Bryant's heads, coming in through the windshield.

Burton floored the accelerator and the motor home shot forward, throwing the Wildmen's timing off. This time, the majority of the outlaw bikers' rounds were late, again hitting the Winnebago's sides or even flying past the rear bumper and missing them altogether. Burton pulled the trigger on his AR-15 again. Then again, and again.

A biker wearing a cutoff denim jacket rather than the leather vests most of them preferred to fly their colors took a 5.56 mm round straight through a patch on his chest bearing the number 13. The Navy SEAL couldn't help but grin to himself. The thirteenth letter of the alphabet was *M* and the patch stood for marijuana. But the biker who had worn it had smoked the last joint of his lifetime and now he fell forward over the motorcycle behind which he'd been kneeling.

Beside him, Burton could hear the *rat-a-tat-tat* of Bryant's own fast-and-steady semiauto fire as more of the 5.56 mm NATO rounds peppered the men on his side of the highway. In between the shots, the reverberation that came from lead striking gas tanks and other motorcycle parts rang out in the night.

Burton fired again, having lifted the barrel slightly and done his best to align it with his left hand while his right continued to drive the motor home. Under current conditions, it was impossible to utilize the sights, and the SEAL was grateful for the time he had spent on the range and in kill houses practicing his point shooting. He had angled the barrel of the AR toward the head of another biker who had turned sideways to the oncoming Winnebago to change magazines in his AK-47. The man wore a patchy beard and sported long brown hair that looked as if it had never been introduced to the concept of shampoo. Hunkered down behind his bright purple and chrome bike, he was struggling with the rifle.

The outlaw biker obviously hadn't practiced enough, Burton thought as the round he had just fired struck the man in the temple, drilling through the matted hair hanging over his ear. A relatively small amount of residual blood spurted out of the entry hole—at least it was a small amount compared to the flood of crimson that blew out of the other side of his head as the bullet drove on. Like a long-range shotgun blast opening up the tsunami-style wave of blood, which had started inside the man's brain, spread ever wider as it distanced itself from the exit wound. The vast majority of it flew directly into the face of another biker who had aimed his own AK at the Winnebago and was about to fire.

The blood from his outlaw brother was like a slap to the face, and suddenly the skin that had shone white in the motor home's headlights turned scarlet. The red-faced biker stood frozen for a second, either not understanding what had just happened or letting the horror of it momentarily paralyze him.

It didn't matter to Burton which had stopped the man in his footsteps. It gave the SEAL time to reorient his AR-15 and pull the trigger once again. The round disappeared into the face already dripping with blood, and the frozen biker suddenly "thawed." He flew backward into the chopper of yet another of his brothers, doing a backflip over the seat and disappearing out of sight.

Bryant, with both hands free, had continued to maintain a steady stream of semiauto fire from his assault rifle. Out of the corner of his eye, Burton had seen several of the bikers on the man's side of the road go down to the barrage. Now he glanced that way in time to see a clean-shaved biker with a cigarette hanging out of his mouth, squatting behind the gas tank of his elaborate Night Rod Special. Burton could even see the smoke rising upward from his mouth in the bright lights of the racing Winnebago.

Burton turned back to his side, fired one-handed again, then suddenly hit the brake. The new change in speed caught the biker off guard. But this time, their rounds were out ahead of the Winnebago and flew past the grille on both sides. Burton took advantage of the enemy's momentary confusion to pull the trigger twice more and send another pair of the bikers flopping onto the grass alongside the highway.

As the roar from his AR died in his ears, Burton turned back to see if Bryant's aim had been thrown off when he hit the brake. It didn't appear to have been, and Burton marveled slightly at how quickly the two men—granted, from very specialized units made up of top warriors but from completely different branches of the service—had learned to anticipate each other's moves. Such was the hallmark of any successful partnership; both partners had to sense what the other was about to do even before it was done.

Bryant's huge shoulders could barely squeeze through the window at his side, and there was absolutely no space around the frame for Burton to see what the Marine was doing. But through the hole where the windshield had once been, he saw the last few inches of Bryant's rifle pointing down at the man behind the Night Rod Special motorcycle, the cigarette still in place. Then that barrel jumped slightly three times as Bryant drilled a trio of semiautomatic rounds into the gas tank just below, and in front, of the biker's head.

A split second later, Bryant fired again, and this time his round caught the man squarely in the forehead. The man's eyes rolled back into his head and the cigarette fell from his lips—directly into the fumes rising from the ruptured gas tank.

"Hit it!" Bryant shouted to Burton. But just as the Recon Marine had anticipated his partner hitting the brake, the SEAL had caught onto Bryant's strategy a tenth of a second before he pulled the trigger, and had already floored the accelerator.

Only two Wildmen still remained standing on Burton's side of the road. They continued to fire as the Winnebago suddenly shot forward. Burton took them out with a double-tap of his trigger, then turned back toward a trio of outlaws still firing on Bryant's side.

The Recon Marine got one of them amid a barrage of rounds that flew toward him but missed. The other two continued to fire at the rear of the Winnebago as it passed by them.

Bryant jerked his bulk back into the motor home, a big grin on his face. "One thousand one…" he counted off. "One thousand two…"

Burton looked up into the rearview mirror just in time to see angry tongues of red, yellow and orange flames leap up and out of the Night Rod Special's ruptured gas tank. The display was accompanied by an ear-piercing boom, and as he continued to watch he saw the flames reach out and engulf the two Wildmen who thought they had escaped death. The duo screamed, dropped their weapons and began running around in pain-maddened circles of fire.

"Okay," Bryant said. "I was guessing it would be on 'three,' so I was off a second. Still a bad way to die." He reached down to grab two more fresh magazines for his and Burton's rifles. "Betcha it hurts like a mother."

"Yeah, well, better them than us," Burton commented. "In any case, I think they're a little beyond the point where 'Stop, Drop and Roll' is going to do them much good."

Bryant filled the AR-15s with the fresh loads then set them back down. Without another word, he jumped up and walked quickly past the front of the Winnebago into the living area. Burton had slowed the Winnebago once they'd seen the last two bikers go up in flames, and now he twisted slightly to see Bryant through the open bedroom door at the other end of the motor home. He was looking out the back window, his bulk completely covering the frame.

The SEAL looked up into the side mirror for what seemed like the millionth time. Far behind them, he could see headlights. They were bobbing around, up and down, and no two were in line as they would have been had they belonged to automobiles instead of motorcycles. The sight caused Burton to frown.

A moment later, Bryant had returned to his seat. "I don't understand it," he said, staring ahead through the nonexistent windshield as the wind continued to rush through and assault their faces.

Burton knew exactly what he had to mean. "Neither do I."

They had driven no more than another quarter mile when Bryant spoke again. "We saw that they had walkie-talkies earlier, and there's no doubt they had cell phones, too. The maggots we shot wouldn't have had a chance to call ahead and warn their brothers they were losing. But the last two guys doing their fire dance might have had a chance to alert their friends down the road that we'd made it past them."

"Maybe, but I doubt it," Burton said. "We kept them pretty busy shooting at us until we passed. And by the time they'd have thought of their radios or phones, they'd turned into human torches."

The man at Burton's side nodded. "But that doesn't mean we aren't going to face at least one more ambush site in a minute or two."

"No," the Navy SEAL said, "it doesn't." He turned his eyes briefly toward his partner, then back to the road again. "And it doesn't answer the other question we both have on our minds but haven't put into words yet."

"So let me put it into words now," Bryant said. "Why haven't the Wildmen who keep following us taken part in this little circus so far? Why do they just keep trailing behind like a pack of hyenas who plan to let the others make the kill then come in to scavenge?" He waited for several seconds.

But Burton didn't have the answer. He had only suspicions.

The lights of Columbus could be seen in the distance, and when they topped another rise in the highway, they saw a third ambush site set up on the sides of the road. It was still away in the distance, but they were moving toward it fast.

"Guess we'll have to wait on the answer until later," Bryant said. "Looks like we've got another fight on our hands."

"Thought you said you enjoyed this stuff," Burton said as he reached down and behind him for his rifle.

"I say a lot of things I don't mean." Bryant grabbed his freshly loaded weapon as well. "People just like the soothing sound of my voice."

Out of the corner of his eye Burton could see the man

grinning, and knew that, as with most warriors, Bryant *did* enjoy combat—if in a strange and unusual way that most men wouldn't understand. He supposed it might be simply the fact that most people took satisfaction out of putting into practice anything for which they'd been trained, and at which they were good.

At least the Navy SEAL knew that was the case with him.

"Oh, I'm soothed, I'm soothed," he said. He lifted his AR-15 and rested the barrel on the dashboard. There was so little glass left in the windshield now that he'd decided to just shoot out through the front of the Winnebago, too, around the sides of the steering wheel. "You'd think after the first two of these ambush sites didn't stop us, they'd change strategy."

"They have, to a certain extent," Bryant said, pointing ahead. "Look at the road."

The Winnebago was less than a hundred yards away now, and Burton could see the bikers' new setup in the headlights. It looked similar to the gauntlets they'd already run, with one exception. Three motorcycles—one with a sidecar—stretched across the pavement, connecting the two clusters of gunmen on both sides of the roadway.

"And that's not all," Bryant added. He swept an arm around the Winnebago's driving area. "Our windshield's gone, we've got more bullet holes in the sides of this tin can than there is body left, and who knows what's going on with the engine." He pointed through the windshield hole to the front of the hood where dozens more bullet holes were sprinkled. "It's only a matter of time before we become inoperable. We're like a wounded wildebeest at the back of the herd being stalked by a lion."

"Or a pack of hyenas," Burton said, glancing into the mirror yet again.

"Hyenas front and back," Bryant agreed.

Then, as if to confirm Bryant's earlier question about the Winnebago's engine, smoke began to trickle up from the hood. A foul stench blew in with the wind, and the motor home began to jerk in spasmodic convulsions as it slowed from sixty miles per hour to forty.

They were almost at the next ambush site now, and both men readied their rifles as the Winnebago chugged on.

"Got any ideas what we're going to do if this thing actually gives out?" Burton asked. He hadn't really expected an answer, but he got one.

"Well, assuming we live through it, there should be a couple of motorcycles still in good enough shape to ride," Bryant said.

"Oh, yeah," Burton said, nodding. "Good plan. They teach you anything about size and space in leatherneck school? We've got *seven million* dollars on board this landlocked ship-on-wheels and there's barely enough room to carry all the money in here. What do you think we're gonna do, toss it all into a couple of saddlebags and ride off into the sunset like Peter Fonda and Dennis Hopper?"

"It's nighttime," Bryant said. "We're more likely to ride off into the sunrise than the sunset." Then he chuckled. "Guess we could call Triple-A if it dies."

"Yeah," Burton said. "You do that. And I'll let you

explain all the bullet holes in this thing." Bryant had extended his rifle barrel over the dashboard yet again, and now he lowered his eyes down to the sights. "Look on the bright side, Shooter. We'll probably get killed and won't have to worry about it."

A moment later, their rifles were jumping in their hands again.

ONE AXIOM OF GUNFIGHTING against multiple opponents had always been that the wise shooter took out the most dangerous threat first. If that meant two men, standing side by side, with one holding a pistol and the other a shotgun, the scattergunner went down first. If both had shotguns, whoever looked faster became the recipient of the first round. The same theory applied to men with rifles over handguns.

In the situation that Bolan now found himself, the men with the heavy armament were either seated on the couches and chairs or standing casually behind Norman. To a certain degree, the man in the double-breasted shirt shielded Bolan from those who were scrambling to get their more lethal weapons into action.

Norman's right hand had already reached the grip on his Glock, and a .45 ACP or a 10 mm was a big pistol round that couldn't be ignored.

So Bolan's first round from the sound-suppressed Beretta 93-R went straight from the barrel, up into the nose of the man in the red shirt. The subsonic hollowpoint round blew the man's nostrils into nothingness before exploding his sinuses and then exiting out the back of his head. Blood, brain matter, shreds of skull and hair sailed out in a stream of mixed colors a split second before Norman slumped to the floor.

And now, there was nothing between the Executioner and his adversaries.

Bolan twisted slightly at the waist, swinging the Italian-made machine pistol to his left but leaving the selector on semiauto. In this confined space, he'd have little to no time to reload. Granted, he suspected he could count on Spike Nash to back him up to a certain extent, but he knew even a top Delta Force operative didn't have the firefight experience that he had. So the Executioner would stick to the ideology that he always employed.

He would assume that he had to kill all the enemy himself. Any help he got from Nash would simply count as gravy.

The Executioner pulled back on the trigger, taking up the slack and preparing to exert the final couple of pounds of pressure needed to discharge the machine pistol. By his count, he had to drop ten more men with the fifteen rounds he had left after using the one already in the chamber to take out Norman. Three-round bursts—if he switched to automatic—would empty his weapon after a mere five squeezes of the trigger. Not only would he not have time to drop the empty magazine and replace it with a full one from under his arm, he seriously doubted he'd have time to even draw the Desert Eagle.

No, Bolan thought as he pulled the trigger again, firing another suppressed hollowpoint round squarely into the chest of a man with a Zapata-style mustache seated on one end of the couch farthest to his left, he could allow only one cartridge apiece to each drug runner. He would have to make each shot count and, assuming each one hit a vital area and he didn't miss any targets, he would have five rounds left to clean up any less-than-lethal hollowpoint rounds that had slowed, but not finished, any of these Morales contacts on the U.S. side of the border.

The 9 mm round the Executioner had just fired had split the Zapata mustache in two, knocking the man's head backward on the couch and causing him to drop the Belgian FN assault rifle at his feet. Tiny bits of white spewed out from below the man's destroyed upper lip with his last breath of life, and Bolan recognized them as the front teeth that had been in his mouth a moment before.

Gripping the Beretta in both hands now, the soldier swung the gun slightly to his right, raising it over what was left of the head of the man with the mustache. Another of the drug runners had been standing lazily against the far wall behind the now-toothless man, an old and battered-looking ChiCom AK-47 leaning against the wall next to him. He had obviously expected no trouble, but now he had found it. His hands shot nervously toward the weapon to his side, but he succeeded only in knocking it to the floor.

Bolan took advantage of the man's loss of small motor skills, skipping him for the time being, and lowering the 93-R to pump a round into the chest of a redheaded man trying to bring an Ithaca 12-gauge pump gun into play. And he wasn't a moment too soon.

The shotgun barrel was already moving in Bolan's direction when the Executioner pulled the trigger. The bullet disappeared inside the shotgunner's gray sweatshirt, the heavy material letting only a small, short and sudden trickle of residual blood squirt out of the entry hole. The real force of the round, Bolan knew, had mangled the heart and sent pieces of it out the back of the shirt.

The man with the shotgun was just as dead as his brothers-in-sin. His death just hadn't been quite as dramatic.

Now, as the man who had fumbled the ChiCom AK-47 finally retrieved it and started to turn his way, the Executioner turned his attention his way. A double-tap of 9 mm bullets struck the man just under the arm as he turned, causing him to jerk spasmodically but not stop. By the time Bolan had pulled the trigger once again, the gunner was facing him. The soldier's next semijacketed hollowpoint round twisted through the guy's nose like an electric drill.

Bolan heard a sudden explosion and turned just enough to catch a now-familiar sight. Nash held a Kimber Ultra+ CDP II pistol in his right hand. His backup weapon—the Ultra CDP II was in his left, and he had just opened fire with both weapons and taken out a blond-haired and bearded Anglo-looking drug runner. The man with the light hair and skin had just risen from his seat with an M-16 in his arms, and was the closest man in the room to Nash but the farthest from the Executioner.

The ghost of a smile crossed Bolan's face. He and Nash hadn't worked together very long, but, already, they were thinking like a team who'd been paired with each other for years. As the man with the M-16 began to fall, the Executioner noted the blond hair and beard. It looked real rather than peroxided, which tended to confirm that the drug runner had come from the Lohman end of the Mexico-America alliance rather than from the Morales Cartel.

Not that it mattered. Both the Mexicans and Americans were dealing death throughout both countries. All deserved to die.

Another American-looking gunner—whose Uzi had leaned against the wall like the ChiCom AK-47 of Bolan's earlier kill—had been almost as clumsy getting his weapon into play as his now-dead ally. But finally finding the grip, fore-end and trigger with the right hand, he twisted back and sprayed a storm of unaimed lead toward Bolan and Nash. The Executioner and the Delta Force warrior squeezed their triggers simultaneously and a 9 mm round and a .45 sped through the air too fast for the eye to follow. Bolan's round ripped through the Uzi-man's throat, exploding his Adam's apple and severing the carotid artery as Nash's .45 caught the man directly in the chin and angled up into the brain.

Both were kill shots, and neither Bolan nor Nash would ever know which one had actually caused the man's demise. Not that it mattered.

The Israeli-made subgun fell to the wooden floor with a dull thud that was barely audible within the roar of the firearms. The man who had released it lived long enough to make one futile effort to halt the blood hosing from his neck, clasping both hands to his throat. But that effort didn't last long.

A second later he dropped to the floor, out of sight behind the couch where the man with the Zapata-style mustache still sat, his eyes staring blankly at Bolan in death.

The Executioner heard another .45-caliber explosion next to him and assumed yet another gunner had been taken out by Nash. But he had little time to contemplate that theory as a man wielding a Calico 9 mm machine pistol, with a 100-round drum magazine, stood up from the other end of the couch next to Mustache Man and cut loose with a wild full-auto burst of fire.

Bolan had used Calicos himself many times in the past and found them to be excellent weapons. Because the massive drum magazines were mounted on top of the pistol itself, they tended to shoot high unless the sights were employed. An experienced shooter could easily adjust to that, and turn it into the deadly weapon it had been designed to be. But a man who hadn't learned of the machine pistol's slight idiosyncrasy, and practiced and prepared to work around it, rarely utilized the Calico to its fullest potential.

The gunman who faced Bolan and Nash with this Calico didn't possess that experience, and his lack of training cost him his life.

As a dozen rounds blew over the Executioner's head, Bolan pointed the Beretta at the man with the Calico and pulled the trigger. One lone 9 mm round struck the inexperienced gunman squarely in the sternum before exploding his heart. The machine pistol fell to the wooden floor, as its operator flipped over the back of the couch.

A mental picture of José Morales and Fredrico Guzman flashed through Bolan's brain and he wondered for a moment where the two men were, and if they were even still alive. He couldn't afford to allow them weapons of any type, so while it had been necessary to bring them into the house, it had been just as necessary to keep them unarmed. If the two cousins had any brains, they would have hit the floor and done their best to roll under one of the couches or find other cover—not that there *was* much cover inside the ranch house living room— and running back out the front door would have been paramount to suicide.

Bolan was convinced, now, that Norman had stationed men to guard the money in the barn. They had to have heard the firefight in the house, and would undoubtedly shoot anyone they didn't recognize.

The Executioner had little time to contemplate the cartel gunners' fate. By now, the rest of the men who were in the house with Norman had accessed their weapons. Bullets were flying throughout the living room thicker than a nest of hornets struck by a stick. Bolan knew it was time to move, and at the same time that thought struck his brain he also thought of another plan.

He could kill two birds with one stone, as the saying went.

The soldier dived toward the couch where the corpse with the Zapata mustache still sat. Hitting the wooden floor on one shoulder, he released the Beretta from his hand as he rolled up to one knee. Before Bolan had even stabilized, his right hand had swept up the Calico machine pistol and checked to make sure the selector was on full-auto.

It was.

His new position slowed the fire from the rest of Norman's pack for the split second the Executioner needed to reorient himself. Two more men remained against the far wall of the room, and now he aimed at their belt buckles, pulling the Calico's trigger back and holding it tight. The rapid-fire 9 mm rounds spit out perhaps twenty rounds in fast succession, as Bolan cut a figure eight back and forth between the men.

One dropped a sawed-off shotgun; the other released a Ruger Mini-14.

Both died on their feet, then fell to the floor.

More fire—four straight rounds—came from Bolan's side. He didn't bother to look that way, hoping that the explosions, which sounded like more .45s, had come from Nash's Kimbers. If so, the Delta Force commando had probably taken out the other gunner on the couch nearest him.

If not, more of those same rounds would probably kill the Executioner in the next second or two.

But Bolan wasn't finished. A final gunner had been trying to clear another M-16 with a stovepipe jam. Now, seeing that his comrades were falling like flies all around him, he threw down the assault rifle and drew what looked like an old Smith & Wesson Model 10 .38-caliber revolver.

Bolan sent a half-dozen rounds from the Calico drilling into the man's face, practically decapitating him and throwing him back into his chair.

Suddenly, the living room of the old ranch house

went silent as the roar from the gunfire died down. A voice inside Bolan's head told him not to drop vigilance.

A second later, Nash started to speak. "I guess that's—"

Those were the only words he had gotten out of his mouth when a head and shoulders—and a pair of arms cradling another AK-47—popped up from behind one of the couches that had been covered by a dirty sheet.

The Executioner turned the Calico that way and tapped the trigger. A quartet of 9 mm rounds struck the last-ditch Lohman's American drug runner in the chest. His Kalashnikov fell over the couch and landed on the sheet. He fell backward, out of sight.

As the roar of gunfire died away, Bolan heard two loud clicks to his side and turned to see that both of Nash's Kimber .45s had locked open, empty. Without hesitation—and looking for all the world as if he'd practiced the maneuver thousands of times on a gun range—the Delta Force commando let both pistols fall to the floor and, in one smooth movement, drew the big CRKT Natural combat folding knife with his left hand and pressed the stud lightly with his thumb. The spring inside the thick handle kicked in to engage the assisted-opening feature, and the blade sprang out with all the drama of an automatic knife.

At the same time, Nash's right hand had accessed his .40-caliber, double-action, American Derringer DA38 and lowered the safety with his thumb.

The weight of the Calico told Bolan that he still had plenty of ammo left in the drum mag. But behind him, he suddenly heard scuffling sounds and whirled. Instead of another threat, however, he saw José Morales and Fredrico Guzman on the floor. Both men were cursing under their breath in Spanish, rolling on the wood and each trying to get beneath the other to use him as protection.

Bolan heard Nash snort. "You two are a couple of brave ones, all right," he said. "I think you can relax now. The fighting's over." Pressing the liner lock to free the CRKT's blade, he folded the weapon back into its handle and returned it to his pants, reengaged the safety on his derringer, then bent forward to retrieve his Kimbers. Producing a pair of loaded .45 magazines, he thumbed the release buttons on both of his pistols and let the empty magazines fall to the floor before stuffing the grips with fresh loads.

Bolan strode quickly to the front window and looked out toward the barn. When they'd come in, the twin barn doors had been fully closed. Now, unless his eyes were playing tricks on him from another angle, the doors looked as if they had been slightly rolled away from each other, leaving just enough room in the center for someone to peer out.

"I'm not so sure you're right," Bolan said over his shoulder.

"What do you mean?" Nash answered.

"About what you just said."

"About the fight being over?" Nash strode forward, joining Bolan at the window.

"Uh-huh," the Executioner said. "I'm not sure it's over at all. In fact, I think it might just be starting."

FIREPLUG BRYANT KNEW that in most situations, semiauto fire was as good as full-auto. For one thing, it conserved ammunition. For another, it tended to make the shooter actually take aim—either by utilizing the old military "quick kill" technique of point shooting with a long gun or resorting to the sights at longer range—rather than firing wildly in what was commonly known as spraying and praying.

But full-auto certainly came in handy when a person wanted to lay down a lot of cover fire fast. And right now, the Recon Marine would have happily traded his semiauto AR-15 for anything that kept firing as long as he held back the trigger.

On the other hand, Bryant knew that the true fighting man made do with what he had, when he had it. He didn't waste time or brainpower wishing he had other equipment.

He kept the barrel of his weapon resting on top of the Winnebago's dashboard, pulling the trigger as fast as he could and feeling the light 5.56 mm recoil bounce softly against the vinyl with each round he sent into the Wildmen bikers on his side of the road. To his side, he saw the now-familiar sight of Shooter Burton doing essentially the same thing—only one-handed. The SEAL's other hand was busy guiding the chugging motor home straight toward the motorcycles blocking the middle of the highway.

Three of the bikers went down like a trio of dominoes standing side by side.

But there were twice as many of the outlaw bikers left standing and firing at the Winnebago. And those were

just the men on *his* side. Burton had his own hands full
with another small army of hard-core Wildmen bikers
across the road.

The rush of air through the front of the motor home,
the roar of the AR-15s inside the small cab area, the
peppering sound of rounds flying back at them in return fire all combined to nearly deafen Bryant. He could
hear Burton say something next to him that sounded
like "Ace-er-sell!" and wondered what that could possibly mean.

A second later, the front of the Winnebago struck the
motorcycles lined up across the roadway and Bryant was
thrown forward, catching himself with his left hand and
somewhat softening the blow as his forehead snapped
down into the dashboard. Only then did it occur to him
that "Ace-er-sel!" had probably been, "Brace yourself!"

Metal shrieked against metal, adding a new noise
to the cacophony as the Winnebago charged and sput-
tered on through the barricade. The sidecar split from
the motorcycle to which it had been attached, tumbling
side over side off the highway on Burton's side of the
road. The bike that had been parked in front of it—an
old restored Indian motorcycle instead of a Harley for
once—did the same, rolling into the other cycles that
stood on the shoulder and then down into the bar ditch,
taking yelling and cursing hardmen with it and becoming the second to have its gas tank burst into flames.

The third Harley—an elaborately painted red-and-
white XL 1200L Sportster—parked directly in front
of where Bryant sat, fell to its side, away from the oncoming motor home. The handlebars got caught on the

bumper and it skidded along the pavement with the motor home, squealing and crunching as the Winnebago chugged on. Sparks from the friction flew into the air and into the cab to land hotly on both the Navy SEAL and Recon Marine as thousands of dollars' worth of motorcycle and customization were destroyed.

Bryant thought for a moment about the pain the bikers had to be feeling as their vehicles were systematically ruined. Their bikes were almost as important to them as the colors they wore on their backs, and a tremendous amount of time and money had gone into making each one just right. Then Bryant remembered that the outlaws had planned on riding away from the Winnebago with millions of dollars, which was far more than enough to replace any of the Harley-Davidsons that had to be sacrificed.

Bullets, still flying in through the open windshield, jerked Bryant back to the present situation.

The Winnebago was lurching more wildly now, whatever part of the engine that had been affected by the enemy bullets threatening to die altogether. But as they passed the third ambush site, the nearly trashed vehicle continued to move forward, if only at half speed.

Bryant stuck his head out his side of the window and saw that this time they had failed to kill all the bikers before passing them. Now, at least a half dozen of them were roaring their bikes to life and getting ready to follow the severely disabled motor home.

Perhaps a quarter mile farther back, the headlights of more Harley-Davidsons continued to bob up and down, back and forth, as the bulk of the Wildmen club continued their maddeningly slow but steady pursuit. As Bryant continued to watch, he was somewhat surprised to see the outlaws still at the ambush site sitting on their motorcycles, waiting for the followers to catch up.

For a few moments, the Winnebago seemed to come back to life, suddenly lurching forward and steadily picking up the pace again. Bryant pulled his head back inside the cab area and glanced over at the speedometer in front of Burton. They were closing in on eighty miles an hour.

"Maybe it just needed a little more juice," the SEAL said out of the corner of his mouth.

Bryant didn't bother answering. Instead, he said, "You saw that the guys we missed still haven't started after us, I suppose."

Burton nodded. "I can see them in the side mirror. They're just sitting there."

"How far are we from the first Columbus exit?" Bryant asked.

"Ten, maybe twelve miles would be my guess."

"Plenty of time for them to catch up for a final attack."

"Right," Burton agreed. "But I'm guessing that's not what they have planned."

Bryant found himself nodding. "I'm guessing the same thing," he said.

"They've got a fallback plan," Burton said as the Winnebago raced on through the night, sputtering occasionally but for the most part running smoothly. "Something they were hoping they wouldn't have to resort to."

"And what would that be?" Bryant queried.

"No way to be sure," Burton said. "At least not yet. "But I've got my suspicions."

"Me, too," Bryant stated. "The only thing I can think of is that whatever it is, using it takes the chance of destroying the money on board."

"My thoughts exactly."

"So what would be your guess?" Bryant asked. "Rocket launcher? Maybe an old bazooka?"

"Something along those lines," Burton said. "Some of these outlaw bikers—the one-percenters as they call themselves—have cut deals with everyone from the IRA to the Mexican and South American cartels. They aren't just in the methamphetamine business anymore. They run guns, heavy armament and anything else illegal that'll turn a profit. They could certainly have something like an RPG in their arsenal."

"Well," Bryant said, "they've got something. There's no other explanation for the tactics they're employing. And it's something that will definitely put a halt to this rig." He tapped the dashboard in front of him to indicate the Winnebago. "But it's also something that risks destroying the money, too. Otherwise they'd have used it first instead of saving it until last." He stuck his head out the window and took another look. The bikers who had survived the last ambush had finally mounted their bikes and were pulling off the shoulder onto the highway to join their pursuing brothers. The Recon Marine pulled his head back inside once more. "Whatever it is, I suspect we're about to find out. How fast are you going?"

"I'm hitting ninety once in a while," Burton replied.

"But we're starting to jerk again. Something's definitely damaged. Every once in a while I drop down to sixty."

"We don't have much longer," Bryant stated. "Whatever it is that's broken under that hood is just giving it one last, final attempt."

"Like a drowning man gasping for air before he goes under for the last time," the SEAL agreed.

Burton turned to face him for a second. "You know we're not likely to live through all this," he said.

"I know."

"So I think you might want to get on the horn and notify our top-secret handlers—whoever they are."

Bryant had the phone in his hand before Burton had finished the sentence. He tapped the speed dial, and several moments later a female voice, which would have sounded sexy under other circumstances, said simply, "Yes, gentlemen?"

The Recon Marine quickly ran down the new developments in their situation, including the facts that they suspected the Wildmen bikers had some sort of weapon that could totally wipe out the motor home, and that even if they didn't, the Winnebago was about to give up the ghost on its own. After a short pause during which the woman on the other end of the line remained silent, he said, "If they don't blow us to kingdom come first, this thing's going to break down and they'll overpower us. There're just too many of them and too few of us."

"Okay," the woman said. "You want the good news or the bad news first?"

"Let's start with the bad," Bryant suggested. "We're pretty much used to it right now."

"Right after your last call, one of our computer experts ran an in-depth investigative search on the Wildmen. They're suspected in the hijacking of a Vermont National Guard transport truck that was transferring rifles, handguns and an RPG."

Bryant let out a breath. "Well," he said, "that confirms our theory anyway."

"But wait. Here's the good news. Our director put a contingency plan into operation right after we got that intel. Help is on its way. You just need to keep going as best you can. Your backup should be there within—" her voice trailed off for a moment, and Bryant pictured the woman looking at her watch or a clock "—just a few minutes."

"Where's all this backup coming from?" the Recon Marine asked skeptically. "Out of the clear blue sky?"

"Exactly," the woman said. "You can look toward the heavens for salvation. Just be ready."

Bryant took a long time to answer, but finally he said, "Affirmative," then ended the call.

As if the Winnebago's engine had been listening to their conversation, it suddenly began to chug and lurch again. Bryant leaned over and saw that they had suddenly dropped to a little under fifty miles an hour. He watched as Burton looked into the side mirror.

"They're gaining on us," the Navy SEAL said.

Bryant stuck full magazines into both of their AR-15s. "Well," he said, "the lady back there at wherever we were promised that help was on its way. But I'll believe it when I see it. I can't see how they're going to get here in time to save our skins. So if this is our last gasp for air before we go underwater, let's make it a good one."

"We'll at least let them know they've been in a fight." Burton nodded. "But it's going to be primarily up to you. I can't really steer this ship and fire behind me at the same time."

Bryant laughed. "Well, swabby," he said as he turned in his seat and prepared to lean out the window with his rifle once more. "Again, look on the bright side."

"Yeah," Burton said. "Maybe this bag of bolts will finally quit altogether and just stop." Now he was laughing at his own upcoming death as well. "Then I won't have any trouble turning around and firing." He paused a moment before adding, "Before we both go under for that last time, of course."

"Well," Bryant said, "it's been nice working with you."

Burton nodded. "So, since we're about to go out together, tell me your deepest, darkest secret."

Bryant grinned. "I always cry at movies about athletes who die of some disease. Like *Brian's Song*."

Burton turned toward him. "Really?"

"No, but I thought it sounded good." Bryant looked at the mirror on his side and saw that the Wildmen bikers were closing in faster now. "So what's *your* deepest, darkest secret?" he asked.

Burton took a deep breath, looked at his own mirror, then said, "I've read all Nicholas Sparks's romance novels and *liked* them."

Bryant sat up straighter in his seat, readying his rifle. "You read romance novels? You're joking, right?"

"Nope," Burton said.

"Don't worry," Bryant replied. "I won't tell anybody."

Both men could hear the roar of the Harley-Davidsons closing in on them from the rear.

"I don't think you'll ever get a chance to."

CHAPTER TWELVE

Bolan remained silent as he continued to stare out the window of the old ranch house. The closer he looked at the barn door, the more convinced he became that it had been opened slightly since they'd entered the house. The more convinced of that he became, the more certain he was that there was an unknown number of men inside the building, guarding the millions of dollars that were hidden inside the Thor motor home.

"Well, Cooper," Nash said as he ran a hand from his forehead across the top of his head. "You're the man in charge of this op. What do we do next?"

"Wait," Bolan replied.

"Wait?" Nash echoed. "Wait for what?"

"For them to make the first move."

"What makes you think they will?"

"Because they had to have seen us enter the house," Bolan said. "And they had to have heard the gunfight. But they don't know which side won, and they're going to get more curious—and more frantic to know where they stand—with each passing second."

Nash nodded his understanding.

Five minutes went by, then ten. Bolan saw no movement through the tiny slit between the sliding doors in the front of the barn. But he hadn't focused solely on the front door, and his eyes skirted occasionally to a second-floor opening to what was undoubtedly a hay-loft. A pulley, with an attached rope that hung almost to the ground—was mounted just above the doorway. It had obviously been used in the past to hoist hay bales up and into the storage area.

The door to the hayloft was wide open, but the hole it exposed was black.

Ten minutes became fifteen. Then fifteen became twenty. Bolan turned slightly toward Nash who was still by his side. "Better tie these two up," he told the Delta Force operative. "We're about to get into another fire-fight, and this time they won't be of any use to us. Besides, we can't shoot and babysit them at the same time."

Nash didn't hesitate. Pulling several sets of plastic cuffs from his pocket, he went to work on José Morales and Fredrico Guzman, who still lay on the floor. A few minutes later, the two men were trussed hand and foot.

Bolan glanced their way. "Better gag them, too," he said. "They'll be trying to play both sides of the fence, and we don't need them shouting out our positions or other intel when it finally hits the fan."

Nash walked immediately toward the closest arm-chair still covered with the dusty white sheets. Produc-ing the CRKT Natural Knife gain, he snapped the blade into place and began cutting gag-size strips from the material. As soon as he'd finished, he tied them around José's and Guzman's mouths. Then, apparently having a sudden thought, he cut more strips from the sheet and used them as blindfolds.

By now, a good half hour had gone by, and Bolan

knew they were entering a phase of diminishing returns. If Norman and his men had come out on top of the gunfight, they would have sent someone to let the guards know what had happened by now. Since that hadn't occurred, it could mean only one thing: the men who had planned on buying the marijuana had been handed the short end of the stick. They were dead, and their comrades in the barn would have had to have had IQs lower than a rock's not to figure it out.

Bolan's eyebrows lowered in concentration. Some plans worked. Others didn't. So it was time to switch gears and begin working out a new strategy.

The area between the house and the barn was mainly open field. There was one lone tree, featuring an ancient, and long-abandoned, wooden swing seat hanging by one strand of a rotten rope tied to an overhead branch. The tree was perhaps twenty yards directly in front of where he stood. The trunk was wide enough to use as cover, and Bolan suspected he could sprint out of the house, leap down the porch steps and reach it before whoever was in the barn had time to fire. But that would get him less than a quarter of the distance to the barn, and would alert the men behind the barn doors that he was on his way.

The only other possible cover between the tree and the barn was a rusty water pump sticking up out of a short concrete wall that circled the well. The wall was only big enough to hide behind if he lay down on the grass behind it. And even then, he suspected he'd still be partially exposed. And from that position, firing toward the barn would be so awkward as to be ineffectual.

Not to mention that it would make for a superslow start when he decided to sprint toward the barn.

There was an upside to it all, however. Not a great upside, but one nonetheless. If he could somehow get from the water pump to the nearest corner of the barn, he'd be out of sight from the eyes peering—and the guns undoubtedly shooting—through the thin opening between the sliding doors. In order to increase their field of vision, the men inside would have to slide the doors open farther.

That would mean better visibility for Bolan as well as them. The open hayloft was a problem, however, and he'd be exposed to it even with his back pressed against the corner.

By now Nash had returned to the window and stood next to him. Bolan turned to face him. "I'm going to see if I can't make it to the barn."

"Are you crazy?" Nash said. "They'll cut you down before you can even—"

"Not if you lay down enough cover fire," Bolan interrupted. He still had the 9 mm Calico in his right hand, its drum magazine nearly full, and now he turned, walking to the dead man whose AK-47 lay next to where he'd fallen. Lifting the rifle, then fishing through the safari-style vest the dead man had worn, he came up with two more magazines. Returning to the window, he handed both the Kalashnikov and the extra magazines to Nash. Then, on second thought, he returned to the corpse. Grabbing both ankles, he dragged the body across the wooden floor, leaving it next to the front door.

"Here's the plan," Bolan stated. "I'm heading from

here straight to the tree. I suspect I can get there before anybody fires at me but even if they do, the shots'll be hurried and likely be wild."

"*Likely* is the operative word, here, Cooper," Nash said. "That's an awful lot of assumption on your part."

"It is," Bolan agreed. "But sometimes a plan has holes in it so big you can't completely plug them. When that happens, you have to just make the best of the situation and do what you have to do. From the tree, I'll be heading to the water pump. They'll be aware of me by then, and they'll be firing. So you've got to keep them humble with the AK. Try not to shoot me while you're at it, okay?"

"Okay."

"When I reach the pump, I'll hit the ground behind the wall."

"The wall?" Nash repeated, shaking his head in dismay. "Let me get this straight. By wall, you mean those little one-foot concrete things that aren't high enough to protect a garden gnome?"

"I think we're on the same page," Bolan agreed. "Like I said, I'm counting on you to keep them busy with cover fire."

"I'm good, Cooper," Nash said. "Otherwise, Delta would have never taken me. But I'm not a super hero."

Bolan couldn't help but smile. "Great," he said. "Because who knows how much kryptonite might be between here and the barn."

"You're flat-out mule-eared crazy," Nash stated.

Bolan ignored the comment. "Now, the last leg is going to be from the water pump to the corner of the barn. That's the farthest—maybe fifty yards or so—and there's nothing to hide behind on the way."

"Yeah," Nash said. "So I noticed. But you can bet your crazy ass *they'll* have noticed *you* by then. And they'll have figured out exactly what you're trying to do. Not to mention the slow start you'll have getting to your feet behind those short little patio stones. You're going to have to get up off the ground and—"

"I know what I'm going to have to do," Bolan told him. "That's why I gave you two extra magazines. You just keep them busy."

Nash shook his head again. "And you're taking that Calico, I assume?"

Bolan nodded. He turned and started back toward the couch where the original Calico shooter lay in pools of blood. He had noticed the man had worn a shoulder rig for the high-firepower machine pistol, and under the weak-hand side of the specialty harness another 100-round drum was secured in ballistic nylon and Velcro.

Slipping it off the dead man's shoulders, the Executioner shrugged into the rig. He wasn't sure exactly how many rounds he'd already fired from this appropriated weapon. Or how many the dead man had used up before him. But he wanted to start fresh, so he switched the drum on top of the weapon with the one in the shoulder caddy and snapped it into place.

Counting the round still in the chamber, the Executioner now knew he had 101 9 mm rounds at his disposal, and at least fifty more cartridges in the partially used drum, which now went under his arm.

He didn't think he'd need them all, but it was always better to have too much ammo than not enough.

"Okay," Nash said when Bolan had returned to the window. "You didn't drag that body all the way across the room for fun. I'm guessing you want me to do something with it?"

"That's affirmative. Like you said, the most dangerous time for me is getting up from behind the concrete wall—"

"I'd call it a curb," Nash said.

"Call it whatever you want to. Getting up, getting started and sprinting the last fifty yards to the barn—that'll be the danger zone. I'm out in the open the whole way and getting closer to the enemy with each step, which makes me a bigger target with each step, too."

"So where's this dead guy come in?" Nash asked.

"As soon as you see me start to rise, I want you to open the door and push him out onto the porch. You'll have to stand him up and brace him against the wall while you open the door with the other hand. Just get him out on the porch, then fall back, grab your rifle again and start pouring rounds into the barn."

"And you think they'll mistake this dead guy for another attacker and it'll draw some of the attention off you?"

"That's what I'm hoping for," Bolan said.

"Yeah, well," Nash stated, "as long as we're hoping, we might as well hope big. So I'll be hoping they think he's one of the walking dead and that they're being attacked by zombies." He stared up into Bolan's eyes. "But I'm not putting much faith in either of our dreams, here."

"Like I said, sometimes you just have to—"

"Go with what you've got," Nash finished the sentence for him. "I still think you're crazy."

"There are those who'd agree with you," Bolan said. "Now, are you ready?"

"Oh, I'm ready," Nash told him. "But then I'm not the one who'll be dangling on the end of a fishhook like a worm now, am I? The question is, are *you* ready?"

Bolan nodded. Then, without another word, he walked to the front door of the ranch house, threw it open, and, with the Calico in his right hand, darted outside. In less than a second he had crossed the porch and leaped down the steps to the ground, then started toward the tree like an Olympic fifty-meter-dash champion.

But the Executioner had been wrong about one thing.

The gunmen in the barn *were* ready for him, and they started shooting at the same time his feet hit the ground after jumping off the porch.

THE WINNEBAGO HAD slowed to forty miles an hour and black smoke was pouring from under the hood like a fireplace whose owner had forgotten to open the flue. And the motor home was jerking back and forth like some giant beast with a bad case of the hiccups.

Burton had been looking back and forth from the mirror to where the windshield should have been for the last mile. The motorcycle headlights behind them were within a hundred yards or so now, but they had leveled off their speed, and were keeping at that distance.

Bryant could see them in the mirror on his own side. Suddenly, he stood and grabbed his AR-15. "I think I'll break out the rear window and take a little target prac- tice. Maybe even wipe out whoever has the RPG."

"Not likely," Burton said as he struggled to keep con- trol of the motor home. "Whoever has the RPG is prob- ably getting it ready right now. It can be done while still riding on a motorcycle—we did it in a training exercise one time. But he'll be at the rear of the pack until the last minute. Just in case you think of doing exactly what you just thought of doing."

"Well," Bryant said, "then I'll just take out as many of the enemy as I can. Up our score as high as possible before they blow us up."

Burton saw his partner's eyes flicker toward the smoke coming out of the Winnebago's hood for a mo- ment. Then Bryant said, "That is, if this pile of still- moving junkyard rubble doesn't blow us up on its own first and save them the trouble."

Bryant disappeared from Burton's sight.

Through the choking and chugging of the motor home, the SEAL could feel the vibrations as his heavy footsteps hurried to the back of the vehicle. A second later, the tinkle of glass breaking sounded behind him, and then the *pop-pop-pop* of 5.56 mm rounds from the Recon Marine's AR-15 sounded.

Burton looked up in the mirror and saw two of the motorcycle headlights twist to the side. Then, in the shadowy light from the other trailing bikers' headlights, he watched both cycles crash.

Two more Harleys went down in their wake.

The other Wildmen bikers dropped farther back.

Bryant returned to his seat but kept the rifle in his

hands, across his lap with the barrel pointing out the window. "It can't be long now," he said, and for the first time Burton thought he might have heard a trace of stress in the man's voice.

He recognized it because he was feeling the same stress himself. It had been a long, tiresome, running gunfight. Even the most hardened warriors had their limits, and Burton knew he and Bryant were getting close to theirs. For some reason, the SEAL's thoughts turned to Matt Cooper and Spike Nash on the other end of this operation. He barely knew either of the men, but his take was that Nash was probably as tough-minded as he and Fireplug Bryant were. It would take a lot to get the Delta Force operative down. Cooper was another story. The big man might as well have had Ultimate Warrior or Toughest Man in the World tattooed across his forehead. There was something about him—something that bordered on the mysterious—that emanated a strength that went beyond anything even the SEALS, the Recon Marines or Delta Force could produce. The simple fact was that Cooper was beyond anything Shooter Burton had ever encountered in anyone else, period.

The brief lull in the shooting gave Burton a chance to gather his thoughts. While he, Bryant and Nash would probably never admit it, he knew that all three elite forces men had the greatest respect for one another. They were the best within their respective branches of the military, and their training and skill levels were similar, if not exactly the same. And all three of them—the SEAL, the Recon Marine and the Delta Force operative—had automatically known they could count on one another.

With Cooper, however, it had been a little different. As easily as the men had accepted each other as equals, they had immediately, and without really thinking about it, deferred command to Cooper. There was just something about the big man's very presence that demanded it.

They were all leaders, but Cooper was a leader of leaders and that was all there was to it.

Bryant broke Burton back out of his brief reverie. "They're gaining again," he said. "My guess is they've readied the RPG and they're preparing to use it."

He pulled the magazine out of his AR-15, checked the remaining rounds inside then traded it for a full magazine from the gunnysack. "In that raining exercise you mentioned earlier," he asked. "Did you guys actually fire the RPGs while you were still riding the motorcycles?"

"Yep."

"I was afraid you were going to say that," Bryant said.

"It's kind of tricky but it can be done," Burton went on. "You have to rest it on the handlebars and—"

Bryant cut him off in midsentence. "Enough. I don't need to know the exact details of how I'm going to die."

"What gets me," Burton said, "is that they're taking quite a chance of blowing up the money along with us. *That,* I don't quite understand."

"I think they've run out of other options," Bryant replied. "And there's always the chance that they can salvage a lot of the money before it burns."

"That's pretty dicey thinking," Burton said as the

Winnebago coughed even louder than before, then lurched forward so hard that both men jerked with it. "But I guess if you've had enough methamphetamine rot out your brain…" He let the sentence trail off.

"They're getting desperate," Bryant said. "We're getting awfully close to Columbus where there'll be more traffic. More cops. None of their ambushes have worked. I guess they've decided the chance of losing the money's a risk that's become worth taking."

Burton nodded. "The game hasn't quite gone their way," he said. "They're ready to take their football and go home."

"Exactly," Bryant agreed. "But they're going to do their best to kill us first."

There was nothing more to say, and the two elite warriors rode on in silence, readying themselves mentally for the death they knew was now only minutes away.

But a moment later, the sound of a low-flying plane cut into their thoughts, drowning out all the other noises that had plagued Burton's and Bryant's ears for hours now. To the SEAL it seemed to be just overhead and when it passed, Burton looked out through the giant hole in the front of the Winnebago and saw that he hadn't been far from wrong.

The fighter jet—it looked like an F-15 to him during the brief second he could see it—was only a couple hundred feet above the ground.

What was even stranger than its altitude was that it bore no markings of any kind.

Burton turned to Bryant. "Did you see that or have I lost my mind?" he said.

"You've probably lost you mind," Burton replied, "but if you have, so have I."

As the two men watched, the unidentifiable F-15 banked to the left in the distance, turned and started back toward them. It was even lower to the ground now.

"Uh-oh," Bryant said. "I sure hope he's on our side." He shook his head. "You don't think the Wildmen could actually have access to a jet fighter, do you?"

"Let's hope not." Burton glanced to his side and saw Bryant looking at his mirror again. "What's wrong?" he asked. "Besides the fact that the pilot appears to have just smoked a bowl of crack and is getting ready to ka-mikaze our butts?"

"Look in your mirror," Bryant instructed him.

Burton did so, and what he saw made even the Navy SEAL's blood run cold.

The picture in the mirror wasn't clear in the flashing motorcycle headlights and dark night. But it was clear enough, and both Burton and Bryant could see the man on the lead motorcycle with the RPG from the National Guard hijacking over his shoulder, preparing to fire.

The roar of the plane caused Burton to look back through the nonexistent windshield just as the F-15 shot back over the Winnebago's roof. The pressure from above caused the motor home to shake, shimmy-ing like some gigantic, crazed, Hawaiian hula dancer and threatening to make the half-destroyed vehicle fall apart into a pile of nuts, bolts and other pieces of metal.

"Look!" Bryant yelled suddenly, and as the word came out of his mouth Burton heard the pounding sounds of machine-gun fire just above them. Looking back into the mirror, he saw the man who had held the RPG only a second before go flying off his motorcycle into the air.

In several pieces.

The rocket-propelled grenade launcher fell somewhere alongside the road, as if it—and certain death—had never been behind Burton and Bryant at all.

But the machine-gun fire didn't stop there. As the Winnebago chugged on, whoever sat at the controls of the F-15 kept firing a steady stream of high-powered rounds into the long line of motorcycles trailing the Winnebago. Burton continued to steer the failing motor home, glancing back and forth from the highway ahead to the mirror just outside his side window.

Outlaw biker after outlaw biker fell to the barrage of gunfire from the plane. A few of the Wildmen bikers escaped the onslaught, but those who did crashed into motorcycles that had fallen in front of them, and went tumbling head over heels into the massive wreck on the highway.

Then, suddenly, as if it had been waiting for just the right moment, the Winnebago spit out one giant flume of black smoke before the engine finally went silent.

Burton let the motor home glide as far as its momentum would take it, then steered it off the highway onto the shoulder. Looking in the mirror again, he saw that at least a half-dozen bikers had been able to guide their Harleys around the clump of their dead or dying brothers, and were now heading straight for the ruined Winnebago. They were too far away to see their faces, but Burton knew that the money was no longer all they were after.

The Wildmen bikers still wanted the money, but now they wanted vengeance, too.

"Well, jarhead," Burton said as he grabbed his AR-15. "Looks like it's just them and us now." He reached for the door handle, ready to drop to the ground and fire as many rounds into the men on the motorcycles as he could before the inevitable happened and they killed him. What he saw on the other side of the cab area stopped him.

Bryant had his head out his window and was looking skyward. "Hang on," the Recon Marine said. "There's another plane overhead."

Burton looked up through the broken glass in time to see it pass over the Winnebago. It was higher than the F-15 had been—high enough, in fact, that he couldn't make out what model of plane it was. But in addition to the aircraft, the Navy man saw tiny black dots drifting down through the sky. As they neared, he was able to see that the black spots were men. About two dozen of them were parachuting to the ground with rifles clutched in their hands.

"Air cavalry to the rescue," Bryant said as he pulled his head back inside. "And not a minute too soon."

The mysterious men, Burton could now see, were all wearing the blacksuits to which he, Bryant and Nash had been exposed when they'd first met Cooper and the others. Burton remembered that the men themselves were simply referred to as blacksuits as well.

"I don't think these are air cav, Fireplug," the SEAL said. "It's more like ninjas to the rescue."

"At this point, I'll take whatever help we can get."

The blacksuits began firing before they even reached the ground, and in the mirror both warriors in the Winnebago saw the final few bikers begin to fall.

"I don't think they should get to have all of the fun, do you?" Bryant said.

"Nope," Burton returned. "I'd say we've earned a bit ourselves."

The two men got out of the Winnebago at the same time.

Burton was a second too slow to catch a biker who was passing the motor home with his door. But he had the presence of mind to duck as the man on the Harley sent a semiautomatic volley of pistol fire into the driving area where the SEAL had been a second before. The enemy's strategy was obviously to pass the Winnebago, skid into a turn, then fire again.

He never got that chance.

The outlaw biker was just hitting his brakes when Burton opened up on him with his AR-15. Pulling the trigger four times in a row, the Navy SEAL sent a quartet of 5.56 mm rounds into the man's colors.

The biker lost control of his bright blue Harley Nightster as the handlebars twisted suddenly to the right, flipping him up off his seat and sending him flying through the air to land on the pavement, dead. His bike fell to its side, skidding straight down the white lines separating the lanes of the highway in a spectacular display of red-and-orange sparks.

So much for shooting people in the back, the SEAL

thought. This was real life, not some B-movie Western. In war, you killed the enemy any way you could.

And this was war.

On the other side of the Winnebago, he heard Bryant's AR pounding steadily, and watched as another of the last oncoming bikers fell to the small-but-deadly rounds. Another pair of bikers, riding side by side, suddenly thought better of continuing the attack and tried to turn around. Unfortunately for them, they turned directly into each other.

Both men tried to get up at the same time, but both fell to the rounds of unseen hands of the blacksuits, who were now almost on the ground.

Bryant's eyes narrowed as he raised his AR-15 to shoulder level and searched for another target, but there wasn't one. Far in the distance—out of reasonable range for his weapon—a couple of shadows turned their motorcycles around and disappeared into the night. Burton watched the red taillights grow smaller then disappear altogether. There appeared to be only two of the bikers left.

The outlaw bikers from Brooklyn were going to have to go into a serious campaign for prospects if they intended to survive.

The blacksuits were on the ground now. Some had already gathered in their parachutes and were running toward the Winnebago. The man in the lead—a muscular man with short, curly blond hair—stopped three feet in front of Burton, gave him a quick salute and said, "We've got to get the money out of here before the cops come."

"It's all on board," Burton said, then turned and climbed back into the motor home, passing across the seat and leading the man in black toward the back of the vehicle. More blacksuits followed, each intent on gathering the seven million dollars hidden inside the Winnebago and getting it out of there.

Bryant joined them, and together the SEAL and the Recon Marine began to pull up the tops of the bench seats, chairs, the table, and the bed and other furniture in the rear of the Winnebago. The blacksuits formed an assembly line not unlike an old-fashioned fire brigade from the back of the motor home to the front, passing the cash along to other men outside the vehicle who stuffed it into a series of black ballistic nylon equipment bags and backpacks.

"This is all good and well," Burton said as they worked their way from the bedroom toward the front of the Winnebago. "But how do you guys plan to get it out of here? Unless you can jump high enough to get back to your plane, it looks to me like we're all on foot."

"Just for the moment." The blond-haired blacksuit grinned. In the better light inside the motor home, Burton noted that the man was young—in his early- to mid-twenties. But he had the charisma of a natural-born leader.

Before more words could be said, Burton heard the distinct sound of a heavy semi-tractor-trailer pulling up alongside the Winnebago. He looked out the window and saw a logo featuring a rooster's head painted on the side. A speech bubble portrayed the rooster shouting out the words *Johnson's Chicken!* The door on the other side of the truck opened up and he heard boots hit the ground. A moment later, the back doors of the trailer ground open with metallic clinks and the blacksuits began carrying the bags of drug money that way.

"Let's go," said the blond-headed blacksuit. "You guys, too…Bryant and Burton, right?"

The two men who had narrowly escaped death nodded. "Or Shooter and Fireplug," Burton said. "I think saving our butts puts you on a first-name basis with us."

The blond man laughed. Rather than passing the last bag of money out the door he lifted it into his arms himself. "I can guess which one of you has to be Fireplug," he said, looking at Bryant.

Then his eyes shifted to Burton. "So, by process of elimination, you must be Shooter. But regardless of what your names are, we need to hurry. So come on." He turned and led the way out of the ruined Winnebago to the rear of the huge trailer.

"Where'd you guys come up with this thing?" Burton asked as he followed the blacksuit to the back of the trailer. "And how'd you get it here so fast?" As he spoke, he pulled himself up and into the cargo area, noting that it was refrigerated, which only made sense, considering that it had obviously been designed to carry Johnson's frozen chickens. As the cooler air hit his skin he felt a sudden chill pass through his body. Goose bumps rose on his arms and the back of his neck. Whether the reaction came from the refrigerated trailer or the fact that he'd just been through several life-or-death struggles, he didn't know. But he did know that inside the trailer there were no chickens—frozen or otherwise to be found. What he saw instead was a quickly stacked pile of money bags, hastily folded parachutes, M-16s and men in blacksuits.

And Fireplug Bryant, who had already boarded.

The blond blacksuit leader closed and bolted the door behind him before he responded to Burton's inquiries. "I'll answer your questions in reverse order, if you don't mind," he said. "You're right. We didn't have time to get a ground vehicle here to cart off the money. But we found this thing—" he indicated the inside of the refrigerated truck with a sweep of his hand "—heading north out of Columbus. So a few of us bailed out there and… shall we say, appropriated it."

"What happened to the chickens and the driver?" Burton asked as the truck's engine, which hadn't shut down, roared louder and they began to move.

"The chickens, I'm afraid," the blacksuit spokesman said, "are well on their way to thawing and then rotting alongside the road. They had to serve a greater purpose."

"And the driver?" Burton asked. "He's not rotting away someplace for this same greater purpose, is he?" The Navy SEAL felt his facial muscles twist into a frown of concern. He didn't mind killing a thousand bad guys—that's what he'd been trained to do and what he was good at—but to take the life of an innocent trucker went 180 degrees against everything in which he believed.

But Burton had learned quite a bit about the mysterious men from the equally mysterious installation where this mission had begun, even if he still didn't know exactly who they were. So, even though he felt obligated to ask the question about the truck driver, he suspected he knew that these black-clad warriors who had fallen from the sky would be as opposed to cold-blooded murder as he was.

The young blond blacksuit laughed. "The truck driver's just fine," he said as they began to pick up speed. "He's tied up in the berth right behind the driver's seat, happy as a clam."

"Happy?" Bryant said. "I can't imagine that having an army of ninja-looking guys with M-16s commandeer your chicken truck would bring joy to most men's hearts."

"No," the blacksuit said, "but the Valium I fired him up with sure seemed to." He patted a pocket in the stretchy black fabric that covered his body. "We carry some with us for just such occasions. Fact is—" the smile on his boyish face widened "—I understand our top man used a little on the other end of this mission earlier. But you probably didn't hear about it yet."

Burton shook his head.

The blond blacksuit continued. "Anyway, when I last saw the driver he was joking and trying not to nod off. By now, however, I'm sure he's sleeping soundly. By the time he wakes up we won't need the truck anymore and we can let him go. His company will be compensated."

"So where are we going from here?" Burton asked.

"Well," said the blond blacksuit. "I could tell you, but it'd be so much more fun just to show you."

CHAPTER THIRTEEN

Novelists and other writers who have never actually been shot at often compare bullets passing close to a man's head as sounding like "angry bees" swarming past. Men like Mack Bolan, who had escaped such barrages of gunfire so many times over the years that he'd lost count of them, knew this to be a fallacy. A person felt air pressure as the rounds zipped past his or her ears. But the only sound actually heard were the explosions from the firearms that had projected the deadly missiles, and the even more distinct crack if the bullets were traveling faster than the speed of sound. Both noises seemed to come at the same time as the lead flew by, but sound being slower than the flight of the bullets, the explosions actually came a split second later.

Hence the old saying "You never hear the one that kills you."

Ten feet from the thick tree trunk, Bolan dived forward into a shoulder roll, the Calico cradled in both arms. As his head went down and his feet came up, the soldier felt the left heel of his hiking boot strike the rotten wooden slat that had served as the seat of the swing hanging from the limb above it. By the time he was right side up once more, he was behind the thick trunk and the weathered wooden seat, as well as the lone rope still attached to it, were swinging back and forth behind him.

Fire continued to come toward him from the barn, but the massive tree trunk absorbed the rounds like a sponge taking in water. Pressing his shoulder against the other side of the living wood, Bolan listened to the explosions of full-auto fire, and felt the vibrations as the tree took each impact. In response Spike Nash fired from the house, laying down cover fire to divert as much attention from the Executioner as possible.

Looking up, Bolan saw that the limb that had supported the swing had been shot off away from the trunk, roughly six feet up from the ground, a little too high for the fork it created to be utilized as a shooting rest for his Calico. He was, nonetheless, able to pull himself erect, hunching only slightly in order to keep the top few inches of his head still behind cover. Then, leaning quickly around the tree, he pulled back on the Calico's trigger and sent a good fifteen-to-twenty 9 mm rounds directly at the barn door.

The gunfire from the barn let up suddenly, telling Bolan that regardless of how many men had been stationed inside to guard the money, most of them were firing through the slit between the twin sliding doors. But fairly regular gunfire seemed to come from the second story of the building as well, from the hayloft door Bolan had noted earlier.

Letting up on the Calico's trigger, the soldier realigned his aim, tilting the machine pistol up toward the hayloft and sending another barrage of rounds that way. The gunfire from that site ceased, as well, as whoever fell back to avoid the Executioner's return fire.

Bolan jerked himself back behind the tree trunk a second before new shots rang out from the split between the barn doors. Once again, he let the thick tree take the attack. But as the striking rounds continued to reverberate against his shoulder like some electronically vibrating massage chair, he couldn't help but let a grim smile creep over his face.

There were either far fewer men in the barn than had been in the ranch house. Or the available space—the slot between the doors and the small window-door in the second story—was so limited in the area that not all the drug runners could crowd in and fire at the same time.

Gunners who were so crowded together that it limited their efficiency was an advantage. Not a big advantage, but an advantage nonetheless.

Taking in a lungful of air, Bolan suddenly shot from behind the tree and sprinted toward the water pump. He waited until he had run a good ten yards before opening up with the Calico. His rounds were more imprecise than they would have been had he been stationary, but precision shooting at this point wasn't his goal.

As 9 mm after 9 mm after 9 mm left the short barrel of the Calico, the Executioner watched them strike the doors in the front of the barn. Bolan cut loose with a sustained burst; slivers of aged wood and chips of long-dried and sun-baked red paint were gouged from the doors and flew through the air. But at least one of his rounds must have found the thin crack between the doors.

Between shots, he heard the sudden scream of a man who had suddenly been surprised with intense pain.

Bolan ran on, hearing more cover fire join his own

continuous rounds as Nash held back the trigger on his AK-47. Then the assault rifle halted for a few seconds, telling the soldier that the Delta Force commando was changing magazines. The man with the spiked hair had been well cross-trained in all major battle rifles throughout the world, however, and it took little more than the blink of an eye for the explosions to break out again. As the AK-47 opened up again, Bolan dived once more, this time sliding face-first into the grass surrounding the minuscule concrete wall around the water pump.

The Executioner did his best to burrow as low as he could into the ground as more rifle fire from the barn skimmed over his prostrate body. The retaining wall had been designed to be decorative rather than protective, and several of the rounds stitched across his shirt and pants, leaving streaks of heat that felt like sudden sunburns on his skin. From this position, firing back was impossible. To do so, he'd have had to lift his head, arms and half his chest above the concrete. Doing that without catching any of the lead flying out from the barn would be all but impossible.

Staying in that position, however, wasn't an option, either. Already the heavy rifle fire had cracked much of the concrete in front of him. In a few more moments, huge holes would be created, making way for a final kill shot.

So, without further hesitation, Bolan scrambled to his feet, hoping that Nash already had the body inside the ranch house in hand and was ready to throw it out onto the porch. As he came to his feet and began the final sprint toward the corner of the barn, he realized Nash had to have acted.

Because the gunfire that had been directed at him suddenly shifted away, the rounds drilling into the front of the ranch house and the columns supporting the porch.

Bolan risked a quick look over his shoulder as he raced on. Behind him he saw that even though Nash had let go of the corpse and ducked back inside the house, the dead drug runner still stood in an upright position. The bullets fired into him from the barn had driven his back against the house and kept him temporarily pinned there on his feet. The man's head and arms flapped wildly in a macabre dance of death as round after round after round pounded his dead flesh.

He finally fell to the ground for the second time as Bolan turned back and continued his sprint toward the corner of the barn.

The diversion the body had created couldn't last forever, however, and as Bolan neared the barn, the men inside returned their attention to him. The Executioner left his feet once again, diving forward as he'd done at both the tree and the water pump, barely evading another cluster of fire that sailed over his back and left sears on his shoulder blades as the earlier rounds had done on the top of his arms and legs. As he rolled back to his feet, he turned first to the hayloft and saw a rifle barrel sticking out of the opening. Just above the weapon was a head wearing a khaki-colored bucket hat.

Angling the Calico that way, the Executioner sent ten rounds upward.

Some of the bullets struck the rifle and sent it spinning out of the hands that held it. The rest of the volley hit the face Bolan had seen above the barrel. The bucket hat toppled off the gunner's head and seemed to float down to the ground next to where the rifle had landed. Finally, the rest of the man—now minus the left half of his head—tumbled out of the hayloft to land with a loud *plunk* as he struck the packed dirt below.

As if directed by some unseen orchestra conductor, all firing suddenly ceased. Considering the angle at which the Executioner now stood, and the slight width of the opening between the barn doors, firing from either Bolan or the men inside the barn would be nothing more than a waste of ammo.

Bolan took a deep, cleansing breath and thought for a second of José Morales and Fredrico Guzman still in the ranch house. As the two men's faces crossed his mind, Bolan couldn't suppress a wry smile that tilted the corners of his mouth.

The situation in which he found himself was often referred to as a Mexican standoff. But when you took into consideration the roles being played by Fredrico and José, and the entire Morales Cartel, Bolan realized that the circumstances he was currently in could more accurately be called a Mexican Mexican standoff.

But, even though there had been a temporary break in the gunplay, Bolan knew it would be short-lived. So something had to be done. Either the Executioner had to maneuver himself into a better shooting position or the men inside the barn had to open the doors wider to take aim at him.

Bolan's brain worked at the speed of light. There was no sense in letting the enemy make the first move when he didn't have to do so.

Firing another burst of 9 mm rounds from the Calico, Bolan turned his attention back to the open window to the hayloft. No more fire had come his way from the barn's second story, which led him to believe there might have been just the one gunman stationed there. The rusty pulley and the attached rope were still where they'd been when he'd first spotted them from the house. But now, the Executioner looked at the weather-beaten hoist system with a new eye.

Would it be possible for him to climb it? Would the ancient and frayed hemp rope—or the long-neglected steel pulley itself—support his weight without breaking? He didn't know, and he wouldn't until he tried it. What he did know, however, was that he stood little chance of entering the barn through the front door without taking a dozen or more rounds from the men congregated there. Far better—if he could pull it off—would be to climb up into the hayloft, then surprise the rest of the men inside the barn from behind.

Bolan's jaw tightened. The hayloft route was hardly without risk, however. There could easily be more men hidden on the second story who simply hadn't shown themselves yet. And they might decide to do just that as he pulled himself up the rope, a task that would require both hands and leave him defenseless until he reached the top.

As always, Bolan weighed the odds both ways then made his decision. With the Calico aimed almost directly overhead, he moved silently across the packed earth until he was directly beneath the window. He stood still for a good thirty seconds, giving any other gunmen who might have accompanied the one splattered on the ground next to him time to expose themselves. Then, with his eyes fixed on the window, Bolan stooped low and grabbed the khaki bucket hat that had fallen next to the body of the man who had worn it. Now heavily soaked with blood, brain matter and other fluids, it was easy to throw upwards, directly in front of the window and just below the mounted pulley.

The sudden appearance of the hat drew no fire—or other response—from inside the hayloft, which proved nothing. The loft might still be filled with well-disciplined gunmen who simply weren't taking Bolan's bait, and he had run out of lures. His gut told him that the man he'd just killed had been alone on the barn's second story and that it was now time to try climbing the rope.

So he would follow that gut instinct.

The soldier hooked the Calico to the end of its shoulder harness beneath his right arm. Then, reaching up and grasping the rope with both hands, he tugged. Several of the smaller threadlike strands—woven together to make up the thicker rope—snapped audibly in the silence that now surrounded the barn. Bolan tugged again and heard similar noises. Whether the entire rope would break before he reached the top was anyone's guess.

The soldier only knew that he had to chance it.

Nash had seen what he was doing from the ranch house, because the Delta Force commando began pounding the barn's sliding front doors with rifle fire once more, doing his best to divert attention from the hayloft and back toward himself.

Bolan reached up and wrapped his fingers around the rough-hewn hemp. Then, slowly, so as not to put any more strain on the line than necessary, he began to haul himself upward, hand over hand.

With each new fistful of rope he grasped, the soldier again heard popping sounds as more strands—weakened by weather, time and now his weight—snapped. Halfway up the side of the barn, the rope suddenly gave partially away and he fell back several inches. But the strands that remained still held, and he began his upward trek once more.

Bolan's right hand was an inch from the pulley when the rope suddenly crackled, then broke completely in two. But as he heard the disintegration begin, the soldier gave a final, mighty tug and got his left hand up and over the steel. Looking down, he watched the now-severed line fall downward to the ground, coiling into its final resting place like a rattlesnake about to strike.

But the rope was no rattlesnake, and it was the Executioner who was about to strike.

The rusty steel of the pulley affixed to the side of the barn creaked audibly as he pulled himself on up and into the hayloft. The effort took only seconds, but considering the fact that with each passing second he expected a gun barrel to appear in front of his face it felt like hours. Finally, however, he was inside the barn on a wooden floor covered with hay strands that had broken off from the bales stacked to both sides of the loft.

He appeared to be alone.

The Executioner wasted no time unhooking the Calico from its shoulder harness. Then, rolling to his belly, he held the 100-round machine pistol in front of him, using his elbows, knees and feet to crawl forward toward the edge of the hayloft. When he had finally reached the end of the upstairs storage area, he looked down to see the Thor motor home Norman had spoken of back in the ranch house.

Ten million dollars should be inside it.

An even dozen guards were crowded around the front door of the barn, proving to Bolan that they had little, if any, military training. Or common sense for that matter. There wasn't nearly enough room at the crack between the two sliding barn doors for that many men to maneuver, and the barn held other areas of possible entry—such as the hayloft—that should have been covered more effectively.

Bolan saw little reason not to take advantage of the drug buyers' lack of experience and stupidity.

Still in the prone position, he extended the Calico over the edge of the hayloft and dropped the sights on the man at the far right of the group crowding the doors. All were facing away from him, waiting. They evidently thought the one man at the hayloft window still had it secured, and were convinced that the next wave of attack would come through the front doors.

It was an incredibly stupid assumption, and it would cost all twelve men their lives.

Taking careful aim, Bolan squeezed the trigger and stitched a figure-eight pattern of full-auto fire into the man at the far right. Then, still holding the Calico's trigger back against the guard, he blasted a continuous stream of gunfire to his left, taking the men out with 9 mm rounds from their hips up to their napes. As the gunners slammed up against the barn doors, then fell backward, their weapons flew out of their hands into the air.

Most of the men died on their feet before hitting the ground, but by the time Bolan had reached the last three men to his left, the trio had had time to turn and were attempting to return fire. So the Executioner cut a figure eight back and forth through the inexperienced gunmen, and the last man fell to the barn's hard-packed dirt floor at the same time the Calico finally ran dry and the bolt clicked open.

Bolan had managed to burn through a hundred rounds since jumping off the porch, but he still had the partially full drum magazine he'd changed out earlier under his left arm, and now he switched the two again as the thunderous roars of gunfire began to subside.

A rotting wooden ladder was nailed to the barn wall to one side of the hayloft, and now Bolan cautiously descended it, keeping his finger on the Calico's trigger and one eye on the mass of dead men by the doors. As soon as his hiking boots hit the ground, he hurried over to check the corpses, pressing an index finger into the throats of the men who still had throats. Those who didn't hardly needed checking.

One way or another, all twelve gunners were dead.

Bolan kept the Calico up and in the ready position as he opened the door to the Thor motor home and climbed aboard. The vehicle was deserted. The Thor was set up differently than the Winnebago, but by starting at the back and working his way up to the cab area, he had little trouble finding where the hiding places had been built into the walls, floor, furniture and other places. With each new secret innovation he found, he counted the money that had been hidden there.

When he finally reached the driver's seat, Bolan

frowned. Returning to the very back of the Thor, he repeated each step, counting again.

And once more, a grimace covered the soldier's face.

Something was wrong.

Jumping down from the vehicle, then over the bodies of the dead men at the front of the barn, Bolan slid the doors farther apart and exited the barn. An expression of concern covered his face.

He, Nash, José Morales and Fredrico Guzman had brought ten million dollars' worth of high-grade marijuana across the Mexican-American border, but there was only three million dollars on board the Thor.

Bolan kept the Calico in his right hand as he twisted the doorknob of the ranch house with his left. There was still seven million dollars' worth of grass unaccounted for, which meant this ranch-house rendezvous wasn't the only stop planned for the Winnebago.

José and Fredrico had some explaining to do.

THE RANCH HOUSE and barn were filled with the bodies of the dead. Dead men told no tales, so Bolan decided their present location was as good as any to check back in with Stony Man Farm. As soon as he'd walked back out onto the porch, he pulled out his sat phone and tapped in the number.

"Hello, Striker," Barbara Price said when the rerouted call finally reached the Farm.

"Hi, Barb," Bolan replied. "We've run into a bit of a snag."

"Okay. Go ahead."

"It appears this ranch house was only the first stop where the grass was to be transferred," Bolan explained.

"In fact, the Lohman's men here were only taking a little less than a third. Three million worth."

"How much is left?" Price asked.

"Seven mil."

"Any idea how many more stops are on the agenda?"

Bolan took in a breath and blew it out through clenched teeth. "If my two informants are telling the truth this time," he said, "just one. It's supposed to be another Winnebago like ours. And it's coming from Lohman's, too."

"Wonder why they're splitting it up the way they are?" Price asked.

"According to José and Fredrico," Bolan said, "there was a temporary cash-flow slowdown at Lohman's. They didn't have the whole ten million on hand yet but wanted to get the Thor on its way. Then, when the rest of the money came back in from their street dealers, they sent the other seven million with Julio and Burton and Bryant. Speaking of Julio, I assume the blacksuits Brognola sent to bail out our SEAL and Recon took care of his body?"

"That's affirmative," Price said. "Jack and Charlie are flying Julio's remains and the blacksuits themselves home even as we speak."

"Good. An army of blacksuits draws too much attention during the day. How are they replacing the Winnebago?"

"Hal decided to just keep them in the Johnson's Chicken truck," Price said. "The driver's still tripping on Valium—he got another injection—and he's coming back to the Farm with the others. Blindfolded, of course. We'll keep him locked in one of the bedrooms until this is all over." The mission controller paused for a breath of air. "He wasn't scheduled to check in with Johnson's headquarters until after he made his delivery down in southern Alabama, so the truck won't be missed for a couple more days."

Bolan realized he was nodding to himself. "Okay, Barb," he said. "That should give us plenty of time. Now, with Julio dead, did Burton and Bryant call back to Moreland to find out where they're supposed to go?"

"They did, but Moreland still doesn't trust them completely. He won't give them their final destination until they're almost there. He's just telling them which highways to take and when to turn."

"Where are they now?"

"Just turned east out of Cincinnati," Price replied. "At least with Julio dead they're able to call in at will now. Have your boys given you the next stop yet?"

Bolan pictured José and Guzman, once again bound inside the ranch house. With all of the bloodshed they'd witnessed it hadn't been hard to get them to talk further.

"Yeah," he told Price. "We're to meet the buyers near Saint Louis."

There was a long pause on both ends of the line, and the only sound was a tiny bit of static now and then. Finally, Price said, "Are you thinking what I'm thinking, Striker?"

"Probably. There's a good chance we're about to do business with ourselves. I didn't think the timing was right before, but things have changed. We may very well be getting ready to meet Bryant and Burton in Saint Louis."

"So what do you want us to do if that's the case?"

Price asked. "We were planning on getting new leads toward the tops of both the Morales Cartel and Lohman's on the other end. If it's just Shooter and Fireplug who show up…" His voice trailed off, turning the statement into a question.

"If that's the case," Bolan said, "we'll just have to play it by ear. At the very least we'll have taken ten million dollars of drug money, and an equal amount of high-grade marijuana, off the streets. And I'll lean harder on José and Fredrico and see what I can find out from them."

"It'll be almost like starting back at square one," Price pointed out.

"Sometimes you don't get all the breaks. It doesn't mean you give up."

"Of course not," Price said. "I'm about to call Burton and Bryant again. Anything you want me to tell them?"

"Just fill them in on what's going on at our end," Bolan told her. "Everything we've just discussed."

"Will do," Price said. "Base out."

"Striker out," the soldier replied. Then he turned back into the house. Inside, he left Nash still in charge of the prisoners as he went searching through the rest of the building. He and the Delta Force commando had begun this mission with plenty of heavy firepower, but they'd been forced to leave it back in Juarez when they'd climbed the wall that surrounded Twin Pines and hadn't had a chance to rearm. Their rifles, extra ammo and other equipment was lost forever.

And it needed to be replaced.

In the closet of a back bedroom, Bolan found what he'd been looking for. The small area was stacked with ammunition and magazines for a variety of pistols, shotguns and rifles. But what caught his eye was an even dozen boxes of 9 mm rounds that would fit his Calico nicely and twenty freshly loaded 7.62 mm magazines for Nash's newly appropriated AK-47.

Bolan clipped the Calico back under his arm and began hauling his find back into the living room. Nash slid the sling of his AK-47 over his shoulder and helped load the boxes of ammo into the Winnebago. Then the two warriors escorted José and Fredrico to the motor home so they could start their journey to Saint Louis.

THE SUN PEEKED over the horizon as the Daybreak motor home rolled down the right-hand side of I-44.

It had been a long night, but Reynaldo Morales couldn't remember any time in his life when he'd felt better than he did at that moment. All his plans were about to work out. All his problems were about to go away. In a matter of hours now, he would become the undisputed Don of the Morales Cartel and Don Pancho would be regarded as nothing more than an old man who had outlived his usefulness and should be put out to pasture.

Or, as soon as Reynaldo could get around to it, put "under" a pasture somewhere. Combined with the massacre at the church, the loss of ten million dollars and the same amount in high-grade marijuana would prove to the rest of the Morales Cartel that the old man no longer had any place within the organization.

Reynaldo smiled behind the wheel of the motor home as he guided it off the interstate at Pacific, Missouri. For miles now, he had seen the billboards advertising

Six Flags Over Mid-America and read the words that promised entertainment and fun for the whole family at the giant amusement park.

Well, Reynaldo thought as he glanced up into the rearview mirror and saw the twenty men crowded into the motor home behind him, his "family" was about to take another hit. But Reynaldo himself—even though the mercenaries behind him knew him as Reuben Ortiz—was certainly about to be amused and have fun personally.

Reynaldo drove slowly through the traffic leading to Six Flags but passed the entrance to the giant parking lots. He was able to pick up speed once the traffic thinned, but he drove only a few more miles on the blacktop before twisting the wheel and turning onto a winding dirt road that led up into the hillside. Now he was forced to slow again. The slight inconvenience did nothing to dampen his mood. It was almost over. In just a few more hours, his—or rather "Reuben Ortiz's"—hired guns would attack both the buyers from Brooklyn and the other Winnebago, which would by now be carrying seven million dollars in marijuana and three million in cash.

Reynaldo glanced again into the mirror. The men behind him had quieted compared to the rowdiness they had exhibited during the drive earlier. They knew the time for battle was almost on them and, like fighting men everywhere, good or bad, they were quietly reflecting on their lives, wondering if they would die, but at the same time contemplating all the things they would do with the money they made if they survived.

Their near silence and concentration made Reynaldo's smile widen. All of them planned on surviving, of course. Few men—and certainly not mercenaries who fought for whoever paid them the most—entered a battle with no hope of winning. And these men were all but assured of a win. Reynaldo's last phone call to Tony Moreland at Lohman's had told him that his man—Julio— had been killed in some random and unexpected attack by a group of outlaw bikers on the road. The Winnebago they'd been driving had been trashed, but two new men Moreland had enlisted had survived the attack, and stolen some kind of refrigerated frozen-chicken truck to complete the journey.

Now Reynaldo actually chuckled out loud at the fact that two drug-smuggling rookies who probably had little to no experience in gunplay would be the only men the mercenaries would face on the Brooklyn end. The hired killers following Ortiz should make short work of them.

A Latino man—a former *federale,* if Reynaldo remembered correctly—with long stringy hair sat directly behind the Daybreak's driver's seat. Evidently hearing Reynaldo's soft laugh, he leaned forward and the soon-to-be leader of the Morales Cartel felt his irritating breath on the back of his neck.

"Did you say something, Mr. Ortiz?' the man asked.

It had taken Reynaldo a while to get used to the Reuben Ortiz name, but by now he answered to it as readily as he did his own. "No," he said simply. "Just thinking." He knew the man behind him, dressed in worn blue jeans, worn cowboy boots and a faded green BDU shirt, was bound to ask him what he'd been thinking, so he cut the question off before it could be spoken. "Just thinking about how I will spend my share of the money we're about to get."

In the rearview mirror, Reynaldo could see the man smile. He could also see the barrel of the man's AK-47 sticking up next to his head. Nothing further needed to be said.

The Daybreak followed the twisting road up into the hills, finally coming to a green sign with white letters. The words read simply *Scenic Turnout* and Reynaldo pulled off the hard-packed dirt onto a gravel-covered area. As he halted the motor home, he looked through the windshield at the lush green valley ahead of him. It dropped a good two hundred feet below the turnout, but Reynaldo knew a little-known back road that led down into the lower plateau. It was this road that the new men from Brooklyn, and Reynaldo's own three younger brothers and cousin Fredrico, would take to make their exchange.

It was also this road that he and his men would follow once the other motor home and the chicken truck had arrived in order to seize both the money and the marijuana.

And kill everyone in the two vehicles.

In the meantime, there was no better place to wait than right here. From this vantage point, he could not only watch the two vehicles arrive, the Daybreak would look no different than a hundred other such vehicles that had brought families to the area on vacation.

Reynaldo laughed again, silently this time so he wouldn't have to respond to any words from the former *federale* behind him. The vehicle's windows were tinted, so no one could see the weapons and other gear that belonged to the men inside. And as long as he kept his window rolled up, no one would notice his costly Western-cut suit, which also looked out of place in this amusement park world of cargo shorts and T-shirts.

Reynaldo considered standing up and giving his mercenaries a final pep talk, then decided against it. All the men knew what they were to do already. Half of them would go after the two new men in the frozen-chicken truck, kill them and take the money they had brought to purchase the marijuana. The other half would attack the Winnebago that had started in Juarez and take possession of the product itself. Then, they would return to the Daybreak and make their escape before authorities were even alerted. And again, the motor home would blend in perfectly with the Six Flags traffic.

Killing Reynaldo's three brothers and cousin was an unfortunate part of the overall scheme. But, if truth be told, Reynaldo had never really cared all that much for his brothers or Fredrico, and eliminating them, here and now, would lessen any possible competition he might face later on for leadership of the cartel. There was a certain Shakespearean aspect to the little minidrama that appealed to Reynaldo, and it brought yet another smile of satisfaction to his face.

He brushed a tiny white speck off the lapel of his suit, reminding himself to get it cleaned before returning to Juarez. He could drop it off at the dry cleaners when he picked up the striped slacks that had been stained by the cigar ash when he'd crossed the international bridge before embarking on this long drive into the United States.

And then, he could go back to wearing the frock coat, paisley vest and cravat by which he was known in Mexico.

It would be good to be Reynaldo Morales instead of Reuben Ortiz once again.

"BETTER MAKE THIS a three-way call, Base," Bolan said as Nash guided the Winnebago onto the exit ramp thirty miles west of Saint Louis. He looked up and saw the sign announcing Pacific, Missouri. "We need to get Burton and Bryant in on this conversation, too."

"Hang on," Price replied and he heard a series of clicks in his ear. Then a deep voice said, "This is Fireplug. Go."

"What's your location, Fireplug?" the Stony Man Farm mission controller asked.

"Still in Illinois but just barely," Bryant said. "We're passing East St. Louis exit signs at the moment."

"What was your last direction from Moreland?" Bolan asked the Recon Marine.

"Into Missouri and west on I-44," Bryant replied. "Supposed to call him back as soon as we've crossed the state line."

"It's what I was afraid of," he said. "He's sending you to buy dope from us."

"Sure sounds like it," Bryant agreed. "We're too close for it to be a coincidence."

Nash had been forced to slow the Winnebago as they'd fallen into traffic headed for Six Flags Over Mid-America. Now the Delta Force operative twisted slightly in his seat and looked over his shoulder at José and Guzman. "We're still going the right way, right?" he asked.

"Yes," José said. He had begun rubbing his wrists where the plastic cuffs had chafed his skin. "Go past the park."

"And you've been there before?" Nash said.

"Many times," José replied. "It is a valley in the foot-hills where we often make exchanges."

Bolan saw Nash nod. "Just make sure we don't en-counter any surprises," he said. "Because you two'll be the first shot if we do."

Bolan held the phone away from his ear for a second. "The only surprise it sounds like we're going to have is that we'll be meeting with our own men."

An irritated expression covered Nash's face as he nodded his understanding. "So what do we do?"

Price evidently heard Nash's words because as Bolan returned the sat phone to his ear, she said, "That's a good question, Striker. What *do* you want to do?"

Bolan hesitated, thinking. He hated to find out that they'd made this trip from Mexico only to take pos-session of a truckload of cash and a Winnebago filled with marijuana. On one hand, at least they'd gotten the dope off the streets and seized a large amount of money used for illegal purposes. But this run was only a small part of the overall operation of the Morales Cartel and Lohman's on the other end, and he'd hoped to destroy the whole organization, not just hamper or slow it.

"Wait until Burton and Bryant talk to Moreland again," Bolan finally said. "Let's make it official. Then we'll go ahead and meet wherever Moreland sends them. Maybe we can gather some new intel. At the very least, we'll be familiar with another of their exchange sites."

"Affirmative," Price said. "Fireplug, you read that?"

"Affirmative on this end, too," Bryant replied. "I'm gonna hang up now. It's almost time to call Moreland back."

Bolan killed the call on his phone and dropped it into his lap. The Winnebago finally passed the entrance to Six Flags, and José directed them onward. They were less than a mile past the amusement park when José instructed them to turn down the first dirt road they saw.

The sun was rising high in the sky, its rays beating in through the Winnebago's windshield, as Nash guided the vehicle downward on a twisting dirt road. Deep ruts—evidence that heavy vehicles such as other motor homes and trucks had used the road during wet weather—caught the tires and made for a bumpy ride. As they bounced slowly along, the sat phone in the Executioner's lap rang again.

"Striker," Bolan said.

"We're on with Burton and Bryant again," Price said.

Bolan waited.

"Moreland's got us getting off at the Six Flags exit in Pacific." It was Burton speaking this time—Bolan recognized the voice. "We take the first dirt road—"

"After you've passed the park," Bolan interrupted. "Be careful. It's got some deep ruts in it."

"I guess it's official then," Burton said, his voice sounding more than a little disappointed. "It's you we're meeting."

The Winnebago made a final twist to the right then came out onto a flat grassy area hidden within the hills. "This it?" Nash asked over his shoulder.

"Yes," José said. "Right here."

"We're there," Bolan said into the phone. "Talk to you when you get here." He pushed the button to end the call and dropped the phone back to his lap as Nash ground the Winnebago to a halt.

The soldier raised a hand to his eyebrows, shielding his eyes from the bright midmorning sun as he surveyed the valley. It appeared to be devoid of livestock or any other animals for that matter. But far in the distance, higher up on a rise, he could see another motor home parked facing the valley.

The sun was too bright to make out the make or model.

CHAPTER FOURTEEN

"He wasn't kidding about this road being rough," Shooter Burton said as the Johnson's Chicken truck barreled its way down the twisting road. "Good thing we're hauling money instead of eggs."

Fireplug Bryant had both arms out in front of him, bracing himself against the dashboard in the semi's cab. "Well, it's almost over," he said, the words coming out in staggered syllables that kept time with the bumps. "Then I guess Cooper will either cut us loose again or come up with some other plan."

"I'd bet on another plan. Cooper doesn't strike me as the kind who quits anything once he starts it."

"I wouldn't bet against you on that," Bryant grunted.

After what seemed like hours but couldn't have been more than five minutes, the truck suddenly emerged into a flat prairielike area. Less than a football field away, Burton saw a Winnebago much like the one he and Bryant had driven until it had been shot to pieces. Twisting the big wheel in front of him, he headed the truck that way.

Bryant sat back in his seat now that the ride had smoothed out. Burton glanced toward the Recon Marine and saw him smiling.

"Something on your mind?" Burton asked.

"Up there," Bryant said. "Looks like some family in a motor home got tired of the rides at Six Flags and came out here sightseeing."

"And *that's* enough to put that gigantic grin on your face?" Burton asked, laughing now himself.

"Cut me a break," Bryant said. "It's been a long couple of days. I was just thinking it might be nice someday to have a family and a motor home that I could load up with a wife and kids and picnic supplies instead of guns and ammo and drugs."

"Keep dreaming, Fireplug," Burton stated. "You'd be bored out of your mind in two hours." He stared up at the ridge his partner had pointed out. "See there?" he said. "Even *they're* tired of it. They're already leaving."

BOLAN SAW the big semi rumble out from the road onto the flat grassland. A second later, something in the corner of his eye caught his attention and he looked that way. For a moment, he saw nothing but the open land and the ridge in the distance. Then it hit him.

At the same time the truck sporting the big talking-chicken logo had appeared from the road, the motor home on the ridge in the distance had started backing up. As his eyes finally focused on the distance, the vehicle turned out of sight.

And something in the Executioner's mind told him to get ready.

Bolan continued to stare at the ridge, the feeling that danger was near flowing through his veins and arteries just as surely as was his own blood. He had never been a big believer in extrasensory perception, but he had firm faith in experience. Experience logged references in the brain. Sometimes the subconscious picked up details—little things the conscious passed over—and combined them with other details to tell the experienced warrior that there had been too many coincidences for something to be a coincidence at all.

Which was what had just happened. There had been too many motor homes involved in this operation, Bolan realized. The Morales Cartel and Lohman's obviously believed in using them exclusively to transport both money and drugs. So it seemed just a little too convenient that yet another one had been waiting there on the ridge where it could view this valley when they'd arrived.

And even more convenient that whoever was in it had decided to leave as soon as the chicken truck appeared.

"There they are," Nash said, reaching for the door handle. "Should we get down and—"

Bolan reached across the seat and grabbed the man's arm. "Get your AK ready," he said as he lifted the Calico from the floor next to him.

"What?" Nash started to say. He was frowning, trying to figure out this sudden change in the atmosphere. "You think it's somebody else in the chicken truck?"

"No, but get ready anyway." The Executioner pulled the bolt back on the Calico to chamber the first round.

"Then what—" Nash started to say.

"Just do it," Bolan commanded, cutting the man off. "I don't have time to explain." Opening his door, he dropped to the ground and started toward the oncoming truck.

It was less than a hundred feet away when the Daybreak motor home came rushing into the clearing behind it.

Burton and Bryant had both been smiling as they neared the Winnebago. Now those smiles faded as they saw Bolan lift the Calico in his right hand and motion past them with his left. Both men looked into the side mirrors on the chicken truck and their smiles turned to frowns.

Rifles were suddenly thrust out the windows of the Daybreak as it continued to speed forward. Guns cut loose, ricochets zinging off the rocks in the distance as bullets whizzed past Bolan. He switched the Calico's selector to full-auto and fired a steady stream of fire that shot back at the motor home like a fire hose. The windshield shattered and several men screamed in pain.

Suddenly, gunners armed with rifles and shotguns poured out of the vehicle's windows and doors. The vast majority appeared on the passenger's side of the vehicle, where Bolan was. There had to have been close to twenty in all, they all swung their weapons toward the Executioner.

The Johnson's truck had ground to a halt and Bolan dived in front of it as a 3-round burst from an M-16 split the grass where he'd stood a moment before. Dozens more rounds, sounding as if they came from every caliber imaginable, exploded a moment later.

Rolling twice, the soldier passed the front bumper of the Johnson's truck and came to rest on his belly, directly behind the left front wheels. Leaning slightly to the side, he angled the short-barreled Calico up on the driver's side of the Daybreak. Only two of the men had exited the motor home on that side. Another half-dozen rounds spit from the Calico pistol and struck the chest of one of them, a Latino with dark stringy hair. The man jerked in a wild dance of death before hitting the ground.

Behind him, the Executioner heard Nash's AK-47 open up. He tapped the Calico's trigger once more and sent more 9 mm rounds into the other man on the driver's side, a gunman toting a Mossberg riot shotgun and wearing a green BDU blouse and khaki work pants. This guy tried to outdo his dancing partner with more gyrations before finally collapsing on top of him instead.

That side of the truck was now clear. The battle was being waged on the other side of the line of vehicles, so the Executioner leaped to his feet. Through the windshield of the chicken truck, he could see Burton behind the wheel and Bryant on the other side. Bryant's attempt to try to get out and join the firefight on his side would have been tantamount to suicide. So, staring at him, Bolan shook his head, silently telling the man to stay put for the time being. Then, turning toward Burton, he waved him out and down.

Burton followed the hand directions, appearing a second later with an AR-15 gripped in both hands. Both he and Bolan squatted next to the cab.

Rifle and shotgun fire continued to explode as the men on the other side of the Daybreak fired at the Winnebago, and Nash returned their fire.

"Stay here for ten seconds," Bolan ordered. "I'm going to try to work my way around behind them."

Burton nodded.

Bolan kept the chicken truck's engine block between him and the men on the other side of the Daybreak as long as he could, finally hurrying past the trailer before darting out from its cover and sprinting across the open gap between the trailer and the motor home. Automatic rounds flew his way, striking inches behind his feet before he dived again, rolling up against the side of the motor home. A Latino wearing fatigue pants and a white T-shirt suddenly appeared at the tail of the Daybreak, wielding a heavy M-1 Garand. Bolan rolled onto his knees and held the Calico's trigger back, sending another half-dozen 9 mm rounds into the gunman. Four of the rounds struck his abdomen and chest. A fifth caught the wooden forend of the rifle, splitting it into pieces.

The sixth performed the same splitting act with his skull.

The Executioner heard movement behind him and twisted in time to see Bryant's big frame drop to the ground with the grace of a cat. The Recon Marine had slid across the truck's seat and emerged on the safe side of the vehicle. In his hands was another AR-15 like the one Burton had wielded, and now Bolan watched as the SEAL and Recon Marine whispered back and forth, working out their own battle strategy within the ongoing onslaught.

Turning back, Bolan was just in time to pull the trigger again as a mountain of a man came around the tail of the Daybreak. He had unusually pale skin and was obviously Caucasian, and as more 9 mm rounds blew from the Calico's barrel the Executioner couldn't help but wonder just who these men were.

Some looked Mexican, others, American. Were they from the Morales Cartel? Lohman's in Brooklyn? Both?

It didn't matter at the moment. Staying alive was the current name of the game. If the Executioner could achieve that, he'd have plenty of time later to find out who was trying to kill him and his men.

Finally reaching the back of the Daybreak, Bolan dropped to one knee and peered around the edge. It looked clear, but the gunfight was still raging behind him and on the other side. So, quickly rising, he let the Calico lead the way as he started to turn the corner and move on.

A split second before he moved behind the truck, he saw a man suddenly drop down from the front of the Daybreak's driver's side. The man wore an expensive-looking black suit, cowboy hat and boots. A medium-frame Glock—either a 9 mm or a .40 S&W—was gripped in his right hand.

By the time the soldier had turned back his way the man had disappeared between the vehicles. Where had he come from? Bolan had looked through the windows of the Daybreak as he passed them. The man had to have been hiding in the bathroom until now.

Bolan moved on, stopping and kneeling again before rounding the Daybreak to the "action side" of the vehicles. When he peered around the corner this time, he saw that the intruders had been reduced significantly. While he couldn't see them, he could hear the full-auto rounds of Spike Nash's AK-47 and the slightly slower *pop-pop-pops* from Shooter Burton and Fireplug Bryant's semi-auto AR-15s.

The Executioner reminded himself that he was almost directly behind the attackers from the Daybreak, and therefore in line with the rounds from his own men.

And there was no such thing as friendly fire.

Still using the tail end of the Daybreak as cover, Bolan raised the Calico to shoulder level before leaning slightly around the back of the motor home. He pulled back on the trigger, sending a spray of death from the high-capacity machine pistol. Rounds struck the back of a Caucasian wearing a hoodie with the sleeves cut off, and the volley practically folded him in two before he fell. More 9 mm rounds cut into the side of a Latino gunman trying to turn with an old Thompson submachine gun. He fell to his death as a moan escaped his lips.

The Executioner continued to fire; men continued to fall. The symphony of violence reached a crescendo, then suddenly all was quiet as the last of the gunfire died down and a strange sort of peace seemed to fall over the valley.

The Calico still held at the ready, the Executioner stepped away from the Daybreak and walked forward. A few seconds later, Nash, Burton and Bryant stood up from behind various spots around the chicken truck and strode out toward him.

The peace didn't last long, however.

Before the three elite warriors could reach the man they knew as Cooper, the sound of the Winnebago's side door opening was heard in the near silence. Footsteps running on the other side of the motor home followed, then José and Guzman appeared, running awkwardly. They disappeared behind the chicken truck for a moment, then reappeared between the truck and the Daybreak.

Bolan and his three fellow warriors turned their weapons their way, but there was no need to fire. The two men had worked the restraints off their ankles, but the plastic cuffs still bound their hands behind their backs.

"Reynaldo!" José screamed. "Save us!"

The man in the expensive black suit Bolan had seen earlier suddenly rose from behind the Daybreak's left front fender, the Glock in both hands. Taking careful aim, he fired a round into José's chest. As the guy fell, the man with the Glock swung the gun slightly to the side and shot once more, this time striking Guzman.

Bolan, Burton, Bryant and Nash all turned their weapons toward the man wearing the cowboy hat and pulled their triggers at the same time. A volley of rounds tore the man's torso apart like some giant meat grinder.

The fancily dressed man fell to his back, his eyes wide open, staring blindly into the bright noonday sun. The black cowboy hat fell from his head and landed upside down on its crown, rocked back and forth several times like a ship adjusting to an ocean wave, then settled into place on the ground.

Bolan and the other men gathered around him. For the most part, the men who had attacked them looked, and dressed, like hired gunmen. They had worn various combinations of well-worn denim and khaki, with touches of military fatigues and other battle wear thrown in here and there.

Nothing fancy. Everything "blue-collar."

This man was different.

"Quite the duds on this Reynaldo guy," Bryant observed, looking down. "Must have been the head dude."

"I wonder who he was," Nash said.

The Executioner looked into the dead man's eyes. "Just another drug-running nobody," he said.

EPILOGUE

It was late afternoon before Bolan learned the identities of the men who had attacked from the Daybreak motor home. He and the hand-picked elite warriors from the various branches of America's armed forces had spent most of the day electronically fingerprinting the bodies that littered the ground in this hidden valley before digitally sending the impressions back to Aaron "the Bear" Kurtzman, the computer wizard of Stony Man Farm.

Kurtzman had run the prints through AFIS—Advanced Fingerprint Identification System—and while a few of the men could not be found on file, most popped up readily as belonging to ex-cops or soldiers from the United States, Mexico and other Latin American countries, which gave the Executioner what he considered to be a 99.9 percent conclusion: someone had recruited experienced gunners from both sides of the border to make up an army of mercenaries. And they were the same mercenaries who had committed the cold-blooded attacks on the church in Juarez, and otherwise harassed the Morales Cartel.

The surprise had been the identity of the man wearing the expensive hand-tailored Italian suit and the custom-made hat and Old Gringo cowboy boots. A search of his body had come up with a Mexican driver's license, passport and other forms of identification that represented him as Reuben Ortiz. But his fingerprints claimed otherwise, and when those results came back from AFIS Bolan had taken a closer look at the man's papers.

The forgeries were good, he saw. Top quality. The kind only a wealthy man could afford, and only a wealthy man who also had good solid criminal connections could obtain. But they were forgeries nonetheless.

The dead man with the chest full of bullet holes was none other than Reynaldo Morales, the second in command of the Morales Cartel.

"The question is," Hal Brognola, Stony Man Farm's director of Sensitive Operations, said into the sat phone Bolan held to his ear, "why would this clown recruit mercs to murder his own people?"

Bolan stood staring across the grassland of the valley, toward the ridge where he'd first seen the Daybreak a few hours ago. "We may never know the entire story, Hal," he said, "but I think the operative word here is *second* in command. Didn't I read something in the file before all this started about the number-one leader of the Morales Cartel? A Pancho or something?"

"Don Pancho," Brognola replied. "Good memory, big guy. But he's in semiretirement. Reynaldo was the man actually running the show. He was the guy with the real power."

"But probably not the real money, Hal," Bolan said. "Or at least not as much of it as he wanted. My guess is Reynaldo resented however many pesos the old don was getting to keep him living lavishly in…" The Executioner's voice trailed off for a moment. "Where did the file say his villa was?"

"Mazatlán," Brognola told him.

"Right. Well, I'm betting that Reynaldo thought it was time he stepped up as *numero uno* instead of two." The Executioner glanced away from the ridge as Fireplug Bryant walked by carrying a case of empty beer bottles they'd found in the Daybreak after the gunfight. The Recon Marine and the other two elite warriors were busy making Molotov cocktails to destroy the motor homes and the marijuana before they left. They'd all take off, with the money, in the chicken truck.

But the mission was hardly over. There were still several loose ends that needed to be cleaned up.

"What's Phoenix Force's status?" Bolan asked Brognola.

"They got in around 0600 hours this morning. Exhausted. They're still asleep upstairs."

"And Ironman and his boys?" Bolan said, referring to Carl "Ironman" Lyons and the other two members of Able Team.

"Radioed in right before you called. Said they were ten minutes out…wait a minute…sounds like they're landing outside right now."

"Great," Bolan said. He turned his eyes toward the Daybreak where Shooter Burton had stuck one end of a short hose into the gas tank, the other in his mouth. Bolan watched Burton's lips tighten as he started the siphon, then saw the man make a face and spit as the gasoline came up through the hose. A moment later, the beer bottles were being filled. "Wake up Phoenix Force and get them headed toward Juarez," he said. "By now, Bear should be able to hack into emails and other electronic communication inside the cartel. Have him come up with a list of the Moraleses involved in the family business and tell Phoenix Force that everyone on that list goes down. I want them to clean house along the border."

"Gotcha, big guy," Brognola said.

"And while they're at it, I'm sure they can glean some intel on where the marijuana crops are being cultivated deeper inside Mexico's interior."

"I'll tell PF it's a priority," Brognola said. "You mentioned Able Team?"

"I did. Give them a few hours of sack time. What I want them to do can wait. Besides, it's going to take Bear and the rest of his computer crew a while to do what I want them to do."

"Which is…?"

"We already know that Tony Moreland back in Brooklyn is dirty, but he's just the rec-vehicle dealership's manager. We need to find out if the owner—the Lohman of Lohman's—is part of this drug pipeline, too. So one or more of Stony's computer team needs to check bank transactions and other statistics for the man. In fact, they need to run similar checks on every employee who works for the dealership."

"That'll take a little time," Brognola pointed out.

"That's why I said you can let Able Team catch forty winks."

"Anything else?" Brognola asked.

"Yeah. Tell Jack and Charlie to go to Juarez with Phoenix. After they've taken care of the Moraleses there, and found out where the growing fields are, I want them to hit the interior as protection for our flyboys. Jack and Charlie are going to do a little weed spraying."

By now, Nash, Burton and Bryant had piled all the corpses into the Winnebago and Daybreak. The Molotov cocktails had been readied, and the three elite warriors each held several in their arms. They stood waiting for the Executioner to end his phone call.

"I didn't ask you where you're going, big guy," Brognola said.

Bolan looked at the men who were waiting on him. They had all done their jobs far and above the call of duty and he'd been proud to work with them. But they had one last leg of this mission to perform before he sent them back to their respective units.

"My new partners," Bolan said, "and I are going south to Mazatlán to find Don Pancho. With all that's happened he's likely to want to come out of retirement and we don't want that. Besides, he might not be too active right now, but in the past he's been responsible for everything from drug smuggling to murder. And there's bound to be a huge group of bodyguards around him. Men who deserve to die just as much as the rest of the Morales Cartel."

"The lowlifes who survive will eventually reorganize, and as soon as they do, they'll be open for business again."

Bolan nodded to the three men holding the bottles and they began lighting, then throwing their homemade bombs through the windows and doors of the motor homes. As he walked toward the chicken truck, Bolan spoke once more into the sat phone. "That's okay, Hal," the man known as the Executioner said. "I'll be open for business, too."

* * * * *